About the Author

Betrayal is David Grant's first published novel after a
lifetime in scientific research. He lives in retirement near
the Peak District of Derbyshire.

Dedication

To the memory of my daughter Gill

David Grant

BETRAYAL

AUSTIN MACAULEY
PUBLISHERS LTD.

A CIP catalogue record for this title is available from the
British Library.

**Company and school names are purely fictional and any
similarity to existing concerns are coincidental.**

ISBN 9781786120953 (Paperback)
ISBN 9781786120960 (Hardback)
ISBN 9781786120997 (E-Book)

www.austinmacauley.com

First Published (2016)
Austin Macauley Publishers Ltd.
25 Canada Square
Canary Wharf
London
E14 5LQ

Acknowledgments

I would like to thank the numerous sources of published information with regard to the nature and geography of Cyprus which forms some of the background to this book. Also some of the material was gleaned from my own experiences on this beautiful island and with the army during National Service.

Chapter 1

Canterbury

A shaft of early morning sunlight crept through a chink in the drawn curtains. Jack Blake blinked as the sudden brightness dispelled his turbulent dream giving way to the surroundings of his bedroom.

He glanced at his bedside clock. Still only seven o'clock.

Tempted as he was to turn over and snatch another hour, he had things to do. He yawned, slipped reluctantly from the warm comfort of his bed, and sat rubbing his face briskly between his hands to gather his thoughts.

'Right, you lazy sod,' he muttered to himself, 'pull yourself together and get your finger out.'

He wandered sleepily over to the bedroom window and opened the curtains, squinting at the sudden burst of brightness from the early morning sun. The majestic towers of Canterbury cathedral loomed in the distance over the nearby housetops. He loved this place, the ancient city with its cherished history and the wonderful Kent countryside with its abundance of fruit orchards and oast houses. It was a typical English summer morning with the birds singing their dawn chorus and from below the sound of a milk float on its early morning round.

As he savoured the scene he realised he was on the threshold of a completely new phase in his life. Now in his mid-twenties he wondered what he had accomplished so far. What prospects did a young man have with no commercial or industrial experience? Could a hard earned general science degree and five years as a junior army officer qualify him for a future career?

He mused about his earlier life. Not a particularly bright student at university, although he had achieved a rather mundane pass degree in general science. An unlikely qualification for pushing the boundaries of knowledge, but maybe sufficient for him to find a good position from where he could hope to progress into management. That's where his main interests lay. After numerous applications it became clear that companies were not interested in new graduates without specialist degrees and no work experience. Possibly also his lack of enthusiasm was only too transparent. The years of inaction had left his body yearning for something rather more exciting than the prospect of a sedentary job in an office or laboratory.

Then he noticed an advert in a national newspaper inviting applications for the Royal Military Academy at Sandhurst. The available positions were for officer cadet training which on completion would enable successful candidates to sign on in the regular army for short service commissions.

He remembered the moment when he had made the impulsive decision to apply. Events had followed swiftly and, after a series of interviews, tests, and an intensive physical examination, he had been admitted to the course.

The training had been arduous but rewarding and he threw himself into the new life with gusto. He was eventually commissioned as a second lieutenant into the Corps of the Royal Engineers. He spent four years in deployment to various overseas posts on routine duties before being dispatched to Cyprus for his final year.

On demobilisation he had achieved the rank of first lieutenant and was given the option of signing on with an immediate captaincy, or to return to civilian life.

Although he had enjoyed the service with its variety, the excitement of never knowing what each new day may bring, and the good humoured banter of his comrades, he chose to return to civilian life.

So here he was once again looking for employment, but now five years older. He would have to be less particular than before and take anything reasonable on offer. He couldn't continue to live off the good will of his parents.

He now had a mature confidence as a result of his five years of military service and he viewed the future optimistically.

But a dark cloud hung over him. It was the memory of that terrible event in Cyprus. It haunted his dreams and tormented him every waking day. It was a mystery that remained unexplained and he was resolved to find answers no matter how long it took and whatever the cost.

Now it was Monday morning, one week after returning to the UK and his army discharge. Since then he had fed on the indulgence of his parents, almost shedding all feelings of responsibility.

He had a number of friends in the neighbourhood, several of whom he had known since schooldays, and for the first few days he had made a point of meeting up with them. Dave Guest who lived only a few doors down the road was one of these. He worked in the computer division of a large company just outside Canterbury.

They had chatted about Jack's prospects in finding a position suited to his qualifications. Dave said that the internet was a good place to start looking. Many companies advertised vacancies on line either directly or via recruitment agencies.

Although Jack had a smart phone he had neither a desktop nor a laptop computer at home and he preferred to look at a bigger screen in the quiet of the local library, and that was where he was resolved to go this morning. He could also check the situations vacant columns in the array of trade journals on the reading racks.

The enticing aroma of frying bacon wafted up the stairs bringing his mind sharply back to the present. He showered quickly and regarded himself critically in a full length mirror on the bathroom wall. A tall slim brown-eyed young man looked back at him. Not bad looking he thought, although he could do with putting on a bit more weight. He ran a comb through his short light brown hair before donning jeans, blue T-shirt, and trainers.

'Morning all!' he called out as he entered the dining room. His father, Fred Blake, was seated in his usual position at the breakfast table, his head buried in a freshly delivered newspaper. He was tall dark man, unmistakably Jack's father, happily married to his wife Dora with silver wedding celebrations still a joyous memory of the recent past.

The other table occupant was Jack's only sister, Jenny, an attractive brown eyed brunette with a frivolous sense of humour. Although she was two years younger than Jack she was pursuing a very successful career having qualified as a solicitor, and was employed by a legal firm in the city centre.

Now she sat with her elbows resting on the white tablecloth she looked up at Jack as he sat down opposite her.

'Hello lazy bones,' she said with a grin, 'condescended to come down and join us then?'

Fred put down his paper and smiled, 'Jen, give your brother a break. He's only just come out of the army. He's entitled to a few days off.'

'Oh, you're always sticking up for him Dad,' retorted Jenny.

The easy banter was simply a sign of the close relationship between the two siblings. Jack had always felt fiercely protective towards his sister and was extremely proud of her accomplishments, and she in turn looked up to her brother and would be quick to turn on anyone who criticised him.

Their mother entered the dining room carrying a large tray. An open-faced woman with twinkling green eyes and pleasant personality, she enjoyed her occupation as housewife and mother although in her earlier days before meeting and marrying her husband she had led a successful career as a medical receptionist at a local GP's surgery. Although both Fred and herself were now approaching middle age they were still an attractive couple.

'Morning everyone, here's your breakfasts,' she said brightly as she joined her family at the table.

'Any idea about what you're going to do about a job son?' said Fred tentatively, glancing towards his son. 'Not that I'm trying to rush you into anything,' he added hastily with a wry smile, 'Just wondered about how you see your future.'

'Funny you should mention that dad,' responded Jack, 'and you listen, too, young lady,' he said glancing pointedly at his sister, 'I'm off to the library this morning to see what jobs are available. A job in a laboratory of some sort is my best chance with my science degree.'

He paused for a few moments and shrugged his shoulders before adding, 'I know it's only a general degree but it should let me get my foot in the door somewhere. I really want to get into management though,' he concluded wistfully.

'Just be patient son,' said his mother with a smile 'I know you too well. I'm sure you'll get want you want eventually but don't try to rush it. You're not likely to walk into a managing director's job straight away.'

Jack laughed, 'No such luck, Mum, I'm willing to take almost anything for a start. Let's just wait and see what I can come up with.'

'I agree with your mother,' rejoined Fred, 'I know you'll be successful with whatever you do in life. You will always have your mother's and my support. In fact maybe I could help in some way,' he added thoughtfully, 'I know a few people who might be able to help.'

Fred was immensely proud of both his children, feeling that they had already achieved so much more than he had although he did hold a responsible position managing a large retail outlet near the town centre.

'No, Dad,' responded Jack, a little too sharply, 'I don't want that sort of help, thanks all the same. I'd rather find a job off my own bat if you don't mind. Don't worry, I'll get something sooner or later.'

'Huh,' exclaimed Jenny who had been listening to the conversation with a mock expression of disbelief on her face. 'Big hero brother comes back from a sunny holiday island, all nicely suntanned, and here's everyone rallying around as if he'd been fighting a war. I don't believe it.'

'That's right, Jen,' said Jack with a laugh, 'and got paid for it, too. What could be better?'

Their conversation was interrupted by a sudden loud knock at the door.

'Hmm, a bit early for callers isn't it. I wonder who it can be,' said Dora.

'OK, Mum, I'll get it,' said Jenny as she jumped up to answer the door.

It was their next door neighbour Tom Charlesworth, who, with his wife Rita, had been close friends of the Blake's for many years. Tom was a well-built hale and hearty man in his late forties. He had short cropped red hair and piercing blue eyes. As an ex-sergeant major in the Scots Guards he was well qualified for his present occupation as head of security at an industrial complex lying just outside of Canterbury.

'Morning everyone,' he said robustly in a strong Scottish accent. 'Sorry it's so early but I really had to pop round to say hello to Jack before setting off for work.'

Tom had been away on a course and had not seen Jack for some time. He grabbed Jack's hand in a vice-like grip and pumped his arm up and down vigorously.

'Rita told me you were back home. Hellfire young man, the whole neighbourhood is really buzzing about you!'

'Mind you,' he added with a grin, 'at one time I thought you were a wee bit soft, you know, long haired student type, but you've certainly proved me wrong. Not that I approve of officers, it's the NCO's who usually have to tell 'em what to do.'

Jack laughed saying conspiratorially, 'never a truer word, Tom.'

'Not so in your case, Jack,' returned Tom, his voice taking on a serious tone. 'When I read about that little escapade of yours I went green with envy, I can't tell you how much I still miss the service,' he finished wistfully.

Tom was referring to those events in Cyprus, the cause of his present depression. The news of the incident had somehow got back to the UK and been reported in several newspapers but it had been blown completely out of proportion by the media, with the most important parts missing.

Jack knew that the praise was unjustified and any mention of it made him feel uncomfortable as it brought back the memory of the events on that fateful night.

'A typical example of press exaggeration,' said Jack dismissively. 'It was a routine patrol and nothing like the way it was reported. The men on the patrol did all the work. I just happened to be the leader that night. It could have been anyone.'

'How's Mary?' he continued, abruptly changing the subject. 'I spoke to Rita the other day so I know that Mary's only just gone back to start the new term. I only just missed seeing her.'

Jenny chuckled, 'Ha, I thought it wouldn't be long before you got around to her.'

Mary was the daughter of Tom and his wife. A year younger than Jack she was a petite auburn haired young woman with an attractive outgoing personality. She was also an intelligent girl having completed a degree in education before qualifying as a primary school teacher. Jack had known Mary since they were both children and they had become very close over the years, always able to share confidences with each other, but perceived each other simply as good friends.

In recent years both sets of parents had quietly entertained hopes that the relationship between the pair would develop into something more but these hopes faded when Jack joined the army and he was forced to be away from home for the last few years.

Jack knew that Mary was no longer living at home. She was now teaching at a school some distance away and rented a small apartment close to her school only returning to her parents' home during holiday times. Even then she often preferred to stay at her apartment to socialise with her circle of friends.

When Jack said he was looking forward to seeing Mary it was a complete understatement. His body ached with anticipation as he realised just how much he had been missing her.

Tom gave Jack a knowing look, a slight smile playing on his face. 'She's fine, but very busy. She's really caught up in her career and doing very well. Yeah, I know,' he said with a laugh, 'I'm her dad so I am going to brag about her aren't I?'

'Any idea when she's likely to be coming back home?' said Jack adopting a feigned casual tone, 'It would be nice to catch up.'

'Not really sure, Jack,' said Tom. 'She's a bit of a loose cannon but there's a good chance she'll come home at half term in October. She knows you're back home now so I think she would be looking forward to seeing you, too.'

He regarded Jack with a curious frown, 'Anyway, Jack, why am I telling you this. Surely you two keep in touch with each other?'

'No, I'm afraid not,' said Jack with a tinge of guilt. 'Don't know why, we just didn't get round to it. After all it's not as if we were engaged or anything, just close friends.'

Jenny intervened with a laugh, 'you are priceless Jack! Close friends indeed. Come on, admit it. You think the sun shines out of that girl. It's as plain as the nose on your face. Oh, and another thing. Every time she's come home while you've been away she's asked after you. Don't you realise she's crackers about you, too?'

'Oh shut up, Jen,' said Jack embarrassed. 'You don't know what you are talking about.'

'Yes, Jenny,' added her father, 'it's none of your business. You wouldn't want any of us making comments about you and Alistair would you?'

Alistair was Jenny's fiancé and worked in the same office. They had been courting for about two years, but had not yet made any plans for a wedding.

'All right, I'm sorry if I embarrassed you,' she said, rising from the table. 'Anyway, I have to get off to work now, enjoy your day everyone and good luck with your job hunting Jack.'

She gave Jack and her parents a quick peck on the cheek before sweeping out of the house to her car.

Chapter 2

Cyprus One Year Earlier

For the final year of his army service Jack was posted to Dhekelia, a British Overseas Territory, one of two sovereign base areas in Cyprus and close to the border with the Turkish occupied part of North Eastern Cyprus. The Royal Engineers camp was part of a garrison of British army units and the area, covering some eight square miles, included all the facilities of a modern town with a substantial population of civilians, and service wives and families.

The camp consisted of multi-story accommodation blocks, stores, workshops and transport centre. Much of the southern boundary faced the tourist area of Larnaca Bay with its rugged coastline of rocky sand dunes, hotels and beaches. The western boundary looked towards the towering grandeur of the distant Troodos Mountains.

Jack was in charge of the workshop, and with his team of engineers responsible for the care and maintenance of vital telecommunications equipment. He settled down well, enjoying the work which finished early each day because of the hot climate. Off-duty times were spent bathing in the nearby warm sea or relaxing at the officer's club. It had its own fenced-off private beach and there was a comfortable bar and lounge area.

One especially hot afternoon Jack wandered into the bar mopping his brow and flopped contentedly into a chair at a vacant table. A waiter came hurrying over to take his order for a cold beer and Jack glanced idly around the room nodding at several of the occupants he recognised.

He noticed a familiar face belonging to an officer of his own unit sitting nearby. It was Frank Delaney who served in the administration block. Jack had become acquainted with him soon after his arrival in Cyprus.

Frank looked over and waved with a smile, then rose from his table to join Jack.

'Hi, Jack, good to see you. It's a bit dead in here, needs livening up a bit.'

'See what you mean' replied Jack as he glanced around the room, 'It's bloody hot today isn't it. It's a relief to get out of uniform.'

'You can say that again,' responded Frank with a grin. 'Still, there are consolations,' he added reflectively holding his glass of ice cold beer aloft to savour its appearance with the condensation trickling down the outside of the glass.

Frank was about the same age as Jack, but a head shorter and with fair hair and bright blue eyes, in contrast to Jack's brown hair and dark eyes and complexion. He had a 'cut glass' accent having attended one of England's top public schools, but had been expelled for some undisclosed misdemeanour.

How he had been accepted as "officer material" was a mystery but probably explained by his easy manner and casual air of authority. His frivolous attitude to life was in complete contrast to Jack's who was more serious and down to earth. Nevertheless their opposing natures seemed to complement each other and over the course of the following few weeks they became firm friends.

One day when they were both off duty they drove up into the Troodos mountains in Frank's rented air conditioned car. Both were dressed leisurely in shorts and open necked shirts and wore baseball caps to protect themselves from the fierce rays of the sun.

They ascended the winding narrow road taking in the neat olive groves which slowly gave way to dense forests of cedars and pines. Steep valleys fell away from the roadside and at one place they saw a monastery seemingly perched precariously on the side of the mountain as if about to slide into the valley below.

A brooding dark cloud clung like a bishop's mitre to the mountain summit but the hot sun continued to beat down and the distant views shimmered in the heat.

'I don't know about you, Frank, but I'm ready for a cold drink,' said Jack

'Agreed,' replied Frank, 'I'll pull in at the next taverna.'

They passed a turnoff signposted *Makarios's tomb* and the *Kykkos* monastery but decided to avoid these attractions knowing that they would be thronging with tourists. Instead they pulled into one of the many roadside tavernas and made themselves comfortable at a wooden table sheltered by a vine covered awning. After ordering a Greek salad and a bottle of the local white wine they discussed their future hopes and dreams.

Jack said his aim was to look for a steady job, preferably in the science area, in a manner suited to his science degree but hopefully to progress into management.

'What about you, Frank?' said Jack. 'What do you intend to do? You told me that your family had a successful business in north Wales. Can't you get a piece of that?'

'Huh, a fine chance of that happening,' said Frank, his voice hardening.

'I don't get on with my parents, well, to be honest...' his voice trailed off momentarily before he continued, 'It's my father really. He has disowned me.' He stopped again and gave a short bitter laugh.

'I'm what is known as the black sheep of the family!'

'Oh, sorry to hear that Frank,' said Jack sympathetically. 'What on earth went wrong?'

'I'd rather not talk about it if you don't mind Jack. Just things that happened in the past and my father is not the forgiving type. In any case I'm not interested in spending the rest of my days running some miserable garden centre for a pittance and under the thumb of my father. I want a bit more excitement in my life and something that pays well, and I intend to get it as soon as I get out of this shower.'

Frank paused as if to weigh up carefully what he was going to say next.

He continued slowly, his voice serious and morose, 'I still have the best part of four years to do and I am sick and tired with this life. Just dreary duties day after day. I don't think I can put up with it much longer.'

'Why Frank, what do you have in mind?' said Jack, regarding his friend curiously.

Frank simply grinned and tapped his nose as if to say, 'You just wait, you'll find out.'

Jack laughed, 'You mean I'll find out that you've become a millionaire? I bet you'll just go home, marry some girl and settle down to a humdrum married life with two point four children and slippers.'

'No chance,' said Frank forcibly, 'anyway, you can talk, that's probably the way you'll end up.'

'OK,' said Jack laughingly, 'you're probably right and I'll wait to see you become a millionaire. Talking about married life I've never heard you mention any girlfriend. Is there one?'

'They come and go,' replied Frank dismissively, 'marriage is not on my list of priorities. What about you, Jack? I would have guessed you had somebody waiting in the wings.'

'No, not really,' responded Jack, 'there is a girl that I'm quite friendly with but it's nothing serious.'

After a few moments of silence Frank said, 'Enough of all that talk. Let's just enjoy ourselves now while we can.'

He raised his glass. 'Here's to us, Jack.'

'Yes, here's to us then, Frank,' responded Jack as they clinked glasses together. 'Here's to our success in the future, and our continued friendship.'

***

During the height of the scorching Cypriot summer the two friends arranged to go on leave to an even more scorching Cairo, an hour's flight away by Cyprus

Airways. They booked two single adjacent rooms at a small hotel near the centre of the noisy bustling city.

They arrived dressed casually, as they were prohibited from wearing uniform in the Egyptian republic. Both opted to wear wide brimmed straw hats to shield themselves from the fierce heat of the sun.

They spent the evening sipping ice-chilled Pimms under the shade of a date palm bordering a pool in the fashionable area of Gezira Island in the middle of the river Nile, easily reached by a bridge from the noisy town centre. As the fierce daytime sun faded and the evening started to cool, Frank glanced at his watch.

'It's early yet', he said, 'I wouldn't mind finding a bit of excitement. Let's go and find a night club of some sort. Who knows? We might get lucky,' he finished with a grin.

'Just watch out, Frank,' responded Jack with a warning glance, 'some of these bints can be a bit iffy, if you know what I mean.'

'Ah, you worry too much, Jack,' said Frank dismissively.

The streets of Cairo were still very noisy at that time of the evening, mainly from the loud cacophonous blasts of car horns which Egyptian drivers seemed to delight in more as a form of expression than for any specific reason.

They wandered randomly through the streets searching for a night club, or even just a late night bar where they could get a drink before returning to their hotel. The street noise began to subside as they strayed away from the main roads and into a labyrinth of poorly lit side streets. They turned another corner and spotted a red neon sign blinking on and off and illuminating some incomprehensible Arabic characters. Outside by the entrance was a board displaying photographs of scantily clad young women in various erotic poses.

As they stood ogling the board a short stout middle-aged man appeared as if out of nowhere and gave them an oily smirk. He was dressed in a dark European style suit with the exception of a red fez perched on his head.

'Ahlan wa sahlan, Hello and welcome gentlemen, come on in. There's no cover charge. I'm sure you will enjoy yourselves.'

Frank glanced enquiringly at Jack.

'Come on, Jack, let's give it a go, no harm in looking. We can easily leave if we don't like it.'

Jack regarded the garish frontage of the establishment with a strong feeling of apprehension, but there was a competing sense of anticipation which quickly gained the upper hand.

'OK,' he said, 'nothing ventured.'

They were ushered into a large dimly-lit room with a semi-circular stage projecting from one wall. It had curtains drawn behind, but it was the performance on the stage that met their eyes as they entered. Two young women were gyrating sensuously to the sound of eastern music, their bare abdomens undulating as they performed their version of the Middle Eastern belly dance. Their dark eyes, made up to look huge by the clever application of mascara, peered out from above their yashmaks.

The audience, consisting mainly of young Arab men, several dressed in their traditional gallibiyas, they took scant notice of the newcomers, their attention being firmly focused on the stage.

They were shown to a table near the stage. It had four chairs around it and no sooner had they sat down when two women appeared as if by magic and without waiting for an invitation lowered themselves into the two vacant places. They were of indeterminate age, heavily made up and exuded a strong aroma of cheap perfume. With the exception of the yashmaks, they were dressed similarly to the two stage performers.

Startled by their sudden appearance of the women the two friends just looked at them wide eyed, but before either could utter a word the woman next to Jack leaned towards him to expose an enticing vista of cleavage.

'Hello, Johnny,' she said in a low husky voice, heavily accented. 'My name is Jasmine. Would you like to buy us a drink?'

The question was superfluous as, without any visible summons, an unlabelled bottle was placed on the table by a large hairy hand extended by a similarly large hairy individual who had been hovering in the background. The other hand appeared and placed four glasses in front of them which were filled to the brim with a sparkling amber coloured fluid from the bottle.

There was a heavy, somehow cloying atmosphere about the place and Jack threw a warning glance towards Frank, who had a glass in his hand, his eyes glued to the floor show. The woman sitting next to Frank had her hand on his thigh.

Apart from the introductory mention of their dubious names, and addressing both Jack and Frank as 'Johnny', the women hardly spoke except for the odd comment to each other in Arabic. They kept refilling the glasses and sipping at them greedily each time and prompting the two young men to do the same.

28

The bottle was soon emptied without having any significant effect on them and Jack already had serious doubts about the alcohol content. Then he felt Jasmine's hand stroking the inside of his thigh.

'We'd better have another bottle of Champagne,' she murmured, and this time she waved her hand to the ever-present waiter who produced another bottle of the insipid brew, and the same ritual was repeated.

The floor show eventually finished for an interval, and the lights were dimmed even further, a signal for Jasmine to move her hand further up Jack's thigh and cover his crotch, producing an instant and involuntary arousal.

'The bottle's empty, Johnny. We must have another one.'

She was just about to beckon the hovering waiter when Jack's common sense suddenly came to the fore. He abruptly pushed her hand away.

'No! Sorry, but we don't want any more Champagne, do we, Frank.'

He kicked at his friend's leg under the table to warn him and prompt him back to reality. Frank looked startled at first but then realisation dawned and the message was understood. Alarm showed on Frank's face.

This was an Arab clip joint!

'No, we've had enough. We'd like to have the bill please.'

Jasmine looked surprised.

'Oh come on, Johnny,' she murmured seductively, 'we've hardly got started. Just think of the wonderful time we can have later.'

She thrust her face no more than a few inches from his and her wide brown eyes bore into him as if to confirm the promise.

Both women tried to work their charms, offering false promises of later delights, but Jack ignored them and turned to beckon the waiter. This was clearly part of a familiar scenario and the two women rose wordlessly from their chairs and disappeared through a door by the side of the stage.

A scrap of paper was jammed down on the table in front of them on which a figure was scrawled. Of course it was an exorbitant sum, artificially inflated by the pretext that they had been supplied with genuine expensive Champagne instead of a local cheap sparkling wine, heavily diluted. The amount was far more than they could possibly raise between them.

The waiter hovered belligerently in front of them as Jack looked desperately at Frank.

'What are we going to do?' he murmured out of the side of his mouth. 'We can't pay this amount and this doesn't look like the sort of place where they'll let you do the washing up instead.'

Frank looked around towards the door that they had come in at earlier. There were now two burly-looking men standing one each side of the exit.

'There's only one thing we can do. Make a run for it. There are two other doors. One where those two women went and there must be another one at the back of those curtains. Let's take a chance with the curtains. When I say 'now!''

With their hearts pounding they made pretence of getting some money out to pay the bill. Then Frank said softly, 'now!'

They jumped up from the table upending their chairs and raced onto the stage and through the red velvet curtains at the back, hearing the sudden shouts of the waiter and the two heavies as they charged after them. The curtains covered an opening leading to a kind of hallway with several doors on each side.

The first door on their right was slightly ajar. They pushed it open and rushed in to see the two belly dancers and their two erstwhile companions sitting at a table drinking coffee. The women looked up startled, then they screamed, frightened that they were about to be attacked. They jumped up from the table, spilling hot coffee everywhere, and backed away from the two young men.

There were several chairs scattered untidily around and Frank grabbed the nearest jamming it under the doorknob as the noise of running feet and shouting followed close on their heels. The door started to shake and vibrate as unseen hands tried to wrestle it open.

Looking around desperately they could see only one escape route. A window on the far side of the room, but it was closed. They rushed over to it but it was jammed solid. Evidently it had not been opened for years. In desperation Jack grabbed one of the chairs and holding it in front of him he charged at the window shattering the glass and splintering the frame leaving the remnants hanging drunkenly.

Flinging the chair aside they scrambled over the window sill and jumped down to the other side landing on some rubbish bins, toppling them over to clatter and roll noisily on the ground, spilling out their foul-smelling contents.

It was almost pitch black but they could see that they were in a passageway at the back of the night club. The shouts suddenly grew louder as one of the women pulled the restraining chair away from the door and the pursuers charged in the room, heading for the window. Jack and Frank could see some bright lights at one end of the passage, hopeful signs of civilisation and anonymity. They frantically disentangled themselves from the foul-smelling mess and ran as fast as they could in that direction.

They emerged into a brightly lit thoroughfare then stopped, panting heavily and listening frantically for any signs of pursuit. But there was no sound. Their pursuers had evidently given up the chase as futile. Nevertheless, just to be sure, they walked quickly to put as much distance between themselves and the scene of their adventure as possible.

They had no idea what part of the city they were in but there were some passing cars and so they were confident that there would be a few taxis about. They waited by the roadside until one came along and they waved it down. The driver looked out at them but as they approached the cab an expression of alarm crossed his face. He waved his arms wildly at them and shouted something in Arabic as if to tell them to clear off, and accelerated away into the distance.

'What the—!' gasped Jack. He looked round at Frank and was surprised to see him grinning all over his face.

'It's us, Jack. Not only do we look as if we've just come through the gates of hell, we stink! It was all that rubbish we landed in. Just look at us. We look a real sight.'

It was true. Their clothes were still covered in the remains of rotting food, some of which was smeared on their hands and faces. Their hair was wet with perspiration and plastered down across their faces.

'There's nothing else for it, Jack. We're going to have to find our hotel ourselves. Come on, look on the bright side. What would have happened to us if they'd have caught us?'

Jack grinned back, 'You're not joking! And what about those two women? Bloody hell, we'd have to be pretty desperate to have gone off with either of those two!'

They strolled casually along the pavement laughing and joking about their experience now that the crisis had passed, but keeping a watchful eye out, and hoping that they would stumble into an area that they would recognise.

'Hey, what's this coming?' said Jack pointing to a lone figure coming in their direction on a bicycle.

It was a man, obviously an Egyptian wearing a suit but with the inevitable fez on his head. He had a black beard but no moustache and was loudly singing a song in Arabic. Jack held out his hand and the cyclist wobbled to a halt and grinned happily at the two. For a moment they thought that he might have been drunk but he regarded them soberly for a few moments then his face took on a look of concern. He spoke in English and with only a trace of accent.

'You are English yes? You look as if you've been in trouble, is that right?'

Frank sighed with relief, ignoring the slight detail that in fact he was Welsh.

'Yes, we have been in trouble and we are lost. Perhaps you could tell us the way to our hotel.'

The cyclist nodded his head and proceeded to give them precise directions. It would only be a twenty minutes' walk from where they were at the moment. After he described the route he continued in a serious vein.

'I work at the offices of British Airways. I work with the British and I can usually recognise British servicemen, even when they look like you two do at the moment. You'd be surprised how many of them get into trouble when they come to this city. If you are staying here for any length of time I would advise you to be very careful.'

'I think we've learned our lesson,' said Frank ruefully. 'We really don't know how to thank you. You've been really helpful.'

The cyclist smiled at them. 'Enjoy the rest of your stay, but remember what I've said.'

He waved and went on his way, picking up his song from where he had left it.

The front door was locked when they reached their hotel but they summonsed the night porter by ringing the bell. He opened the door and let them in, wrinkling his nose at them as they brushed quickly past and hastened to their separate rooms. They lost no time in casting off their foul clothing to lay contentedly, eyes shut, soaking in steaming hot baths.

They spent the rest of their leave following the usual tourist trail. The Egyptian museum with its indescribable Tutankhamen exhibits, then the Sphinx and Pyramids sited just outside the city centre. One day they took a taxi down to Memphis, the ancient capital of Egypt, and the burial chambers of Saqqara with its many tombs including the five thousand years old Step Pyramid of the pharaoh Djoser.

'Whew,' said Frank after a particularly active day, 'I've got culture leaking out of my ears. Can't wait to retire to the bar for a long cold beer.'

***

An unfortunate feature of life at the base was the theft of items from the *NAAFI* with its stocks of tobacco, alcohol, and other valuable items from the supermarket section where items of electronic equipment, such as computers and cameras were prized items on the black market. The thieving took a more serious turn however when some rifles and ammunition started to go missing from the camp armoury. All these buildings were securely locked when not occupied and subjected to frequent guard patrols.

All camps in the base area employed many civilians particularly in food areas such as the NAAFI and general catering. Civilian workers outnumbered military personnel in the base and were thought to be the main culprits but all possibilities were being considered. Arrests were made throughout the base area from time to time but the charges were usually trivial, relating to no more than the stealing of petty cash, cigarettes and other minor items. There had been no evidence of any background organisation, just opportunist thefts carried out by individuals.

All the buildings in the camp were connected by a network of roads but they were widely spaced on flat terrain covered with dense scrub. The whole perimeter was floodlit and separate security lighting was fitted to the entrances of all buildings so intrusion from the outside seemed unlikely, particularly as the perimeter boundary had been minutely examined and appeared to allow no means of access.

Extra patrols were consequently organised and within a week of returning from leave Jack was ordered to command a Saturday night patrol. He was given a group of three other men, Sergeant Smith, Corporal Benson, and Sapper Brown. They were all equipped with L2A3 Sterling sub machine guns, hand held AN/PRC-148 radios for communication with each other, and powerful flashlights.

Sergeant Smith was an experienced soldier and tended to look critically upon young officers. He quite liked Jack Blake however and had to admit that he was a very capable young man.

The instructions were clear; the areas at risk must be patrolled in a highly visual manner to deter potential raiders. The patrol should remain together as any separation was deemed to be dangerous if the raiders were armed.

Jack decided on his own initiative to try a different approach which he explained to his group in a short briefing.

'Our patrols haven't had much effect so far,' he said, 'the thieves seem to know when and where they are and time their operations accordingly. It's as if they know the camp procedures. Just think of all the space there is here between buildings, it takes ages to get from one building to another. I want to try a different approach. I would like to catch the blighters, not just frighten them off.'

'Right Sergeant,' continued Jack turning to Sergeant Smith, 'I want you to take cover near the NAAFI building with Sapper Brown. There is an outbuilding about thirty yards from the NAAFI main entrance where you can position yourselves in its shadow. It should allow you to overlook both the main front entrance and the rear door. If you see anything at all keep hidden and inform me over the radio immediately and I will decide on what to do. Corporal Benson and I will concentrate on the quartermaster stores and the armoury next door.'

Sergeant Smith looked dubious. 'Excuse me, sir, but isn't that going against our orders?'

Jack shook his head, 'Not really, Sergeant,' he said, 'the orders are provisional and I think we have enough scope to use our initiative here. Don't worry, I will take full responsibility if there were to be any repercussions. Oh, and another thing,' he added, turning his attention to the other two men, 'don't try stepping out in full view and shouting that 'halt who goes there' crap. These bastards could be armed and if they see you in the moonlight they'll blow your fucking head off as soon as you open your mouth!'

The moon was in its first quarter, eerily outlining the buildings against the star spangled sky, the all-pervading silence broken only by the incessant chirping of the crickets. Because of the vastness of the camp area there was little artificial lighting except around the main perimeter and the entrance to the more important buildings including the NAAFI.

In the early hours of the morning a silver coloured van was seen to move slowly into view from Sgt Smith's and Sapper Brown's position near the NAAFI building. It was clearly visible in the bright moonlight and was being driven slowly. Traffic of any sort would be rarely seen at that time on a Saturday night so Smith immediately reported the sighting to Jack Blake. Jack told them to stay under cover until he and Corporal Benson could join them.

The van came to a stop and two shadowy figures emerged and approached the rear entrance which was in the moon's shadow and could not be clearly seen from the patrol's position.

'I recognise that van sir,' said Sgt Smith when Jack and Benson had joined them. 'It's the Mercedes Benz Sprinter that the NAAFI manager normally uses.'

'Yes, I think you're right, Sergeant,' said Jack. 'Could be that someone's hijacked it for the night.'

'We can't see the rear entrance from here, sir,' said Sgt Smith. 'They must have entered the building so they must have known the entry code for the door lock.'

'Quick, let's get over there now while they are still inside but I don't want them to see us,' said Jack urgently. 'I want to give them sufficient time to actually put whatever they've got into their car, and for God's sake keep quiet. They mustn't hear us approach from where they are inside.'

Jack's patrol quickly doubled to the building and took position in the shadows near the robber's car and from where they could see the now wide open door. The patrol waited their guns cocked and ready, the tension showing on their perspiring faces.

After what seemed to be an interminable time the two men emerged from the building carrying several boxes of goods intent on heading back towards their car. They had left the NAAFI door open so they clearly intended to return.

'Shouldn't we just grab them now, sir?' whispered Sgt Smith.

Jack raised his finger in an expression of caution, before whispering back. 'Wait until they have put the goods in their van, Sergeant.'

The two figures were seen to place the various items into their van and then start to return to the NAAFI.

'Stop!' shouted Jack from his concealed position, 'Stay where you are!'

He turned on his flashlight and directed the beam towards the two men. He could see that they were apparently civilians wearing hooded jackets which covered their heads and much of their faces.

The abrupt command and the blinding light caused the men to stop and to look around frantically to see where the shout had come from. They turned and started to run back to their car.

'Stop!' bellowed Jack again.' Stop now or you will be shot!'

The warning had the desired effect.

Both men froze in their tracks and raised their hands as they turned to face their captors.

Jack approached the two men cautiously in case they were armed, followed by the rest of his patrol. He gave them a quick body search as his patrol kept them covered but they seemed to be unarmed then he pulled off their hoods to reveal their stricken faces. A strangled gasp escaped Jack's lips as he recognised the men, both of whom lived and worked on the base. Andreas Christakos was the civilian manager of the NAAFI and Dimitri, his younger brother, worked as an assistant in the Administration department.

'Andreas,' he said at last, his face twisted by puzzlement and confusion, 'and you, Dimitri, what the hell's going on here? You've been caught red-handed with stolen goods. Do you realise how serious this is?'

Christakos remained silent, a mixed expression of defiance and remorse on his face as he glared back at Jack.

'You realise that you have betrayed your position as a senior employee at this camp,' said Jack, 'I have no option but to hand you all over to the appropriate authorities and you will be charged accordingly. In the meantime you will be escorted to the guardroom and held until you are arrested. Have you anything to say for yourself now?'

Christakos shook his head then, surprisingly a slow smirk crept across his face.

'Yes, Mr Blake,' he said. 'It's true you have caught us red-handed but if you do arrest us there are things that will come out that will be very embarrassing for the British army here. I know that you will be reporting this to the orderly officer when we get to the guardroom but I suggest that you let me talk to him before you do anything more.'

'Embarrassing for the British army?' responded Jack. 'What the hell do you mean? Anyway it doesn't matter what you've got to say. You have been caught red-handed in the course of robbery from NAAFI stores. You can say whatever you've got to say to the orderly officer before we hand you over to the Base police.' He turned to Sergeant Smith, 'Sergeant, escort these men to the guardroom and—'

His voice was cut off as Christakos uttered a strangled low cry and crumpled to the ground.

Sergeant Smith moved quickly to the prone figure.

'Sir,' he rasped urgently, 'Christakos has been shot! There's blood coming from his head.'

There was a loud cry of anguish from Dimitri who rushed over to the prone figure of Christakos.

'Andreas! Oh God, no, Andreas!'

'Everyone stay low, don't move,' ordered Jack.

'He is my brother,' moaned Dimitri.

Jack's first action was to phone the camp medical officer, then the orderly officer from the list of emergency numbers he routinely carried when on duty. The orderly officer immediately ordered the base to be sealed, emphasising that nobody was to be allowed to exit the base until further orders. He then rang the emergency number of the commanding officer, Lieutenant Colonel Maynard, who lived with his family several miles away.

'I'll be there forthwith,' said Maynard after the Orderly officer had told him the news.

In the meantime Jack and Corporal Benson were ordered to remain at the scene until further orders, but for Sergeant Smith and Sapper Brown to escort the distraught figure of Dimitri to the guardroom to await custody by the Base Police.

The Medical Officer arrived quickly at the scene shortly followed by the Orderly Officer. It was quickly ascertained that the cause of death was by a single gunshot wound to the head.

Christakos had been murdered.

When Colonel Maynard arrived he immediately declared the area as a crime scene and ordered that nothing must be touched or disturbed. The first priority was to contact the Provost Marshal's department at the Garrison's Royal Military police headquarters informing them of the situation and stressing its urgency.

Several officers from the special investigation branch of the Military police arrived in due course. Captain Hague, the senior officer, introduced himself to Colonel Maynard and told him formally that the military police would be taking charge of the investigation. Hague assured him of their full cooperation and that any of his personnel would be made available for interrogation.

Hague's first action was to order a thorough search of the area. He then rang the Base hospital to arrange for the removal of Christakos's body to the morgue and to await a post mortem.

Colonel Maynard turned towards Jack. 'OK, Lieutenant Blake, well done tonight. It's unfortunate that it's ended in this way, but you and Corporal Benson can go off duty now but you and the rest of your patrol will have to keep yourselves available in the morning for interview by these officers.

Jack was in a sombre mood after the night's events. He could barely believe what had happened. He tried to snatch a few hours of sleep but with the appalling events of the night playing on his mind he was restless.

The following morning Jack was summoned to the administration block to face Captain Hague where he gave a full account of the night's events leading up to the shooting of Christakos.

'I understand that there was no indication of where the shot came from, and you heard nothing, is that right, Lieutenant?' said Hague.

'There was no sign of there being anyone else around,' replied Jack, 'the shot must have come from a silenced weapon.'

'Yes, that's obvious,' said Hague. 'We have to await the Coroner's report and of course the bullet will go to our forensic unit to identify the type of weapon that was used. We do know that the shot man, Andreas Christakos, with his brother, Dimitri, was in the process of carrying out a theft from the NAAFI stores.'

Hague paused before adding reflectively, 'This is something of a problem for us at these bases. People have been arrested but usually they seem to be opportunist thefts with no real suggestion of any sort of network or organisation.'

'I'm just shocked,' said Jack. 'I've got to know The Christakos brothers over the past few months. I liked them both and would never have thought that they would be involved with this kind of activity.'

'No,' replied Hague, 'you never can tell what people will do if there is a fat payment behind it. Anyway Lieutenant, you've been very helpful. You will be required to attend a court of enquiry but now you can relax and enjoy what's left of the day. Incidentally I have already spoken to the other members of your patrol, but we've not really been able to come up with anything new.'

Later as Hague sat in Colonel Maynard's office they discussed the night's events.

'My men have carried out a thorough search of the area but fruitless I'm afraid,' said Hague. 'We have a rough idea of the direction the shot came from judging by where Christakos was standing and the position of the entry wound. We believe it came from a small storeroom about a hundred meters away so it was almost certainly a high powered weapon that was used, although that will be ascertained by the forensic examination of the bullet. The storeroom does have a very convenient window facing in the right direction but the door was locked as it usually is. It looks as if the shooting was carefully planned, and that brings us to another very significant point. The first thing we did was to check with the guardroom whether anybody had either entered of left in the time leading up to the shooting. They said that one of your officers, Lieutenant Delaney, had driven out only a few minutes before the base was sealed and he seemed to be in a bit of a hurry. He was driving his rented car, well known to the guards, and he was dressed in civilian clothes as he was off duty. The only unusual feature was the time of night. Four o'clock on a Sunday morning is not a time that most people choose to go out.'

'My God,' said the Colonel, 'surely not one of my officers. Of course you have my permission to check his quarters, but I can't believe that Lieutenant Delaney has anything to do with this. He was off duty and free to come and go as he wishes. He is on duty tomorrow so he should be coming back to the base sometime today. If not then he would absent without leave and that would give us grave cause for concern considering the circumstances.'

'We can't delay, sir,' said Hague. 'We must start looking for him immediately. If he returns here then well and good but if he is responsible for the shooting he would certainly desert and go into hiding. I will start that process now.'

Colonel Maynard nodded resignedly. 'Yes you're right of course, Captain. Please do whatever you need to do.'

'Another thing,' added Hague, 'We have searched the civilian accommodation where Christakos and his brother lived but nothing was found. Whatever goods they were stealing were obviously disposed of very quickly. It would be particularly easy for Christakos because as the NAAFI Manager he would often collect supplies from the base central supply depot. He would obviously know the security keywords for the doors and he had use of the Mercedes van for his day to day duties. The van has been examined and was found to have a cleverly concealed partition in the floor where they would have stored their stolen property. It wouldn't be difficult to find someone in the area willing to do this kind of work for a price.'

'I would assume that Christakos disposed of the stolen goods by just driving out of the base with them concealed in the van and taking them to sell outside, possibly in Larnaca or Nicosia.'

'I agree,' said Colonel Maynard. 'Vehicles drive in and out of the base all the time and it would be impractical to stop and check every one. Military personnel and civilian employees in positions of trust such as Christakos would not normally be checked as they would be recognised by the guard. They would be used to seeing him driving in laden with fresh supplies.'

News of the night's events spread quickly throughout the base and when Jack got to know of Frank's absence he was devastated. The only possible reason for this is that Frank must also have been involved in the thefts from the base and that he had killed Christakos to prevent him talking. But that didn't make a lot of sense. Surely running away would implicate him anyway. There had to be more to it than that.

Jack shook his head in frustration. How could Frank have been involved with such criminal behaviour and yet give no hint of his activities. In spite of their friendship Jack knew that Frank was a bit of a wild card but surely not capable of cold blooded murder.

In the evening Jack headed for the mess where groups of officers were standing around talking. As soon as he entered several of his fellow officers came over to discuss the night's events. He was complimented on his actions in stopping the robbery and arresting Dimitri but it was the shooting of Andreas that received the most attention. Everyone knew the Christakos brothers and they were well liked both by the military and the other civilian employees at the base.

He ended the evening a little bit tipsy as drink after drink was bought for him, and eventually he was glad to escape the constant attention.

The following day Jack received a message that Colonel Maynard would like to see him. He approached the CO's door, knocked and entered in response to the peremptory voice commanding him to enter. He saluted, and stood to attention in front of the Colonel who regarded him quizzically for a few moments.

'Relax, Lieutenant Blake. I just wanted an informal word with you. Captain Hague interviewed you yesterday and you gave him a written report of your patrol's activities leading up to those tragic events. I understand that you decided to interpret your orders in a rather more inventive way than those given you. That's correct, isn't it, Lieutenant?'

'Yes, sir, I decided to take a course of action that would be more effective for catching them.'

'Lieutenant Blake, there is a very thin line between being court martialled for disobeying orders and being commended for initiative. This time you've been lucky and your action has resulted in the apprehension of two criminals, even though unfortunately one of them has lost his life. If the four members of your patrol had stayed together it's quite possible that you would have been in another part of the base and you would not have been in the vicinity of the NAAFI to apprehend these men. The other aspect of this sorry business is that Christakos would still be alive but you can hardly be blamed for that.'

'No, sir,' responded Jack, 'but I don't feel very happy about it, and I am worried about Lieutenant Delaney. I think you know that he's a friend of mine.'

'Yes, I know that Blake, but that is a mystery which still has to be cleared up. Unfortunately he has not reported for duty today and he has not returned to the base so now he is absent without leave. I'm sorry that he is a friend of yours but things do not look very good for him. If he did do the shooting then he almost certainly has deserted and if caught could be on a murder charge.'

The Colonel then visibly relaxed as he smiled, saying, 'Lieutenant Blake you've had a stressful time over the past day or two and I commend you for the way you carried out your duties. I will see you in the mess tonight, if you will invite me of course, and I would be happy to buy you a drink.'

Back in Canterbury a headline in the local paper read:

Greek Cypriot civilian killed and another one arrested while attempting to raid British army camp. Local officer was in charge of patrol which led to the capture.

Fred Blake started to read the article with marginal interest until his eyes lighted on his son's name and he jumped up excitedly.

'Dora, come and look at this! It's about our Jack.'

Of course, the description of events that night were grossly exaggerated and distorted and there was no mention of Frank Delaney due to tight censorship by the Ministry of Defence.

The shooting of Christakos coupled with the disappearance of Delaney initiated an intense search of the sovereign base area. His abandoned rental car was soon found but it gave no hint as to his whereabouts. Forensic examination of the bullet that had killed Christakos showed it to be from a Kalashnikov automatic weapon fired as a single shot.

The weeks and months passed without Frank Delaney being found. He had effectively vanished from the Island in spite of all the intensive efforts to locate him.

Jack's life otherwise proceeded uneventfully until the time came for him to return home for demobilisation. He arrived back in the UK fit and well and deeply tanned from the Mediterranean sun but still deeply troubled by that night's events.

Chapter 3
Delaney

The Delaney family lived in a modest mansion in the leafy setting of rural North Wales. They were a prosperous family thanks to a string of garden centres distributed throughout the Lleyn peninsular and Anglesey. The family's Irish name had been inherited from the family's forebears who had crossed the Irish Sea a generation earlier.

The family was headed by Patrick Delaney, a short robust cold man with thinning fair hair and piercing blue eyes. His wife, Dorothy, a slim attractive woman, was devoted to her husband but had a warmer character.

Frank was the middle member of the family, with an older brother Cyril, and a younger sister, Rose, but he was regarded by his parents as the least achieving one. There was no doubt that Cyril and Rose were the favourites.

Cyril had gone to university after leaving public school and had succeeded in passing a degree in business studies with first class honours. He now ran the company head office in Caernarvon. Cyril was very much like his father but Rose, heading for a career in medicine, was an attractive girl and close to her mother in character.

From the very start Frank had been a disappointment. He had been a troublesome boy in his earlier years, getting into frequent fights with other boys and showed a rebellious streak at his prep school.

He was expected to enter the family business eventually to join his brother and, in accordance with family custom, was enrolled at Buckinghurst, the prestigious public school attended by his forebears.

His academic achievements at the school, while not outstanding, were reasonably satisfactory for a while. He settled down well and his wild nature seemed to become subdued. He now got on well with other boys and his athletic build gave him a considerable advantage in sporting activities so he was a popular choice for the school cricket and rugby teams.

Inevitably this humdrum way of life began to bore Frank towards the end of his school life. He was maturing into a young man and anxious to get out into the real world to make his mark. He knew that he was attractive to the opposite sex and had already made conquests with some of the local girls but such extra-curricular activities cost rather more than his meagre allowance could support.

Consequently he tried to augment the shortfall by making frequent trips to the local bookmakers but this did not produce the required results so he quickly found himself in debt to local shopkeepers who had given him credit. By itself this was not unusual as it was the custom for the shopkeepers to give Buckinghurst schoolboys credit for short periods as they knew that the debts would be settled when they received their monthly allowances.

It quickly became clear in Frank's case that this was not going to happen. When he defaulted the shopkeepers complained to the Headmaster.

Frank was duly summonsed to the head's study and quizzed as to why he had incurred the debts but he simply shook his head saying, 'I just don't understand it sir. I suppose I just lost track of how I was spending my allowance. I'll be more careful in the future.'

'Well Delaney,' said the Head sternly, 'I am not very convinced about that as an explanation but in any case I think you need to have a word with your father. I have telephoned him and you are to ring him back now.'

Frank groaned inwardly. He could just imagine what his father would say and he would probably have a very good idea about the reasons for Frank's cash shortage.

It was as he expected. His father ranted at him at length, and warned him to curb his expenditure and show some responsibility; otherwise he would be taken away from the school.

This did not deter Frank in the least. He felt no sense of shame about his actions and so he started to think of other ways of supplementing his income.

One day the school was due to play an important cricket match with St Peters school in the next county and Buckinghurst was the visiting school. It was a long ride by private coach on a hot summer's day and they were glad to reach their destination where they were given refreshments in the cricket pavilion. Afterwards, in the joint changing room, Frank noticed that one of the boys of the home team slipped a high end mobile phone into his school jacket pocket before hanging it up on one of the pegs.

The home team won the toss and Buckinghurst had to field first. Then during his team's innings, Frank, batting at number three, was bowled out for a respectable score and he walked back to join the rest of the team on the veranda outside the changing room.

After changing his pads he excused himself briefly and went into the changing room on the pretext of getting a towel to mop his brow as it was such a hot day. There was nothing unusual about this as boys would often go in and out of the changing room during the match to retrieve various items.

The room was deserted and Frank went straight to the jacket, took out the mobile phone, and pocketed it in his white trousers before re-joining his team on the veranda.

After the match he showered then swiftly rolled up his white cricket gear and put it in his holdall, then moved out of the pavilion to board the coach back to school. He tensed as he waited for the rest of the team, expecting to hear an outcry from the changing room but all seemed to carry on normally.

The coach moved off and Frank relaxed as he realised he had got away with it. He knew the phone was top of the range and he was sure that he would get a good price for it. However, when the coach pulled into the school gates he was shocked to see the headmaster and several of the housemasters waiting outside the main entrance. The headmaster boarded the coach as it came to rest, his face grim.

'I'm afraid we've had a serious complaint from the headmaster at St. Peters school. He phoned me to tell me that one of the boys in their team has reported that his mobile phone has gone missing. He remembered quite clearly putting it in his jacket before the match but it had gone when he changed later on after the match. They have carried out a thorough search of the premises and the other boy's possessions but without success. Obviously I am reluctant to believe that anyone here could be responsible but I have to ask you on your honour as members of Buckinghurst School if anyone knows anything about it.'

There were murmurs of protest from the assembled boys, and George Clayton, the team captain spoke up on behalf of them all.

'None of our team would do anything like that, sir,' he said, 'we visit other schools a lot and there's never been any complaints until now. I'm sure it must be some kind of mistake. Perhaps he didn't have the phone with him in the first place. I bet it turns up.'

The Headmaster grunted, 'I hope you are right Clayton. I wouldn't want to go to the lengths of having you all searched.' He turned and left the coach abruptly.

Frank's heart was beating fast. That was a narrow escape, he thought. However he had forgotten that it was customary for the captain to collect all the whites for laundry. George Clayton stood up and shouted, 'right lads, don't forget to leave your gear in the basket outside the coach as you get off.'

As they all fumbled in their holdalls to pull out their cricket whites Frank wondered desperately how he could transfer the phone from the pocket of his white trousers without being observed. Perhaps with a bit of manipulation he could get it out while his hand was hidden by the holdall then simply leave it in the bag.

But it wasn't that easy as the trousers were tightly rolled up and he had to fumble for some time before he could get his hand in the pocket. He felt the hard outline of the phone and gripped it firmly then he let it fall randomly inside his holdall as he pulled out the trousers followed by his shirt and finally his socks. As he pulled out the second sock the phone had somehow got caught in it and it came flying out of the bag and landed on the coach floor in full sight of everyone.

For a few moments there was a stunned silence as the boys all looked first at the now dormant phone and then at Frank's flushed face. Finally George Clayton spoke up, his voice bitter and accusing.

'My God, is that the phone that went missing and that everyone's been looking for? You took it didn't you Delaney?'

He bent down to pick up the phone which appeared to have suffered no damage. Then his voice turned to anger, 'so that's what you are, a petty thief! You've let the school down and us, your team mates. We'll be lucky to get invited to play against another school ever again. Come with me to the headmaster now!'

Clayton grabbed Frank's arm and jostled him down the aisle of the coach towards the exit to shouts of 'Get out Delaney, stinking thief!'

He was violently pushed from behind causing him to stumble and fall face forward onto the hard floor.

Clayton shouted, 'There's no need for that! He'll get his just deserts. Just let him get off the bus.'

Inevitably Frank was severely reprimanded by a red-faced headmaster and summarily expelled from the school. His parents were notified and his father arrived on the same day to collect him. He stood confronting his son, his voice trembling with fury.

'So, you've turned out to be a common thief. You have disgraced our family name and you have disgraced this school, a school that this family has served with honour. That honour is now lost forever. I will never forgive you for this and you can forget any further support from me. You are on your own. You can stay at the house until you find a job, then I want you out. Is that clear?'

Frank nodded glumly. He knew that he had done wrong but he was incapable of feeling guilty. His mistake was in being caught. All's fair in love and war, he thought, and he knew that if he ever saw a chance to make a quick profit again then he would take advantage of it, no matter who got hurt.

In any case he was nearing the end of his school life so he felt little sorrow at leaving a bit sooner than intended, but the prospect of finding a job and earning a living was a different proposition. His aim had been to sponge off his family while looking for a lucrative source of income not involving too much hard work. That idea was now a non-starter so what prospects did he have now?

He decided to apply to Sandhurst Military Academy, an idea supported by his father who simply wanted to get rid of him as soon as possible. He was just old enough at seventeen to be eligible and fortunately his privileged education was a strong asset. His recent misdemeanour was kept quiet as his recent school didn't want that kind of publicity, and so he was accepted for training as a cadet.

Time went by uneventfully and he was popular with his fellow cadets. He also did well in his training and in due course received his commission and posted to a Royal Engineers unit at Catterick Garrison.

His military career progressed unremarkably, his only successes as usual being on the rugby and cricket fields, but as time went on he again became restless. His desire for more excitement in his life stretched his army pay. One area where he did achieve success however was with several of the young ladies who lived near the Garrison who found him to be an amusing and attractive personality.

After some two years of uneventful army service and with a further five years to go of his seven years enlistment Frank received a posting to the Dhekelia Garrison in Cyprus to work at the Royal Engineers base.

He soon became bored with sitting behind a desk dealing with mountains of paperwork and yearned for some form of escape. Although he had a gregarious nature he had no close friends. He found most of his fellow officers to be only interested in the army and in furthering their careers.

He managed to put up with this boredom for a year but then his level of malcontent increased to the point where he longed to find a way of escaping the army altogether. The opportunity to do this came along almost by accident.

In his off duty times Frank liked to get away from the British controlled zone and go to the tourist area at the coast near Larnaca. He particularly liked a hotel near the beach where he would sit with a cold beer and chat to the resident tourists.

One off duty day as he was sitting in his usual favourite spot near the window a middle aged man entered the bar and sat down at an adjacent table. He ordered a lager from a hovering waiter then raised the glass in Frank's direction, smiled and said conversationally, 'I've been waiting all day for this. It's like a furnace outside. You here on holiday?'

Frank smiled back saying, 'No such luck. I'm in the army.'

'Should have known,' said the man, 'in fact you look like a typical British army officer, I'm right aren't I?'

'God, is it that obvious,' replied Frank laughingly, 'yes, I'm in the army but I do like to get away whenever I can. Hey, come and join me. It's nice to chat with someone, particularly a fellow Brit who I assume is not in the army?'

The man took his beer and shuffled over to Frank's table.

'No, I'm too fat, old and bald for that lark,' he said affably. 'My name's Len by the way-Len Parker. I live here near Larnaca.'

'My name's Frank, Frank Delaney,' responded Frank.

The two men chatted away casually for a while, exchanging their varying points of view over the Island and its various areas of interest.

'You got much longer to serve then Frank?' said Parker casually.

'I've got a few years to go yet,' replied Frank, but there was a note of bitterness in his voice that Len was quick to pick up on.

'You don't seem to be too happy about it,' he said. 'Can I ask why?'

'I was stupid enough to sign up for seven years most of which I still have to serve, and I hate it. Day after day I sit at a desk filling in forms. It's so boring. I just want a way out to do something more exciting.'

Parker was silent for a few moments and regarded Frank reflectively,

'You work in the admin office at the Royal Engineers base,' he ventured. 'You must find that very dull.'

Frank looked up at Len sharply. 'How do you know that?'

Len smiled knowingly. 'There's not a lot I don't know about what goes on in this neck of the woods. I do happen to know something about you from a friend of mine who works with you.'

Realisation suddenly dawned on Frank. This was a setup!

'You've contrived this meeting, haven't you?' he said accusingly. 'Why, what earthly interest can you have in me?'

'Yes, I admit it,' replied Parker in a contrite tone. 'I do know a lot about you, and for very good reasons which may be to your advantage. Do you want to continue this conversation at my house?'

Why would Parker be interested in me, thought Frank? And how could Parker possibly know that he was going to be here at this particular time, and what was it that could be to his advantage? His curiosity aroused, he decided that there could be no harm in at least finding out what Parker had to say to him.

'We'll go in my car,' said Parker after Frank had agreed to accompany him. 'I'll bring you back here to collect yours after we've had our chat. 'That OK with you?'

Parker's house turned out to be a villa perched high up and overlooking Larnaca bay. Frank gasped in astonishment as they drew up in the drive.

'That's some house,' exclaimed Frank, 'you must be doing pretty well to have a place like that.'

'I don't do too badly,' responded Parker, 'and you too could have something like this if you take up my offer,' he added meaningfully.

Parker led Frank through the house and to an outside terrace by a large swimming pool. There were steps leading down to a small anchorage where Parker told him that he had a powerful boat moored. The house, the mention of the boat, and the open topped BMW car that Parker had used to drive them, were all deliberate attempts to impress Frank, and possibly soften him up for what he intended to propose.

Parker poured them two ice cold beers and they made themselves comfortable at a table overlooking the bay. As a major holiday destination Larnaca bay was alive with all kinds of tourist activity, with boats of all descriptions, water skiers, and wind surfers.

It all had an almost hypnotic effect on Frank. This was the kind of life he dreamed of. Sheer luxury and indulgence.

But how? Was this man about to offer him that chance?

'The first thing I want to know, Len, is how you set me up,' said Frank. 'Someone who knows me must have given you that information.'

'Before I say anything to you,' said Parker, 'I must emphasise that this conversation is to be in strict confidence. You can choose to walk away now and forget that you have been here but I must warn you,'– and here Parker's voice took on a more serious tone, 'if you ever mention what has happened here you will be in serious trouble. I belong to a widespread organisation which is very powerful. However from what I've heard about you I think that you will be very receptive to my idea, particularly as you have agreed to come here to my house.'

He stopped and regarded Frank intently. 'Have I made myself clear?'

Although Frank had no idea about what this man was about to reveal, Parker's tone sent a chill through his body, but he had an impulsive nature. The promise of wealth and excitement to relieve the humdrum life he was living was an addictive proposition.

'That's no problem for me, Len,' he replied. 'I know how to keep my mouth shut. Just tell me what this idea is of yours?'

'Ok,' said Parker, 'you asked me how I know so much about you. It may surprise you to know that one of your colleagues at your base is also a friend of mine. His name is Andreas Christakos.'

'Christakos!' exclaimed Frank in astonishment. 'How and why?'

'We'll come to that in a minute,' responded Parker. 'But he knew you were going to that hotel bar from a chat you had with him before you went there. He told me about that and also a lot about you. After all you have spent quite a lot of time together over the past few years.'

'Yes, that's true,' replied Frank, 'I like him and regard him as a friend. We play chess together sometimes, but why would he be telling you about me?'

Parker regarded Frank intently for a few seconds as if weighing up what to say next.

'Christakos is not a friend of mine. He actually works for me.'

'Works for you?' responded Frank curiously. 'I don't understand. Christakos works for the British Army. How can he be working for you?'

'He extricates certain goods and materials from the base which he sells to me which, in turn, I sell on at profit.' said Parker bluntly, then, before Frank could respond, he added quickly,

'That's where you come in, Frank. Christakos only has access to the NAAFI and whatever he gets from there is pretty small beer. You would be able to get access to more valuable materials. I'm thinking of the electronic and communications equipment locked away in a high security storeroom at your QM stores. I know that as an engineering unit you will have cameras, computers and all types of surveying equipment. These things are in high demand—'

'Just hold it there,' interjected Frank. 'You're telling me that Christakos is thieving from the base where I am stationed as a serving officer – and you want me to aid and abet!'

'Oh, come off it, Frank,' returned Parker. 'I know all about you and I know you are craving some excitement and that you'd like to get your hands on some extra cash, and I hear you can't wait to get away from the army.'

'Oh yes, but not by going to prison,' retorted Delaney. 'What guarantees would you give me for my protection?'

'Yes, Frank,' responded Parker. 'It would be dangerous and I don't think it could go on for than a few months. If there was any possibility of discovery I would arrange for your immediate escape.'

'That's reassuring,' said Delaney with a touch of irony, but my priority is to get out of the army as soon as possible, well before any suspicion falls on my head.'

'Don't worry, Frank,' said Parker in a reassuring tone. 'That will be arranged whatever happens. In fact the main reason for my interest in you is that you could be more help to me outside the army than in it but we'll talk about that later.'

Parker paused and looked fixedly at Frank. 'I need your answer, Frank, yes or no?'

Frank's heart raced as he realised the enormity of what he was being asked to do. If he accepted the offer he could look forward to a considerable source of extra income, as well as the chance to escape the army, but that had to be balanced against the risks. Discovery would certainly lead to a hefty term of imprisonment. However he had never been averse to taking risks in the past and the attractions seemed to outweigh the potential for disaster.

'All right,' said Frank after a lengthy pause. 'I'll do it for a while, but my priority is to get away and be free to live my own life,' he said slowly.'

Little did he realise that by accepting Parker's offer he was committing himself to a life of crime and subterfuge.

Within weeks of this encounter Frank first met Jack Blake in the officer's mess and what started out as a casual conversation soon developed into a close friendship, but in spite of their closeness Frank gave no hint of his involvement in the thefts from the base.

Delaney's first task after a briefing from Parker was to inform Andreas Christakos of the new arrangement. Christakos lived with his younger brother Dimitri in accommodation provided for civilian workers at the base. Andreas assured Frank that although Dimitri aided him in the raids he knew nothing of Len Parker and would know nothing about Frank's role.

Andreas had been pilfering cigarettes and alcohol items from the NAAFI for several months and passing them on to Parker who was able to fence them through various outlets for profit, some of which was passed back to Christakos.

Andreas was visibly pleased with the new arrangement as Delaney, being a British officer, would have right of entry to those buildings that were inaccessible to civilians.

The conversations between the two men took a more dramatic turn when Christakos mentioned that there was a more lucrative market to be had in small arms trading. He assured Delaney that weapons could be sold for vast profit to Parker who he knew was already involved in arms dealing. Delaney preferred not to dwell on the prospect of stolen weapons being sold to enemies of his country and he demurred at this prospect for a while but he had few moral scruples. He thought about the lucrative returns that would result and eventually greed overcame him in spite of the attendant risk.

One of Delaney's regular duties was to take his turn as orderly officer. This entailed checking all storage areas during the night and for this he had the temporary possession of a master key which allowed him to enter and check most premises except for the armoury. He lost no time in taking an impression of the key which he passed on to Parker who was able to make an exact duplicate.

Delaney then proceeded to put his plan into action. Christakos, choosing his times carefully, and using information provided to him by Delaney, would enter and steal items of potential value. This was always during the night and away from any patrols. His brother Dimitri, who was not aware of Delaney's part in the operation, helped him only on infrequent occasions.

The same technique was used for the more dangerous part where rifles and ammunition were the prime targets except that Andreas carried out the thefts alone to protect his brother in the event of discovery. The armoury stored a large number of these weapons and checks were carried out infrequently as it was thought that any illegal entry would be too difficult. It had a solid metal door with a secure locking mechanism which required a separate key from those used for other buildings. One key was kept in the guardroom and the other in the camp orderly room, both of which were permanently occupied. The only people with access to the keys were the duty orderly officer and the armoury senior NCO. Delaney copied this key also using the same technique as for the master key.

He soon found that his personal wealth was increasing in a very satisfactory way. All money was paid to him in cash by Parker and he kept it carefully concealed in his quarters. He felt that he could soon make a small fortune but it could only be for a short time in view of the attendant risks. He became increasingly aware of the need to escape from the army before those risks became too great.

The day before that fateful night of the shooting Parker summons Frank to his house.

'I've learned on my personal grapevine that things are hotting up. The base police and the camp commandants have stepped up surveillance and instigated increased patrols during the night. They are particularly alert to all vehicles leaving the base camps and are instigating detailed searches so it's very likely that they will catch Christakos before long. If they do then I've no doubt he would implicate both you and me. The situation is becoming very dangerous for both of us so I think it's time for you to get out.'

'Good,' responded Frank, 'I can't wait. What do you suggest?'

'No suggestions, Frank,' responded Parker, 'a definite plan, a part of which you will not like. I want you to set up a fake operation with Christakos to raid the NAAFI on a Saturday night. Christakos of course will think that it's genuine so he will carry it out but you will know precisely when it takes place and where Christakos will be.'

Parker paused, looking at Frank intently knowing the enormity of what he was about to say.

'Frank, you must get rid of Christakos. I've just told you what would happen if he's caught with stolen property in his van. If you were to leave suddenly without telling him I'm pretty sure he would panic and confess.

Frank's mouth dropped open in horror as he realised what Parker was proposing.'

'What do you mean "get rid of Christakos?" he spluttered. Do you expect me to kill him? He's a friend! I couldn't possibly do that. I know I've done a lot of wrong things but I stop short of cold blooded murder!'

Parker smiled grimly. 'I'm afraid you have no choice. If you refuse I can assure you that not only will you not escape but your part in all this will be revealed. OK, you could then tell them all about me but do you really want that? It wouldn't change what would happen to you. There wouldn't be any slap on the wrist and be told to be a good boy. It's more likely that you'd be using a walking stick by the time you got out.'

'Isn't there any other way?' said Delaney desperately. 'Couldn't you just give him a good pay off?'

'I can't risk that,' Parker returned. 'He would remain a permanent risk to me once he found he was of no further use. He knows me and where I live. Not only that, he could tell the army all about your part in the thefts from the camp. Do you want to risk that?'

'No,' responded Delaney, 'but surely my desertion straight after the shooting is going to incriminate me anyway.'

'That's true, Frank, but it could be interpreted as a coincidence. It's not proof but Christakos's statement would definitely incriminate you.'

Delaney shook his head slowly as he realised that he really wasn't being given any choice. He had to kill Christakos.

'Ok, I'll do it,' he said slowly. 'What plan do you have in mind?'

'I've thought about this in some detail,' said Parker beckoning Delaney over to a table where there was a rolled up plan of the Royal Engineers camp. 'You will shoot Christakos from a concealed position in line of sight of the NAAFI rear entrance. That position will need to be some distance away and of course it will be dark apart from the moonlight.'

He pointed to the position of the NAAFI building and then to another building some one hundred metres away from it.

'That building is used as a general store room for bric-a-brac so it will be unoccupied. It's up to you to make sure beforehand that you have a key to it. It has a window facing in the direction of the NAAFI so you will get a good view from there.'

'That's a long way away from the NAAFI,' said Delaney, 'how do I do that, and in the dark?'

'You will have a silenced Kalashnikov, an AK47 equipped with an infra-red sight. That should handle it nicely provided your aim is good, and it had better be!' Parker concluded grimly.

'Where do I get such a weapon?' queried Delaney. 'We don't get issued with that kind of equipment and even if we have them in the armoury they won't be equipped with silencers.'

Parker gave a humourless laugh. 'I will provide you with the weapon. Make sure you lock it securely in the boot of your car.'

'Yes, what about my car?' said Delaney. Assuming all goes well, all hell will be let loose and the first thing they will do is to close the camp exit to prevent anyone from leaving.'

'Look at this again Frank,' responded Parker pointing to the camp plan. 'Not far from your position there's a small parking area, just one of many at the base. You leave your car there and you can get back to it within a minute of you doing the business. You could be well clear of the camp well before it's closed.' Parker paused looking intently at Delaney before saying, 'Remember Frank, you will do this. You have no choice.'

'But what then?' said Frank. 'I'd have to get out pronto and without discovery. What do you have in mind?'

'This is the good part for you,' replied Parker. 'You must be dressed in civilian clothes and drive out of the base. But you must do it quickly. It will take them possibly ten or fifteen minutes to get organised and close the camp exit, and don't forget to bring your finances with you. You will certainly need them in the weeks to come.'

'This plan is scheduled for a weekend and you will be off duty so you would be entitled come and go from your base as you like, just like any other day. The difference is that it will be in the very early hours of the morning but it will be a Sunday morning so you could easily be setting off early for a full day out.'

'The guard on the main gate will of course recognise you but there would be no reason to stop you provided you get out quickly before the news get out. You then drive to an agreed position well outside the base area and I will meet you there. You will abandon your car and we will come back here. After a suitable period of time during which you will lie low here you will be equipped with a false identity and returned to the UK.

The plan proceeded as expected, the only hitch being the presence of Jack Blake's patrol at the scene. Delaney's expectations of the freedom he would have chilled his emotions to the point of evaporating all human feelings for Christakos as he pointed the weapon and pulled the trigger. As soon as he saw Christakos fall Delaney wasted no time in carrying out the next part of the plan. He carefully closed the window, relocked the door before doubling back to his car parked nearby.

Within three minutes he had driven out of the camp and on to the scheduled meeting point with Parker.

Chapter 4

Escape from Cyprus

For the weeks after his desertion Delaney, now in hiding at Parker's villa, was instructed to let some facial hair grow and to start wearing a pair of plain glass spectacles.

He was given a new identity. Henceforth he would be known as *Alan Birch*, and an appropriate counterfeit passport and other papers were expertly produced by Parker's shadowy associates.

He whiled away the time by familiarising himself with his new identity or idling on Parker's patio. He was under strict instructions not to go out of the villa but he kept a close watch on the television news reports which merely stated that a man identified as Andreas Christakos had been shot by an unknown person. An intense search of the area was being made but the assailant had not yet been found. There was no mention of himself, but it was likely that the army had requested for his name not to be mentioned at this stage. Nevertheless Delaney had little doubt that both the army and the Cypriot police would be very active in searching for him.

During the days Parker was usually away carrying out his business in the organisation of thefts from various camps, both British and Cypriot, throughout the island. In consequence he had many visitors to the villa, presumably to deposit goods in a secure vault built into the basement. Delaney was instructed to keep himself in his bedroom during these visits so he never saw them come and go. Then there were the mysterious trucks that came during the night and Delaney surmised that these were to transfer stolen property for distribution to their ultimate sources.

Eventually the time came for the next stage of the plan as Parker delivered further instructions to the new *Alan Birch*. This was a very different Parker to the amicable character that Frank had first met. Now he was confronted by a serious man with a dark edge to his voice.

Delaney was to be driven across the Turkish controlled border to Famagusta and thence by ferry to Mersin on the Turkish mainland. He would then be expected to travel to Istanbul and onwards to the UK by scheduled airline.

Naively, Frank had a vision of being free to run his own life once he got back to England, but Parker's next words caused him to freeze inwardly.

'You might be wondering why I have taken all this trouble to get you out,' said Parker coldly. 'Well, that's easy to explain. All this has not just been arranged out of the kindness of my heart. In fact it has been a joint effort with other colleagues both here on the Island and in the UK. You have effectively become our property and hereafter you will do as instructed. Any failure for you to play your part, or if there is any suspicion that you are betraying us will result in your immediate elimination.'

Frank stared back in horror as he realised what Parker had just said to him. The price he must pay for his escape from the army and a charge of murder was to be blackmailed for the rest of his life into doing whatever he was commanded to do.

'Oh, and another thing,' added Parker. 'Don't think of trying to run away between here and the UK. You would be tracked down. Our organisation has a very long reach.'

Delaney stared back at Parker, speechless, his mind in a turmoil as he realised that he had been completely trapped. There was no way out.

Parker's voice relaxed a little as he smirked grimly, 'Look at it this way Frank- oh sorry, *Alan*. Accept your situation, work hard to do as you are required, and you will do very well out of it. You will be able to live a lucrative lifestyle.'

Several weeks later the new *Alan Birch* arrived at London Heathrow by an early morning flight. He was a very different character to the one-time fresh-faced young army officer. Now bespectacled, with long hair and smart trimmed beard and moustache, and wearing a well-tailored suit, he could be taken for a wealthy business man.

As he exited customs to the arrivals hall he saw the usual forest of placards being waved to receive various arriving passengers and prominent among them was one emblazoned with the name *Alan Birch*.

'Hello,' said Delaney, 'I'm *Alan Birch*.'

'Ah, Mr *Birch*, glad to meet you,' said the man with the placard. My name is Norman Longford. I've been told to meet you and take you to the boss's office.'

Delaney regarded Longford with interest. He was a tall angular man of dark complexion and a hard face. Someone you would not wish to argue with. He turned and led the way with Frank following with his luggage trolley.

'Who is your boss and where is his office?' said Delaney as they reached the car park

'I can't tell you anything more at the moment,' replied Longford coldly. 'I just work for him but you'll find out everything that you need to know when we get there.'

As they drove through the busy roads of west London Delaney was filled with a mixture of excitement and trepidation. Who was this mysterious character who was obviously linked in some way to Parker in Cyprus? It had long since dawned upon him that he was not dealing with some tin pot organisation run by one man. This was much bigger than he had ever imagined, spanning several countries. What its main purpose was he had no idea but it surely went a lot further than simple burglary from army camps.

Eventually they reached their destination, somewhere in the northern suburbs of London. It was a street with multi-story office blocks on one side and various shops on the other. Longford parked the car outside one of the office blocks and pressed the intercom button at the entrance. A female voice bade them to enter after Longford had identified himself and the new *Alan Birch*.

A lift took them to the third floor and to a door marked with a board proclaiming it to be the offices of Brevington Recruitment Agency. The young woman who had answered the intercom was waiting for them inside.

'She smiled as she opened an inner door marked *Hans Schmitt Managing Director*.

'Mr Schmitt is waiting for you *Mr Birch*. Please go straight in.'

Delaney found himself confronting a short bald rotund figure seated behind a large oak desk. He was wearing a pair of wire framed pince-nez spectacles which he peered over as he stood to proffer his hand.

'Ah, *Mr Birch*, I'm pleased to meet you at long last,' he said with a slight smile. 'I feel I know you already from the information I've received, but now we need to talk. Please take a seat.'

Schmitt had a high pitched voice and an accent which Delaney judged to be of German origin.

'Hello Mr Schmitt,' said Delaney warily, 'I understand that you hold my immediate future in your hands but I have no idea about what you are expecting me to do.'

'Of course you don't *Alan*, that is if you don't mind me calling you by your first name. First you will need somewhere to live. That has been arranged and as soon as we have finished talking, Norman, who you have already met, will drive you to the address. It's near Hastings, a semidetached house which you will rent. An advance payment has already been made in your name.'

'Hastings!' exclaimed Delaney. 'Why Hasting?'

'You'll soon know the answer to that but let's first get down to what I want you to do. From now on you are effectively in my employment, and I know it's been made very clear to you that you have no choice about this,' and here Schmitt's voice took on a warning tone, 'I am completely aware of your past so you will do whatever task I require of you.'

Delaney nodded submissively. He was now resigned to his fate whatever it may be.

Schmitt continued, 'I do know you have substantial funds of your own which you accumulated from your activities in Cyprus. Then, provided the missions I give you are concluded satisfactorily, you will earn bonuses depending on the value to us of the information you get.'

'Information?' responded Delaney. 'What sort of information?'

'Ha, now we come to the crux of the matter,' said Schmitt. 'You will work as an agent for us but I'll give you more details about all this at a later meeting. Just get yourself settled first. Now let's concentrate on the reason why I want you to live in Hastings.'

'The research division of a large pharmaceutical Company is based there. It's called Brouchers Research and Development Division. They develop new drugs for a range of debilitating diseases, before moving them on to their production plant after they have been approved for use. One drug is of particular interest to us; its code name is EDF301 but my informants tell me that it is one of a whole new range of antiarthritics they are developing. EDF301 is in the middle stage of development and is said to be the new miracle drug for the treatment of Rheumatoid Arthritis. As you might well imagine there would be an enormous interest in it.'

'There's a queue of competing companies who are willing to pay dearly for any information about this research. If we were to be instrumental in getting any of this information it could be worth millions to us alone, never mind what a competing company would make by producing a competitive product.'

'I've heard about this sort of thing,' said Delaney. 'It's called industrial espionage I believe.'

'That's right,' said Schmitt, 'that's what it's called and you probably also know that it's not strictly illegal unless criminal acts such as theft of materials or patent infringement are involved. It's a very grey area and if a competitive company comes out with a similar product it is very difficult to prove any wrongdoing. Also Companies that have been sabotaged are rarely willing to publicise the fact.'

'Well that's all very well,' said Delaney, 'but how am I expected to get his information without actually working there? And it's very unlikely I could just walk in and help myself.'

Schmitt laughed, 'of course not, but you do have to use your guile and charm to get someone on side. Someone who already works in their research labs and holds a trusted position.'

'If they hold a trusted position then it's very unlikely they would tell me anything,' said Delaney dryly

'Nobody said that this job was going to be easy,' responded Schmitt grimly, 'but we have taken a great deal of trouble to get you here because we believe you can do it. Most importantly you have a considerable flair in dealings with the opposite sex. You will have to exercise that flair in the plan we have put together. My people have done a lot of research on the people who work in the labs and have settled on one person in particular who you may be able to influence. That person's name is Paula Kendrick. She's a biochemist and works in the laboratory that is chiefly responsible for the development of this range of drugs. We want you to get to know her, form a relationship, and from then on it's up to you. Of course if you find another way of doing it then feel free, so long as you get the goods. Oh, there's one more thing you need to know. She comes from a wealthy family so you will have to work particularly hard to persuade her to do what we want.'

'No pressure then,' said Delaney in sardonic tone, but in a way he felt a sense of slight relief that what he was being asked to do did not appear to be illegal. 'Just one question Mr Schmitt,' he continued, 'how do I recognise her among the hundreds of people who work there?'

Schmitt opened a drawer of the desk in front of him and took out a photograph. It was a picture of a young lady walking on a pavement, certainly taken using a long focus lens. Clearly attractive, she seemed to be tall with short blonde bobbed hair.

'Do you think you will be able to recognise her from that?' said Schmitt.

'I think so,' said Delaney reflectively after he had studied the image.

'OK, *Alan*,' said Schmitt, 'I expect you to brief me regularly on my mobile. There's nothing more at the moment. Just get home, rest well and think deeply about what you have to do. Hire yourself a car tomorrow. My people have already prepared a driving licence with insurance papers for you and you can pick these up from Norman. Goodbye for now and good luck.'

Longford was a man of few words with a sombre outward attitude so the ninety minute journey southwards was made in silence while Delaney brooded about the task that he had been set. He had a great deal of confidence when it came to women but this was different. Even if he succeeded in cultivating a friendship with this Paula Kendrick how could he convince her to betray her integrity and steal secrets from the company that employed her?

He shuddered at what would almost certainly be the cost of failure.

They eventually drew up outside a modern semi-detached house on the outskirts of Hastings. It was set in a pleasant tree-lined avenue and had a garage offset from the house with a gate and pathway between them leading to the rear.

'Here's the keys and a pack of all the papers you will need,' growled Longford. 'Make yourself at home.'

With that final comment he drove off as soon as Delaney had exited the car.

'I'll bet you're a bundle of laughs at a party,' said Delaney to himself as he watched the car disappear into the distance before walking up the drive and letting himself into the house. It was fully furnished with a plentiful stock of food in the refrigerator and freezer and, as the weather was now turning colder with the inset of autumn, he quickly found the central heating controls.

There is something rather disturbing about all this, thought Delaney. From Parker in Cyprus to Schmitt in London no expense had been spared to ensure that he would end up in this position. It looked as if his assignment was expected to bear rather more fruit than he could imagine.

He started to think seriously about the possible effects of industrial sabotage. Most major companies, such as those engaged in the production of new drugs, agricultural products, petrochemicals, and everyday commercial products. In fact it would be difficult to think of any aspect of modern life did not depend on research and development by large companies. It followed that these companies made huge profits from their research and if some of their vital secrets were stolen by competitors then similar products could be marketed. This would be done by agents working as intermediaries or by employees who could be swayed by the promise of a substantial reward.

Delaney realised that he had now become such an agent and that potentially his function could be worth literally millions to Schmitt's organisation. As he looked around his comfortable surroundings he thought that the cost of all this would be trivial compared to what he was expected to deliver. It was clear to him that he would not be the only one. Schmitt would have to have a network of similar agents working though out the country.

He now realised the true magnitude of his situation. His unwritten contract with Schmitt's organisation was non-negotiable.

There was no 'in' or 'out' clause.

Chapter 5
A New Liaison

Early the next day Delaney rented a car then drove to Brouchers. The research centre was situated in a large industrial area away from the main town but bordering the sea. It was surrounded by a high brick wall with an entrance on a side road leading to a security gateway. A gatehouse was situated to one side and there was a parking area just outside the entrance.

Delaney took a mental picture of the site as he drove slowly past before carrying on for a few hundred yards until he saw what he was looking for. A public house stood by the roadside which proclaimed itself to be called *The Flying Horse*. You can bet your dear life that's the local for Brouchers's employees, thought Delaney.

It was still too early for the pub to be open so he returned to his house to work out a plan of action. He examined himself in the mirror and smugly gave himself a nod of approval. His fair hair was longer than in his army days, and cultivated to accentuate a carefree look which he knew would attract the opposite sex. He had discarded the spectacles worn for his escape from

Cyprus, and his new designer stubble and vivid blue eyes completed the picture.

Later the same day Delaney returned to the Flying Horse and sat alone at a table near the bar. It was mid-week and there were few customers so early in the evening, but shortly after five o'clock a group of men and women came in and stood by the bar chatting. They were all dressed formally, clearly enjoying a relaxing drink after finishing work and Delaney surmised that they would have to be from Brouchers.

Delaney went up to the bar to order himself another drink as an excuse to talk to them. 'Excuse me' he said. 'Do any of you happen to know a Paula Kendrick, she's a friend of mine and I happen to be staying in Hastings for a while. I thought I'd call in on the off chance of seeing her as I know she works at Brouchers.'

One of the women in the group answered. 'Paula? Yes I know her. I often chat with her over lunch. I'm afraid you won't see her in here today though, she just goes straight home to her flat after work. She does come in here after work on Fridays before driving to her parent's house for the weekend.'

'Oh, what a pity,' exclaimed Delaney. 'Never mind I'll catch up with her then.'

The woman smiled, 'I'll tell her you were here. What name is it?'

'Just say *Alan* and tell her I'm looking forward to catching up with her,' said Delaney.

Inwardly Delaney guessed that Paula would wrack her brains trying to remember an acquaintance of that name and would certainly be curious.

Friday came and Delaney arrived to sit in the same place he had occupied before. As before the same group arrived but augmented by several other members of the staff all clearly relishing the thought of a weekend off.

Delaney recognised Paula immediately from the photograph in his possession and the woman he had spoken to earlier directed Paula's attention to him as soon as she saw him. Paula looked over to him and a puzzled frown crossed her face as she tried to recall any recognition of Delaney.

She detached herself from the group and came over to his table.

'Are you *Alan*?' she said.

'That's me,' replied Delaney with a smile.

'Diane said you were a friend of mine, but I don't know you. I can't remember ever having seen you before. What's your surname? That might ring a bell,' she said curiously.

'It's *Birch, Alan Birch*,' returned Delaney with a smile, 'and I do know you but you obviously don't remember me. If you sit down and let me buy you a drink I will explain.'

Paula looked dubiously at this strange man, a very attractive man she had to admit. He had a cultured voice and a charming manner, and there would be no harm in talking to him.

'You must have some reason to go to this trouble *Mr Birch*,' she replied, 'but OK, I'll hear what you've got to say.'

She sat down at the table as Delaney went to the bar to buy their drinks.

'I suppose I'm being very foolish,' said Delaney in his most ingratiating manner. 'But I do know you from university. I was there on a different course from yours but I often saw you around on the campus or the refectory and I found you to be very attractive. I would just be a face in the crowd to you so you wouldn't remember me and I suppose I didn't have the bottle to talk to you in those days.'

Paula had to admit that she was flattered and for several moments was at a loss for words. 'I'm sorry, *Mr Birch*,' she said eventually, 'but I can't recall ever having seen you, but there were hundreds of students there and the only ones I got to know well were the ones on my course. Anyway, why would you go to all this trouble now to speak to me?'

'Because you've been on my mind ever since,' said Delaney adopting an engaging voice. 'I know it's a thin hope but would you agree to join me for a meal sometime?'

His blue eyes had an almost memorising effect on her and she felt herself being drawn into the magnetic personality of this strange man.

Paula allowed herself to give him a slight smile as she nodded. 'All right, *Mr Birch*. When do you suggest?'

'For a start you can call me *Alan*,' said Delaney, 'and I'll call you Paula. Is that OK?'

Delaney suggested that they meet in the Flying Horse on Monday evening of the following week, and they would go on to a Chinese restaurant in town.

During the weekend Paula Kendrick had time to muse about the strange encounter with *Alan Birch*. She was a bright lively young woman with a close group of friends and enjoyed having a good time. She had had several brief affairs and was no vestal virgin, but no serious relationship had so far come her way. *Alan Birch* was undoubtedly attractive. In fact he had affected her in a strange unaccountable way which excited her so she was looking forward to Monday and to see what it was to bring.

As Paula relaxed in the comfortable surroundings of her parents' house she counted herself to be very fortunate to have been born into a wealthy family. Nevertheless, although an only daughter, she had never been over indulged. Her parents had brought her up to believe in the principle of working to be self-sufficient in life. This attitude had paid off if her track record so far was anything to go by. She had achieved an honours degree in biochemistry and then secured a good position at Brouchers. Even now she preferred to pay rent out of her salary for her modest lodgings in Hastings even though she knew her parents would have readily helped her financially if she had preferred to rent one of the more expensive flats near the sea front.

Monday evening progressed exactly as Delaney had planned. He knew exactly how to win over members of the opposite sex and had no difficulty in applying his well-practiced technique of false charm and attentiveness.

He also knew that he couldn't rush things.

Within a few weeks they were meeting every evening and very soon Delaney knew he had Paula in the palm of his hand but he carefully refrained from taking things further than a goodnight kiss. For her part Paula realised that every day she looked forward to the evenings with excitement. She became bewitched by this man, swamped by feelings she had never before experienced. Then, one evening, he took her hand and gazed into her eyes, saying gently, 'Paula, you must know that I am in love with you.'

It was a masterpiece of deception and Paula was completely taken in. 'She looked back at him and replied softly, 'I know, Alan. I feel the same way. I love you, too.'

In a matter of days she moved in with Delaney to begin what she imagined would be a life of bliss. She stopped going to her parents' house at weekends, much to their disappointment, but after she had explained to them that she had met someone who was making her happy they reluctantly accepted the new situation.

It was during one of their conversations that Paula asked Delaney what he did for a living as he had not been very open about his life. In fact he was still very much of a mystery and Paula had become intrigued. He said that he had dropped out of university and taken a range of part time jobs, but his response had been very vague, saying airily that he worked for a large business concern in London.

His attitude suggested that he was not keen to enlarge on this and so Paula let it go not wishing to annoy him. Gradually she sank into a state of complete adulation of this new man in her life while Delaney gave no hint that he was merely playing a part. His intimate relations with her were tender and gentle and she responded passionately in a way she had never before experienced. In fact he had no feelings for her whatsoever, just a pawn in the game he was expected to play.

He was also under persistent pressure from Schmitt who phoned him constantly to hear of any progress. Then he was instructed to report in person to Schmitt's office.

'OK, Alan, you have managed to cultivate a relationship with this girl. Well done there, but how quickly can you get her onside and start procuring some of the stuff we want?' said Schmitt pointedly.

'I'm working on it,' replied Delaney, 'and I do have a plan which I think will work. By the way, Mr Schmitt, I've been doing my homework on this company and I know they make millions from the new drugs they develop. I can understand your interest in company, but surely I'm not the only finger in the pie?'

Schmitt laughed. 'You're right, *Alan*. Of course you're not, but I work on a 'need to know' basis. It's not necessary for you to know who else works for me, nor indeed for them to know about you. That way we are all that bit safer. However this brings me to the reason why I have brought you here today. You've seen that we have spared no expense in helping you escape from Cyprus, especially after what you did, right?'

Schmitt looked enquiringly at Delaney, his eyebrows raised above his spectacles, in expectation of an affirmative nod in response.

Delaney returned with the expected nod and with a humourless smile said, 'Yes Mr Schmitt, I am grateful for that, but I was hoping that perhaps after one or two jobs I would be free to get on with my life in my own way.'

'Very sorry to disappoint you, *Alan*, or should I say *Frank Delaney*,' returned Schmitt with a grim smile. 'That's your correct name and it could be made known to the Military authorities should you ever think of letting me down. Ah, and before you butt in and say that you could tell them about me in return let me tell you about your predecessor who worked for me.'

'His name was Gordon Partridge and his job was to act as a 'collector' for me by going round to a number of my information providers to collect whatever material they had and return it to me. Unfortunately we found that he was creaming off some of this information and selling it privately.'

Here Schmitt paused shaking his head in mock sorrow before continuing,

'So sad, he was found drowned in his car after he drove it in the river.'

Delaney froze inwardly as he heard these words, then he remembered Parker's warning in Cyprus about the likelihood of repercussions should he defect in any way. It seemed so much more sinister coming from this man.

'You said *my predecessor*,' said Delaney. 'Do you mean that my main function is to replace this Gordon Partridge?'

'Yes, *Alan*,' responded Schmitt brightly. 'You've hit the nail on the head. That's exactly what I expect you to do. You didn't think that I've laid out all this cash, provided you with a house, and so on just for you to sit around on your backside all day. OK so you have an important priority job to complete with Brouchers and I'll be happy to get a result from that, but you have to travel around and do precisely what Partridge did, except for the "helping himself bit", of course. You are pretty well settled in now so it's time for you now to concentrate on the main part of your job. To get started I'll give you a computer memory stick with the details of the people who were Partridge's contacts.'

Schmitt turned to the desktop computer in front of him and keyed in a few commands before taking out a memory stick from his desk drawer. He inserted it into one of the USB computer sockets and transferred some of the displayed information. He disconnected the memory stick and handed it over the Delaney.

'Take good care of that, *Alan*,' he said meaningfully. 'Make sure that it doesn't fall into the wrong hands. I suggest you copy the contents to a laptop using software that can only be accessed by three layers of passwords. Then destroy the memory stick. If you don't already have a laptop then get one.'

'That's no problem, Mr Schmitt,' said Delaney. 'That was one of the first things I bought. It also has a very powerful database installed.'

'Good,' said Schmitt with a smile of approval. 'That's the sort of thing I want to hear from you. Now,' he went on, 'outwardly you will be employed by me quite legitimately, with a bank account but in the name of *Alan Birch*, and you will pay your taxes and National Insurance. It's not unusual for employees to be paid on a commission only basis. Officially your title will be liaison officer to Brevingtons Recruitment Agency. As you probably know already we are a legitimate employment agency, and the company's income is based on the success we achieve in finding positions for professional people. We have many people on our books and they provide the company with a steady income.'

'Hold on,' interjected Delaney, 'so I collect this stuff from the contacts stored in this memory stick, but what do they get in return? I assume they want money for what they do. How do they get it?'

'You don't have to worry about it,' responded Schmitt. 'I see to all that once I have evaluated their diverted material, and I make payments directly to discreet accounts in their name.'

Schmitt rose from behind his desk and went round to shake Delaney's hand. 'I think that's all for now,' he said. 'Don't forget, you may feel as if you have been trapped but look on the bright side. You could become a wealthy man if you stick to your guns, keep your nose clean and do as you are told.'

As soon as Delaney left his office Schmitt turned to his desktop computer and clicked on the particular file he needed to access. It requested two security passwords which he entered.

The file contained the names and details of men and women he used for his so-called 'Liaison Officers'. He entered a new name with the comment, *Frank Delaney, known as Alan Birch. Replacement for Roger Partridge.*

Chapter 6
Canterbury

Jack Blake's first action on visiting the local library was to book a seat at one of several desktop computers aligned on desks at one side of the reference room. He logged on and used the browser search engine to flag up situations vacant. This brought up a bewildering array of sites but none of those he tried seemed to be related to his own qualifications and job requirements. He rejected the idea of trying a recruitment agency as they would require applicants to have previous experience, and they cost money in terms of commission.

He turned his attention to the magazine racks which kept an up-to-date collection of all the prominent trade journals. Jack grabbed all of those concerned with the chemical industry from the rack before making himself comfortable at one of the tables.

There were plenty of vacancies listed but most were for people with professional experience or specialist degrees. As a graduate with no experience and only a general science degree his options were limited.

He made a note of all the likely prospects and returned home to start writing out job applications. He realised that his period of army service could turn out to be a disadvantage as prospective employers may well question his commitment to a more humdrum life working in a laboratory. On the other hand he was now more mature than the average inexperienced graduate, and as an officer he had become accustomed to being in command, albeit at a junior level. He had earlier prepared a CV outlining his education and qualifications and had run off a number of copies on the Xerox machine at the library.

Days later he received several letters in reply, mostly to thank him for his interest and to say that they would keep him in mind for the future. Others to whom he had applied simply didn't bother to answer.

The question of Frank's sudden disappearance and the dreadful events of that night in Cyprus still tortured Jack. He knew that the army would have made considerable efforts to locate Frank but, as far as he knew, he was still at large, so during this period of waiting for responses to his many applications Jack decided to start looking for his erstwhile friend in his own way.

He still could not bring himself to believe that Frank could have committed the murder of Christakos but he was not really surprised that Frank had deserted. He had told Jack many times how much he hated the army and would find some way to get out. Jack was convinced that the murder was a coincidence, and that it was carried out by a jealous rival. If Frank had been involved with the thefts from the base then killing Christakos would have made no sense because, as a deserter, he would have been a hunted man anyway.

Jack recalled the outcry at the base afterwards and, although Frank's desertion was not made public, an intensive search for him was instigated. Dimitri, the distraught younger brother of Andreas, had been closely interrogated, but he clearly knew nothing about any of the other thefts from the camp. He had just gone along with Andreas once or twice to earn himself some extra pocket money. Also there was no evidence that he was connected in any way with the more serious thefts from the camp. As punishment for his part in the NAAFI raid he had been summarily dismissed from his employment.

But where to start looking, pondered Jack? The only thing he could remember was Frank's comments about his parents and that they owned a chain of garden centres in North Wales. He cast aside the thought that the police would have already checked the parents' home address.

Jack soon found the address of the nearest centre and a telephone number by an internet search. He rang the centre and asked to be connected to the Manager after explaining that he had a matter of importance that he wished to discuss. After a short wait a male voice came on the line. 'This is Mark Taylor,' the voice said with a strong Welsh accent. 'How can I help you?'

Jack explained that he had an urgent matter to discuss with Mr Delaney, the owner, and would like to speak to him.

'I'm afraid Mr Delaney doesn't normally take calls in this way but if it really is that important I could give you the number of his son, Mr Cyril Delaney who is our General Manager in Caernarvon.'

'OK, that would be helpful,' responded Jack.

Jack dialled the new number and was eventually transferred to Cyril Delaney.

'Mr Blake, I understand you have some important matter to discuss with me. What can I do for you?'

As soon as Jack mentioned Frank's name Cyril's voice tightened. 'I'm sorry, Mr Blake, Frank has disgraced this family in many ways. We no longer have anything to do with him so we cannot be of any help. In fact if we knew where he was we would inform the police immediately. They have already visited my parents' house in their hunt for him and that has left them very distressed. You say you're a friend of his, but if you'll take my advice you will forget him. He's simply no good and never has been.'

'I can understand your attitude, Mr Delaney, and I'm very sorry for what he's put you all through,' said Jack, 'but this is something I must do. I've explained to you how I was involved that night so I just can't let it go.'

A touch of empathy entered Cyril's tone, 'Well, I wish you luck, Mr Blake, and if you do happen to find Frank then I think you know what you must do. You would be wasting your time by approaching my parents. In fact I really don't want you going there and upsetting them but you could talk to my sister, Rose. She has always been much closer to Frank than me for whatever reason. I can give you her address and mobile number. She lives in student accommodation in London as she is attending University College.

Jack promptly rang the number.

'Hello, is that Rose Delaney?' he asked.

'Yes, who am I talking to?' said Rose in a pleasant and well educated voice.

After Jack had told her about his friendship with Frank and that he was now looking for him there were a few moments of silence before she responded.

'I've heard of you, Mr Blake,' she said. 'Frank often mentioned you in texts to me. You may be a bit surprised to know that even though my family had disowned him we remained close. We are brother and sister but I know what he's like and I hate some of the things he has done, but I personally could never disown him.'

'Look, Miss Delaney, I would really like to meet you to talk about this. You may remember something that could give us a clue as to his whereabouts.'

They arranged to meet at a cafe near to her student's flat the following day. As soon as Jack entered the cafe he spotted Rose sitting by herself at a table drinking a coffee. She was busy operating a laptop as were several other students, the cafe obviously being a popular Wi-Fi hotspot for them. He was quick to recognise the Delaney family likeness, an attractive girl with long cascading blonde hair, blue eyes and wearing a minimum of make-up. She was wearing a casual top, loose floppy woollen jumper and blue jeans.

She stood up as he approached the table and smiled as she proffered her hand.

'Good to meet you at last, Mr Blake,' she said.

'Call me Jack, and I'll call you Rose if you don't mind,' said Jack. He took an instant liking to this girl. She had a pleasant open manner, very reminiscent of her brother, but hopefully with very different moral standards.

'I've been thinking a lot about what you said yesterday,' said Rose. 'As you can imagine, the fact that Frank has deserted, is on the run and is suspected of murder is very distressing for me. It almost certainly is for the rest of my family, but they refuse to talk about it or even mention Frank's name.'

'I suppose I can understand their attitude,' responded Jack. 'I must admit his track record leaves a lot to be desired. I really can't explain why we became friends, but he was such fun to be with.'

'Yes, I know,' said Rose, 'he has the charm of the devil. Obviously I would like to know what has become of him but I don't feel very optimistic.'

'No, I suppose your right,' sighed Jack, 'but this is something I feel compelled to do. Frank must have escaped the island under a false name but how I have no idea. He couldn't have done it alone so there must have been help there. The authorities in Cyprus have not been able to come up with anything. Frank seems to have vanished completely and without trace.'

He shook his head in frustration before continuing,

'If only there was some sort of clue. Let's assume he had made it back to England, then he must be living somewhere. Now I'm working on the theory that a man in that situation would not be able to resist going to familiar places. I'm thinking particularly of London where almost anyone can become anonymous. Can you help me there, Rose? Can you think of any places that he visited and where there could be a possibility of him going back to?'

'He used to like his good times,' said Rose thoughtfully, 'and he was very popular with the ladies. I do know that before he was posted abroad he often used to come to London but I was away at school then in Gloucestershire so I didn't get to see him very often. One time I do remember was just before he was posted abroad. He was on embarkation leave and staying in London and he wanted to see me before he went as I was the only family member who would have anything to do with him. I was only fourteen at the time, but I took the train up here and Frank met me at the station. I was due to catch a later train back, but I really enjoyed chatting with him and we had a great meal together. He then took me back to the place where he was staying which turned out to belong to a young lady who I was introduced to.'

'You're probably wondering why I'm telling you all this, but something she said stuck in my memory,' Rose gave a little chuckle. 'Obviously I twigged straight away that she was his current interest, but I can't remember anything about her or where the place was, except for one particular thing. While she was quizzing me about my life and interests she told me that she worked in a wine bar in Chelsea. I think it began with a 'G' or a 'J', was it Joan's bar, or something like that?'

'Now I know it's a thin hope but Frank almost certainly met her in the wine bar. Hang on a mo, I'll have a look on the laptop.'

She keyed "Chelsea wine bars" in the computer search engine to bring up a list.

'That's it!' she said pointing to an entry listed as "Jago's wine bar". 'I remember it now, it's quite an unusual name.'

'Ah, that's a start,' said Jack. 'I think there's a good chance that the Frank I know would return there. I'll be checking it out anyway.'

'I wish you luck, Jack,' said Rose. 'Please keep in touch and let me know if you find out anything.'

Jack had to delay any further efforts in tracing Delaney due to the pressure of finding a job. He applied for positions ranging from lowly paid junior office work to middle management. When he did receive a reply it was usually to tell him that either he was too highly qualified, or that he didn't have the necessary experience. Nevertheless he was not deterred and a regular trip to the library became part of his daily routine.

When he did get invitations to attend for an interview he always found himself in a queue of other applicants desperate to find employment and so far he had not been able to get on any short list.

Chapter 7
Reunion

Delaney left Schmitt's office in something of a daze as he realised the depths of what he had got himself into. He desperately needed to go somewhere to relax for a while to think things over. Then he remembered one of his old haunts in London. It was a wine bar in Chelsea where he had met some of his old flames before being sent abroad. He remembered it was called "Jago's wine bar" and hoped that it was still there after the few years that had passed

He found the bar which hadn't changed significantly apart from a recent facelift. He knew he was taking a risk but felt sure that his appearance had changed sufficiently in the intervening years for him not to be recognised. It probably arose from a basic human need to connect in some way with his past.

He donned the plain-glass spectacles that he always carried around for additional insurance, entered the bar, ordered a half bottle of white wine, sat in a corner seat facing the door and opened a daily paper he had purchased earlier.

It was early afternoon with a scattering of other customers mostly in groups of two or three enjoying a lunchtime drink. It was a peaceful atmosphere with just background murmur of voices and Delaney felt some of the tension leaving his body.

Then he had the shock of his life. A figure entered the bar who he recognised immediately.

It was Jack Blake!

In panic he raised the paper to cover his face and hoped fervently that Jack had not spotted him, but to no avail. Jack had not simply wandered in for a casual drink. He had a purposeful look about him and as he entered he carefully scanned the bar occupants. As soon as he saw the furtive figure in the corner trying to hide behind a paper he approached saying, 'Excuse me, sir!'

There was no immediate reaction, so Jack moved over to stand immediately in front of Frank who now had no option other than to lower the paper and reveal his face.

'Yes?' said Delaney, 'are you talking to me?'

'Frank! It is Frank Delaney isn't it?' said Jack.

'Who?' responded Delaney, 'I think you have made a mistake, sir. That's not my name.'

'Come off it, Frank, I'd know you anywhere. It is you, isn't it?' said Jack firmly.

Delaney looked back at his erstwhile friend in desperation. He really didn't know what to say or how to react. He knew it was futile to continue denying who he was. After a long silence he said in a low voice,

'OK, Jack, of course it's me, but please keep your voice down and sit here with me and I'll try to explain everything.'

Jack immediately sat down at the table, a look of relief mixed with concern on his face.

'Oh, Frank,' he said, 'what the hell's been going on? I've been worried sick about you. What's happened to you?'

'Let's get one thing clear,' said Delaney. 'I'm using a different name now, being a deserter. I'm known as *Alan Birch* so please call me *Alan*. Anyway how did you find me?'

Jack explained how he had tracked him through his sister. He had gone to several wine bars in the Chelsea district before coming across Jago's bar and remembering what Rose had said.

'One thing I really need to know,' said Jack looking intently at Delaney, 'Did you shoot Andreas?'

'Of course I didn't,' replied Delaney abruptly, 'you know perfectly well that I was desperate to get out of the army and I had planned my escape well before those events. I was horrified when I heard about Christakos but then I realised that the army would jump to the conclusion that I did it, but it was a sheer coincidence. It must have been a rival in the camp who shot him, perhaps to get rid of any opposition. The trouble is the army will have coupled me with it so I'm in double trouble if I'm caught.'

'I never for one moment believed that you shot Andreas,' said Jack, 'but do you think it was wise move for you to desert? I mean you will have to be on the run for the rest of your life. Wouldn't it be better for you to give yourself up and face the music?'

'Face the music?' replied Delaney through gritted teeth. 'You mean face a courts martial, be cashiered and chucked out in disgrace, that's assuming of course that they don't connect me to the killing of Christakos. Then the Greek Cypriot authorities will step in and crucify me.

How could I prove I didn't do it?' He paused then went on his voice faltering, 'If I'd have known that someone was going to be shot at almost the same time that I left, then of course I would not have done it. It was just a bloody coincidence.'

'Another thing came out during the investigation,' said Jack. 'Christakos was behind most of the thefts from army stores at the base, but even worse, the army believe that he was stealing weapons from the armoury and passing them on for arms trading. I don't know all the details because I'm not in the army now but finding Andreas was behind the NAAFI thefts of course led to him being the prime focus of suspicion.

'Good God!' said Delaney. 'I hope you don't thing that I had anything to do with that, do you, Jack?'

Jack regarded his old friend with a searching look. 'I couldn't bring myself to believe that, but there was a lot of chatter at the time you went astray to suggest that you were the one behind it all, even though there was never any proof.'

A look of horror crossed Delaney's face. 'I'd never do anything like that, Jack,' he said, 'and I had nothing to do with any of the other thefts. My only purpose was to get away from the army, nothing else, and you have my word on that.'

'No,' responded Jack with shake of his head. 'I couldn't believe any of the chatter. It was just gossip, they had nothing to go on in spite of the investigation. I know they interrogated Andreas's brother Dimitri but he was just being used as a pawn by his brother and clearly knew nothing about the armoury thefts nor who Andreas was dealing with outside. He was eventually just dismissed from the base with no charge.'

'What about you, Jack?' said Delaney. 'They knew we were friends. They must have given you a grilling.'

'You bet they did,' said Jack with a smile. 'I couldn't tell them anything. After all I didn't know you were about to desert, did I?'

'No,' said Delaney, 'of course you didn't but did they ask you if you knew that I was dissatisfied with the army, or that I had any intention of departing?'

'Certainly not,' replied Jack. 'I told them the truth. We were close friends, but that's all.'

Jack's tone changed as he continued, 'You must know that I've been worried sick about you. We were good friends in Cyprus. What are you doing now?' he added curiously. 'How do you make a living?'

'Oh, I manage,' replied Delaney dismissively. 'Let's just say I live on my wits, anyway, enough about me. What about you? What are you doing these days?'

'Well, I haven't been out long and still trying to find a job,' replied Jack. 'Not much success so far,' he finished wistfully.

'Yeah, difficult times, mate,' said Delaney. He regarded Jack thoughtfully for a few moments. Now that Jack had recognised him he really needed to get him to stay on his side. 'Tell you what,' he went on, 'I might be able to help you. I happen to live with a girl who works for a big pharmaceutical company down in Hastings. Her name is Paula Kendrick and I could ask her to put a good word in for you if there are any vacancies. Are you interested, Jack?'

'The way I feel at the moment I'd accept a job digging latrines,' replied Jack dryly, 'but yes, if there's anything going I would certainly be interested. Anyway Frank, err sorry, *Alan*, you've nothing to fear from me. I went to a lot of trouble to find you but there's no way I would give you away. Just as long as you are not involved in anything criminal.'

'No,' replied Delaney with a short laugh. 'You know me, Jack. I may be a bit of a maverick but I wouldn't go around breaking the law. After all, if I were to be caught my life wouldn't be worth a nickel.'

Jack was convinced that Delaney's only crime was that of desertion, a military offense, so as a civilian he believed he was not legally obliged to inform the authorities.

Delaney's offer to help his friend was very atypical of him when his general attitude to people was self-serving. Of course he could assume a false attitude of bonhomie with people and was very gregarious in public, but it was all with the aim of achieving his own ends. But then, who knows if Jack was also working at the same place as Paula he could come in useful too.

'There is one thing you could do for me in return,' said Delaney. 'You said you found me after talking to my sister. Could you let her know that I'm fine and well and I will contact her very soon. You can tell her that I did desert from the army and it's vitally important that she doesn't tell anyone that I've been found. Assure her that I had nothing to do with the death of Andreas Christakos. I think she'll understand.'

'I'll do that for you anyway, *Alan,* whatever happens about the job,' responded Jack.

Later that day Delaney mentioned to Paula that he had met up with an old friend who was looking for a job. He asked her if she knew about anything going at Brouchers for someone of Jack's qualifications.

'They are always advertising for staff,' she replied. 'I'll certainly mention his name if I hear of anything.'

Several weeks passed before Paula was able to tell Delaney that a position had come up in the security department that might suit his friend. It demanded a good knowledge of science, at least to general degree level, and supervisory experience.

Delaney immediately phoned Jack who lost no time in applying for the position. For her part, Paula mentioned to the centre's personnel officer that someone she knew was interested and had applied. She knew that one of the realities of life was that applicants who received personal recommendations from trusted members of existing staff always gave them a head start.

Jack duly received an invitation to attend for interview. The position looked very promising but he had no illusions. He knew that with his complete lack of any previous industrial experience he would be a disadvantage, and even if he was successful he would be starting at the bottom of the ladder. Nevertheless he had to start somewhere, and this looked like as good a place as any.

He arrived at Hastings station on the appointed day and used one of the many taxis at the rank near the station exit to take him to the research centre. The site, surrounded by its high brick wall and high security entrance, was as he expected for a place of such importance.

He presented himself to a uniformed guard at the gatehouse window and was issued with a card marked 'visitor' which he pinned to his lapel. He was asked to wait in a designated area attached to the gatehouse while a telephone call was made to the appropriate department.

In due course a young lady dressed in a dark coloured business suit arrived to conduct him to the interview.

'Mr Blake? My name is June Clarke. I work in the personnel division. Would you please come with me?'

They passed through the security gate and Jack was confronted by a complex of modern buildings connected by an internal road system. He conversed with his guide as they walked, learning that there were several hundred employees working on the site.

They headed towards a large building which appeared to be the administrative centre. The reception area was a vast circular cathedral-like hall from which various passageways led off in different directions, and where his identity was once again checked. They took one of the passageways which led past numerous offices until they reached a small room where several other nervous looking characters were sitting, obviously other interviewees. Jack wondered if they were applying for the same job as himself or if they were there for other vacancies.

At last his name was called and he entered an adjoining room to be faced by two men sitting behind a long table. One of them who appeared to be in his mid-thirties gave him a pleasant smile. The other, a middle aged man with greying hair regarded him with obvious interest. Both wore business suits, evidently managers of some sort. The older man beckoned him to sit in a lone chair on the opposite side of the table.

'Hello, Mr Blake,' said the younger man. 'Thank you for attending for interview. My name is Nigel Brody. I am the personnel manager here, and my colleague here is Jim Dawson who manages the security department.'

Although Jack felt slightly nervous it didn't show. His commissioned rank during his period of army service had given him a great deal of self-confidence, so he was able to answer the questions thrown at him quietly and honestly. Some of the questions were about himself and his hobbies but some related to his interests and qualifications.

'Thank you, Mr Blake,' said Brody finally, 'We will let you know the outcome of your application within the next two weeks. Please see the secretary in the office next door for a reimbursement of your expenses.'

One week later Jack was overjoyed when he was phoned with an offer to join the Company as assistant to Mr Dawson. He didn't need to consider it. He accepted the position immediately. He lost no time in telling Delaney that he had got the job at Brouchers, who in turn informed Schmitt. Schmitt smiled grimly to himself with the realisation that perhaps he had another way of getting his foot in the door of Brouchers. He promptly phoned one of his female operatives whom he had used on similar occasions. It was a routine he always used when he got to hear of new employees at research centres such as Brouchers. Usually it didn't work, but there were the odd occasions that it paid off and he enrolled another informant.

Jack's first task was to find somewhere to live in the Hastings area and his prospective new employers gave him a list of possible addresses where he could find lodgings. One was in a pleasant area close to the sea and as he did not yet possess a car it was only fifteen minutes' walk from the research centre. It was owned by a pleasant middle-aged widow, Mrs Wilson, and the rent would be well within his capacity once he started to earn his salary.

With a week to go before starting his new position Jack was delighted to see Mary return at the mid-point of the autumn term. Mary was equally excited. She deposited her bag in the hallway, said a quick hello to her parents and rushed round to the Blake's house where she hugged Jack affectionately.

'Let's go outside,' said Jack. 'We've a lot to catch up on.'

As it was a Saturday both of Jack's parents and his sister were at home. Dora smiled tolerantly, saying, 'yes you two get off. I'll brew up.'

Jenny grinned mischievously but refrained from making any comment.

They sat side by side in the late autumn sunshine on a wooden bench seat at the far side of a lawn covered by fallen leaves from the lone apple tree in the middle of the garden.

It was two years since their last meeting and as they sat chatting Jack was aware that his heart was beating a little faster than usual. He'd had several girl friends in the past, one or two of which had developed into more serious relationships but none of them had lasted for long. In truth he had always felt a bit awkward with girls and had never been able to talk freely with them.

It had never been like that with Mary. They had always been able to confide in each other without any hint of awkwardness.

'Mary,' he said, eyeing her appreciatively, 'I've missed you so much. It seems ages since I last saw you'.

'I know, Jack', said Mary with a smile, 'it is a long time, and in the meantime you've become quite a hero I hear.'

Her comment brought back in his mind the whole unhappy affair and he was anxious to change the subject as he always did whenever it was brought up. Now, as he took in her features it was almost as if it were for the first time, her wide brown eyes looking up at him from an open friendly face and her full lips. Her auburn hair was neatly bobbed and she wore warm pullover over her dress as air was quite chilly.

'Don't believe everything you hear,' said Jack with a smile, 'I'm more interested in you. I know you're teaching now, but what other news have you got?'

'Oh, not much,' she replied. 'I lead a pretty dull life on the whole, nowhere near as exciting as yours, but I do enjoy my job. I really love teaching, and I have a few friends I spend time with.'

'What about boyfriends?' said Jack apprehensively, dreading to hear what may be her response. 'An attractive girl like you, there must be someone special?'

She did not answer him for several seconds. Instead she looked away and a slight blush appeared on her cheeks.

'I've got a few male friends,' she said eventually, 'there's one in particular I like and we do go out together. His name's Ben. What about you?' she added, a bit too quickly.

This was just not what Jack wanted to hear but he tried to respond casually,

'No, 'fraid not, no such luck. Er, this Ben of yours, I suppose it's serious?'

Mary's voice faltered, 'He is serious about me. He wants us to get engaged.'

Jack was inwardly devastated and for a moment he was lost for words but then assuming an attitude of camaraderie, he said,

'Oh Mary, that's some news. What about you. Is that what you want?'

A few moments of silent awkwardness followed and for the first time since they had known each other they were both lost for words. Then Jack noticed that there were tears in Mary's eyes.

'Mary, what's wrong,' he said softly.

'Oh, it's nothing,' she replied. 'I just feel a bit down that's all. Probably just the pressure at work.'

Jack turned towards her and putting his hands on her shoulders he lowered his head to look into her eyes. 'Mary, we've known each other too long. It's more than that. What's wrong?' he said gently.

'I told you it's nothing. Nothing that need bother you,' she persisted and attempted to turn away from him, but he continued to hold her firmly.

'Oh no you don't, my girl,' he said fiercely. 'I just don't buy that. Do you really believe that I don't care about you?'

'I don't know what you think about me, Jack,' she said slowly, 'but I do know what I think about you. You just asked me if I had a boyfriend and I told you about Ben. We are good friends, but I don't love him. I only mentioned his name to see what effect it would have on you, but it didn't seem to matter.'

She hesitated for a moment then added softly, 'Why are you so blind, Jack, don't you know? It's you, it's always been you.'

She turned away from him saying abruptly,

'There, now you know how stupid I am. Why don't you run away while you've got the chance!'

Jack immediately pulled her close to him. 'Oh, Mary,' he whispered, his voice choking with emotion. 'It's me who is the stupid one. I thought about you all the time when I was away. Of course I love you. I always have. I suppose it's because we have always been so close that I was afraid to put it into words in case you thought that we were just close friends and that it would spoil things between us.'

Later when they re-entered the house hand in hand, their new found happiness radiated from both their faces, Jack's parents regarded them both quizzically, while Jenny just looked at them wide eyed before a knowing smile crept over her face.

'Hello,' said Fred with a smile, 'what have you two been up to? You look remarkably pleased with yourselves.'

Jack smiled broadly at his parents barely able to contain himself.

'Mary and I have something to tell you all. Mary has agreed to become my wife. We are engaged!'

Dora gave a gasp of surprise and jumped up from her chair to embrace them both.

'Oh, darling,' she said breathlessly. 'You don't know how much your dad and I have dreamed of this moment. Congratulations to you both. What about your parents then, Mary. Do they know yet?'

'No,' replied Mary, her face beaming, 'we are just off to tell them.'

Jenny jumped up to embrace them both affectionately. 'You two are crafty,' she said, 'We had no idea that you were going to come up with this whopper. Best news I've had in a long time, it's certainly made my day. Congratulations to you both!'

'I'm really pleased for you both,' said Fred. 'Just hope you'll be as happy as your mum and I have been all these years.'

Chapter 8
Brouchers

The Research and Development division at Brouchers consisted of three main sections, one for fundamental studies where basic chemical structures were synthesised and tested for pharmacological effects, one for studying methods of synthesis and isolation of potential drugs, and finally a pilot plant where methods for ultimate full scale production were designed.

The first two of these three sections were laboratories housed together in a single block with a common entrance, whilst the third, the pilot plant, was housed in a separate tall building. Other buildings on the site included a large administration block situated facing the main entrance, a staff canteen, a maintenance unit, and a security building where Jack was to work.

On his first day Jack was introduced to other security staff, comprising some twenty men and women ranging from uniformed guards a secretary, a computer technician, an electrician, and a photographer. Jack's position was to act as an assistant to Jim Dawson.

Dawson himself turned out to be a pleasant personality, quite different from the image that he had presented during the interview. He was quick to put Jack at ease and insisted that they used first name terms. Dawson then personally conducted him on a tour around the site and the various research laboratories.

Jack learned that the security division was a highly important section of the Centre. Dawson himself had a Master's degree in Science, and assured Jack that his science degree would be essential in his duties as he would have to have a broad understanding of the nature of the research going on. One of their duties was to visit the various laboratories periodically to examine sensitive areas and to ensure that the security procedures were carried out to the letter. As such they had access to all confidential files and intermediate products.

Jack was amazed at the variety and proliferation of instruments scattered around the benches that he was able to recognise. Microscopes, ultra violet and infra-red spectrophotometers, atomic absorption, gas chromatographs and the latest equipment for High Performance Liquid Chromatography. A mass spectrometer and an electron microscope occupied separate adjoining rooms. There was obviously no shortage of money here and it was easy to see why the drugs developed at this centre were so expensive.

Jack was anxious to meet Paula to thank her for her help in him getting the job, and he knew that she worked in the biochemical research laboratory.

He was introduced to the head of the laboratory, a Welshman named Dr Ronald Jones, who occupied a small office next to the laboratory. He was a middle-aged man with short dark hair and a serious expression. He wore large horn-rimmed spectacles and had a gruff manner, accentuated by his habit of peering over the top of them as if to accentuate his superior position.

The next most senior staff member in Jones's laboratory was Tom Fields, a tall fair-haired young man still only in his mid-twenties but already with a PhD. He was gifted with a brilliant mind and was already credited with several of the successful formulations that had been put out by the company. Jack took to Tom immediately, who was quick to put him at his ease and to wish him all the best in his new position. He asked Tom to introduce him to Paula after explaining the reason for his interest.

Paula was busy working at a desk in the corner of the lab as Tom introduced Jack to her. Jack was careful to remember Frank's alias as he knew that Paula would have no idea bout Frank's previous history.

'Hello,' he said, 'nice to meet you at last? I've heard quite a bit about you from *Alan*.'

Paula smiled back at him saying, 'Good things I hope. Anyway Jack, if I can call you that?'

Jack nodded, 'Of course you can. We shall be colleagues in a way.'

She went on, 'Yes *Alan* did tell me about you. I know you had been good friends in the past. Was it from university days?'

Jack had to think fast. There was no way he could let any of Frank's past life slip. He nodded with a vague reply.

'Yes, anyway Paula, pass on to him my best regards and hope to see him sometime.'

The development of new drugs had a high priority status here and pressure was high to achieve targets. As a new employee Jack had to spend several weeks in learning about the company and modus operandi of all the departments. It was exciting but demanding work and the security he had first encountered now permeated every aspect of his new life.

On his first day he had been asked to report to the personnel office where the secretary June Clark clarified his terms of employment. He had been employed on a six months' probation term to assess his suitability for the job after which the Company would have the option to terminate his employment if he failed to reach the requisite standard. Then he had to sign a confidentiality document which forbade him to discuss or disclose any information relating to his work to outsiders. Failure to do so would result in instant dismissal without references.

In the laboratories all sensitive material was kept under lock and key. Only senior laboratory personnel and named security staff were allowed access.

All prospective new drugs were produced in the laboratory by a process of synthesis involving a number of stages whereby intermediate compounds were formed. Secure refrigerators were used for storing synthesised intermediates. Most of the information with regard to formulae and chemical processes was stored in a computer database only accessible by a complex system of passwords.

All this Jack had to assimilate during his first few weeks, but he enjoyed the challenge and soon settled in well. He was quick to make friends with his colleagues, particularly Tom Fields who lived with his girlfriend, Sally, at a rented flat on the outskirts of town.

Jack's new lodgings were comfortable and as weekends were free he was able to travel home to Canterbury to stay with his parents, and to spend time with Mary when she was at home. On occasions she travelled to Hastings to spend time with Jack and was promptly introduced to Tom Fields and Sally, and before long the four of them became firm friends.

The days were becoming colder with the onset of winter and Jack started to go for walks during his lunch hour, partly for the exercise and partly to get some fresh air and escape from the rather cloying air conditioned environment of the lab. There was a small park nearby and he found it to be very relaxing to stroll and savour the peace and quiet, and to let his mind roam free.

Shortly after starting his new position he heard some footsteps coming up behind him. He glanced around to see a young woman obviously trying to catch up with him.

'Hello,' she said with a smile. 'You're Jack Blake aren't you?'

Jack looked at her with a puzzled frown. 'Yes, that's my name, but how do you know that. I can't remember having met you before. Do you work at Brouchers?'

'No, she said, 'but I do happen to know that you've just started working there. That's right isn't it?'

'Yes, that's right. Why, who are you? How do you know so much about me?'

'I know a great deal about you, Jack. I know where you live and that you are very ambitious. I am right aren't I?' She regarded him quizzically.

'Look, who are you?' said Jack angrily. 'What has my private life got to do with you?'

'Never mind who I am, but I do have a proposition for you. Do you want to hear what it is?'

'I don't know that I want to hear any more from you. What earthly proposition could you make that would be of any interest to me.' In spite of his anger Jack was curious. Was she about to offer him another job?

'I represent a large pharmaceutical company. Its name is unimportant. You have just started to work for Brouchers on their experimental drug programme. Have you ever stopped to wonder at the millions of pounds in profit the company makes?'

'Of course it does,' retorted Jack sharply. 'That's why it's in business.'

'But who gets the lion's share of the profits? Not you, Jack, it's the big bosses and the shareholders. But you and your colleagues do all the hard work. Do you think that's fair?'

'Look,' said Jack, losing his patience, 'I don't know who you are or what all this is about and frankly I don't want to know. I demand to know who you are and what you are getting at. Stop beating about the bush!'

'OK, Mr Blake, I know roughly what you earn. If you agree to work with us then you could increase that several times. Just think what a difference that would make to you and your fiancée.'

Jack stopped in his tracks and looked at the woman open mouthed.

'How the hell do you know how much I earn? In any case what are you talking about! I've just come out of the army, and although I have a degree I have absolutely no experience. Why would you want to offer me a job at that sort of salary? I'm not that naive, I couldn't be worth that much to anyone particularly as I work in security and not in the labs.'

'Yes, I know that,' she responded, 'but it means that you have access to most places, especially those where confidential information is stored. All we want you to do is to pass some little bits of that information to us now and again, and each time you will get paid very generously.'

The truth hit Jack like a sledgehammer. He was being asked to indulge in industrial espionage! Although he'd heard about this form of piracy he never thought that he would come across it so soon. And what better time to get a new recruit than now. He was a young person just starting his job, too early for him to have an established loyalty for the company, and still only earning a very modest starting salary. Many would jump at the chance!

Jack turned furiously on the woman, his face flushed.

'You know what you can bloody well do with your offer. Fuck off! If you think I've spent all this time and energy getting a degree and a job that I really want just to end up by being a bloody stool pigeon for you and your sodding paymasters you can forget it! Go on clear off and don't come near me again!'

He turned and walked quickly away back to the lab.

Schmitt's female operative was quick to inform her boss of this encounter. 'Oh well, never mind,' he said, 'I expected as much from what I've heard about Blake but it was worth a try. There will be other fish to fry.'

The day following his encounter in the park Jack was requested to attend the personnel department to sort out some paperwork in the main administration block where he had first attended for his interview.

He found the office he was heading for. It was just a routine matter dealt with quickly by June Clark, the young woman he had first met when he attended for his interview, but as he was about to leave he saw the inner glass panelled door leading to the Personnel Manager whose name was marked clearly on the door. He made a quick decision.

'Would it be possible to talk to Mr Brody? It's rather important.

"I don't know,' she said, 'but I'll see if he's available at the moment.'

She spoke into her internal desk phone then smiled at Jack. 'You're lucky, Mr Blake, you can see him now. Just go in.'

Jack recalled Brody as the pleasant man in his mid-thirties from his interview. He gave him a friendly smile as he beckoned Jack to sit down.

'Hello, Mr Blake. Are you settling in all right? Any problems?'

Jack proceeded to tell him all about the incident in the park,

Brody sat regarding Jack for a few moments, a serious look on his face.

'I'm afraid that this sort of thing happens very often, particularly with new members of staff. There's a whole pack of vultures out there who swoop down to try to get you to betray us in the hope of getting information about our work. I'm glad you have told me about this as it adds to our trust in you. This company, and others like us, lose millions through industrial espionage. In fact it is a very widespread problem. Our company invests huge amounts of money in research and development. You've seen for yourself that no expense is spared for the purchase of modern equipment, and we employ only the best scientists to do the work. Disreputable companies are willing to pay those people handsomely to steal the fruits of this research and then they market similar products under their own brand names.'

'The problem with industrial espionage is that there is very little we can do about these vultures because much of what they do is not strictly illegal. It's a very grey area really. Some of the methods they use are illegal such as when blackmail is involved, someone gets hurt, or where there is an infringement of copyright or patent. We just put our trust in the people we employ and I must admit we are not always successful. In spite of our security measures sometimes we fail, and when we do we don't like to publicise it because that could do even more damaging to the company.'

He paused for a few moments as he regarded Jack standing in front of him before continuing, 'of course as Jim Dawson's assistant you will be in the frontline in helping to prevent this kind of activity. I think you should discuss this matter with him. After all it is his province as head of security. Don't forget, Mr Blake, my door is always open,' he concluded with a smile, 'if you have any problems at all don't hesitate to come and see me.'

Chapter 9

Contacts

When Delaney returned to his house after the shock reunion with Jack Blake his mind was filled with a confusing mixture of emotions. A part of him had been pleased to see the familiar face of his friend and he was confident that Jack wouldn't betray him so long as he believed that he wasn't engaged in any criminal activity.

But he knew Jack Blake only too well. He was a straight as a dye and wouldn't hesitate to go to the police if he found out the truth.

Then there was the matter of his function in the Schmitt organisation and the stark warnings associated with it.

His first action was to scan the memory stick given to him by Schmitt. The contents were protected by a password which Schmitt had given him during their meeting. It allowed him to open a database file listing names, contact numbers, and affiliations.

Delaney promptly set about contacting the people named on the list. As some time had elapsed since they had last been in contact with Roger Partridge, he had no idea what their reactions would be. If they were still employed by the same companies they must feel by now that they were safe from the danger of exposure. A complete stranger contacting them now after all this time and claiming to take Partridge's place might be regarded as suspicious so things would have to be handled very tactfully. However Delaney intended to make a success of his new venture and he did have a natural gift of persuasion when dealing with people. If he could get some of the names on the list to cooperate it would be a start. He could then add to it by making personal approaches at other promising sites.

He decided that the best time to ring would be in the evening when people were likely to be at home and away from work.

The first name on the list was Pamela Cartwright, a development chemist at a well-known cosmetics company. The telephone number next to her name belonged to a domestic landline as there was no mobile contact number listed.

Delaney was slightly taken aback to hear a male voice answer the phone. A television could be heard playing in the background.

'Hello,' he said. 'Could I speak to Pamela Cartwright please?'

'I'm her husband,' replied the voice, 'Who is this and what's it about?'

Delaney realised that there was a certain challenge to be met here. Most husbands are not keen on strange males ringing their wives.

'I'm one of her work colleagues. I just need to talk to her about something.'

'Hold on, I'll pass you on to her,' said Mr Cartwright, obviously disgruntled at the intrusion into his domestic life.

'Hello, who is this?' said his wife when she took over the phone.

'My name is *Alan Birch* Mrs Cartwright.' I'm ringing on behalf of a friend of mine, Mr Partridge who I think you know.'

Delaney heard Mrs Cartwright draw in her breath sharply at the mention of Partridge's name. 'Hold on a minute *Mr Birch*,' she said. 'I need to continue this call in another room.'

She turned to her husband, 'sorry darling, it's about something very important we are doing at work and I do need peace and quiet.'

'Mr *Birch*, what is this about?' she said apprehensively, 'I heard that Roger had died in a terrible accident.'

'Yes, that's true I'm afraid,' said Delaney adopting an appropriately pious tone, 'I know that Mr Partridge was your contact with regard to certain communications between you and I suppose you will have been worried about your own position. I want to reassure you that he did not reveal your name, nor that any of the others he was working with. I won't bore you with all the details but I was entrusted with a list of his contacts and your name is on it. I have taken Mr Partridge's place now and my purpose in ringing you to invite you to continue with me as you did before.'

Delaney could hear her breathing at the other end of the phone. It was several seconds before she replied, 'Mr Birch, I've no idea who you are. How do I know I can trust you? You could be anybody.'

'What earthly reason could I have in betraying you, Mrs Cartwright. You haven't actually done anything criminal,' said Delaney, 'I'd like to come and see you to convince you that I am to be trusted. Is that OK with you?'

There were a few moments of silence before she replied tersely, 'All right, Mr *Birch*, the best time would be during my lunch break. There is a coffee shop nearby.' She gave him the address of the coffee shop and they agreed a date and time for a meeting.

'Another thing, Mr *Birch*,' she said in a low tone of voice, 'I must ask you not to ring this number again. I have a mobile phone so you can ring that if you really need to. My husband has no idea about any of this so please only call me if you really need to when he is out. He goes for a drink with his friends on a Friday night so that would be the best time.'

This was just the first of several other conversations Delaney had over the course of the next few hours. Some refused to cooperate professing that they had no knowledge of a Roger Partridge. Delaney then adopted a more aggressive tone, hinting that unless they continued to cooperate their past would be revealed to their employers. Others, relieved that a new paymaster had appeared on the scene, were only too willing to continue in their former role. He received no response at all from at least half of the names on the list due to extinct telephone numbers or changes of affiliation.

In one case Delaney received a very unexpected response when he rang the mobile number of a particularly important informant who worked at a nearby electronics company. His name was Dr Osbourne who answered the phone with a gruff, 'Osbourne speaking.'

Delaney started to talk to him as he had with the other calls but Osbourne cut in with an abrupt, 'Look, I don't know who you are or what you're talking about. I don't work for that company any more. In fact if you must know I was sacked so now I am not only unemployed but as I have no references I can't get another job. That Partridge bastard you've been talking about was responsible for it all by coercing me by blackmailing me over something he had found out about my private life.'

Shocked as Delaney was on hearing this his concern was whether or not Osbourne had told anyone about Roger Partridge after he had been found out. That could lead further to Schmitt, or even himself.

'I am so sorry, Dr Osbourne,' he said, 'but were the police involved at all? I think you can understand my concern about this.'

Delaney heard a short humourless laugh at the other end of the phone.

'Oh yes, Mr *Birch*,' said Osbourne, 'I'll bet you are squirming. However, I'm no stool pigeon, and apart from that I do tend to value my life, what's left of it that is. No, the police were not involved because my company did not want that kind of publicity. Also I never let on about Roger Partridge, and when I heard about what had happened to him I was hardly wracked with grief. Please don't contact me again as I can't be of any use to you now.' With that comment Osbourne abruptly disconnected the call.

Delaney was particularly interested in those names in the list that had the single letter *(c,)* standing for *computer,* written alongside them. This meant that the individuals had access to confidential computer files where it would be a simple matter to smuggle out their contents on a tiny memory device.

Delaney was amazed at the range of companies and organisations included in the list, including police stations, local government offices, manufacturing industries particularly in areas of the food and drink, textiles, chemicals, pharmaceuticals, and cosmetics. One of the names worked for a well-known car company and Delaney realised that passing on information about the development of new models could be very rewarding to competitors.

He noted that one particularly lucrative activity was within local authority offices. Construction work proposed by councils was normally put out to tender so interested firms could bid for the work allowing the council to pick the most economic option. It was not unknown however for the bids to be leaked illegally allowing a particular firm to make the most attractive bid. Some of the names on the list were of corrupt local officials who were prepared to do this.

The day after their telephone conversation Delaney kept his appointment with Pamela Cartwright and assumed his most friendly persona quickly convincing her that he was a reliable contact.

'Just carry on what you were doing before,' said Delaney. 'Whenever you get to learn of new perfumes or other cosmetics your company is working on, just let me know and I will take care of it from that point. There is no need for you to know what happens to it but you will get paid just as you did before. Whenever you have anything worthwhile I will meet you in person at a place of your own choosing for you to hand it over.'

Within weeks Delaney was making a round of those contacts he had been able to enrol in this way and to pick up information which he passed on to Schmitt. Some of the information was quite trivial and Delaney wondered at times if it was worth passing on but Schmitt assured

Delaney that all information, no matter how unimportant it may seem at the time, would have a commercial value.

Delaney was not concerned about being observed when he delivered the material directly to Schmitt's office as he was, after all, a bona fide employee, but he was careful to use a discrete bank account for his bonus payments.

There was one thing that intrigued him however. He knew that as an intermediary between Schmitt and the individuals who stole their company's secrets, he was effectively shielding Schmitt from any direct contact with them. There must be other "liaison officers" like himself who were playing a similar role, so how could he get to know who they were?

Such knowledge could be useful in the future if anything should happen to Schmitt, and Delaney was ever the opportunist. Schmitt would certainly not divulge this information and he was hardly likely to run into any of the other intermediaries by chance. All meetings with Schmitt were carefully scheduled to avoid such a possibility.

Chapter 10
MI5

The Security Service MI5 has its headquarters at Thames House at the corner of Millbank and Horseferry Road in central London. It overlooks Lambeth Bridge, a few hundred yards south of the Houses of Parliament on the north bank of the Thames.

In his fourth floor office Senior Agent Tony Brent sat behind his desk looking pensively through the window at the view. The serene waters of the Thames replete with its usual conglomeration of pleasure boats and small river craft.

In front of him was a brown folder marked in large red capitals as *Top Secret.* It was entitled,

Report on a probable security lapse at the Hammond Grange Military Research Establishment [HGMRE]

The report was based on information received from an overseas agent that a certain foreign power had developed a new long range anti-tank weapon with a highly sophisticated guidance control system. Further examination of the software by MI5 showed it to be identical to that recently developed at the HGMRE. This went beyond mere coincidence and it was concluded that there must have been a leakage of information from the research centre.

Tony Brent was appointed as the senior agent responsible for the investigation. He was a tall lean man in his mid-thirties, with light brown hair tinged with grey, a pleasant quite handsome face and brown eyes topped rather incongruously by a pair of thick black eyebrows.

Having read the report in detail Brent now sat considering his course of action. So far this breach of security had not been leaked to the outside, and certainly not to the HGMRE itself. He also knew from previous experience that there was never a single leak. It would always be followed up by further leaks until the source was discovered.

As a matter of course, and with the authority of HM Revenue and Customs, the bank accounts of all staff working on the project had been surreptitiously checked but Brent knew that the culprit would cover his or her tracks with a great deal of care.

The report contained resumes of the qualifications, experience and background of all the staff at the centre. The head of HGMRE was the research director Dr Caldwell, and he oversaw many research projects of variable importance. Each project was headed by a capable scientist, and Dr Jenkins, an expert in ballistics, was the group leader for the project now under investigation. He had been with HGMRE for twenty years and was highly regarded in his field of expertise. He seemed to be financially secure, happily married with a family, and Brent considered him to be low in his list of suspects.

Other members of the group were two senior scientific officers, four scientific officers and several assistant scientific officers.

Look for the weakest link, thought Brent as he perused the report. This was most likely to lie with one of the more junior staff, but on the other hand it had to be someone with sufficient knowledge and understanding of the project to be able to understand and communicate the information. This made it more likely to be one of the scientific officers, two of whom were men, and two were women, all in their early to mid-twenties.

None of this group appeared to have any obvious financial difficulties. They were well paid with good prospects for future promotion in the Scientific Civil Service.

Brent, with his extensive experience, knew how to look below the veneer of appearances. The only way to delve beneath the surface would be to carry out a personal investigation. He rang to make an appointment with the Research Director, knowing that it would be given top priority. Government Institutions were very unhappy about any intelligence intrusion into their affairs with its attendant implication of security failures, but they had to be seen to be fully cooperative.

He drove to the centre the following morning and was shown into the Director's office. Dr Caldwell was a smartly dressed man in his mid-fifties with a bearing that suggested a military background. His tone was brusque as he shook hands with Brent to greet him but there was a puzzled look on his face as he wondered what the purpose of the visit could be. He had no knowledge of the security breach as very few people outside the

Ministry of Defence and MI5 would have been aware of it.

As Brent summarised the facts Caldwell stared back at him unbelievingly.

'I find it difficult to believe that there has been a security breach here Mr Brent,' he said. 'We have very stringent precautions to prevent any possible leakage of restricted information, and all our staff are very reliable. They are thoroughly vetted before we employ them and then they have to sign the Official Secrets Act. They know that any breach of this undertaking would have dire consequences for them.'

Caldwell paused and his eyes narrowed before posing the question uppermost in his mind, 'are you absolutely certain that this apparent leakage is not just an unfortunate coincidence?'

Brent shook his head as he responded, 'I can understand you wanting to believe that Dr Caldwell and I wish that were the case. I have to say that it is very rare for secrets to be leaked from government establishments so we are taking this matter very seriously. Our experts have looked at this in detail and according to them the chances of any coincidence are very unlikely considering the complex nature of this software. It's not just that the two systems are similar, certain critical features are identical.'

Caldwell nodded reluctantly to say, 'Yes, we of course designed the software and the hardware that it controls. The system is very innovative and I must admit the chance of an identical system being developed independently is virtually impossible. I suppose the question I am asking is how do you know so much about this foreign system? After all, that country will attempt to safeguard their secrets just as we do, even though they may have stolen them from us in the first place.'

Brent laughed mirthlessly, 'we have agents, too, Dr Caldwell. It didn't take us long to get every detail about this foreign system. The software matches ours in every respect.'

The initial doubt in Caldwell's attitude faded to be replaced by a feeling of intense anger as he accepted the high probability of the presence of a traitor in his department. He leaned forward assertively. 'Mr Brent, you will have my full cooperation. We will do whatever is necessary to find the source of this leak before any more damage is done.'

'Of course Dr Caldwell,' said Brent brusquely, 'I would expect nothing less considering the type of work you do here. Any leakage of information from this site poses a serious threat to our national security. I am here to inform you that MI5 in cooperation with Special Branch will be taking over further action in this matter. It is vital that you and your team carry on as normal. We don't want you to do anything that might raise the culprit's suspicions. I'm quite sure that he or she will continue to try to pass information and that will give us our best chance of catching the person.'

'Yes, I understand Mr Brent,' said Caldwell, 'we will carry on as normal but I still can't understand how on earth this information was smuggled out. As a matter of course we do random searches of personnel when they exit the centre. That is another condition of their employment here.

'We don't think that the information is being smuggled out as paper files,' said Brent, 'that would be far too risky, and the use of mini cameras and microfilm takes up too much time. It's is a bit old hat in this day and age. These people are far more sophisticated now we are in the age of computers. Vast chunks of data can be moved about easily and in seconds. We believe that in your case the smuggling was done by copying information to small memory devices which are very easily concealed. Of course it would have to be done by someone with access to confidential information on your computer system.'

'Yes, I must agree with you,' said Caldwell, 'it's the only possible explanation. Memory devices could be smuggled out in a variety of ways, even in intimate parts of the body, but we could hardly carry out intimate body searches every time employees go out of the gate.'

'No,' agreed Brent with a smile, 'one of the problems with modern technology.'

Caldwell's voice slowed down as he added reluctantly, 'It seems almost certain that it would have to be one of the more qualified members of the group.'

Brent nodded in agreement, 'Yes I'm afraid so Dr Caldwell. Perhaps you could tell me something about this group. I understand that the head of the group is Dr Jenkins, is that right?'

'Yes,' replied Caldwell, 'Dr Jenkins is one of our most experienced and highly qualified people. I have the utmost trust in him. Do you want me to inform him about what we are doing and to ask him to keep a watchful eye open on his subordinates?'

'No,' responded Brent emphatically, 'that's the last thing I want. I agree that he's an unlikely suspect but we could probably say that about all the other team members, so we can't take risks. We often find it's the most unlikely people who do things like this, either

133

because of the lure of large sums of money or if they are being blackmailed.'

Caldwell gave a wry smile, 'what about me then? How can you be sure that I'm not the culprit?'

Brent laughed briefly. 'We could have proceeded with our plans without informing you Dr Caldwell, or anyone else on this site, but we decided that as the research Director it would be better to enrol your participation. Obviously we did vet your background first so we have three very good reasons to be sure of your personal integrity. First your army record is impeccable, secondly your personal circumstance don't indicate any desperate need for any financial boosts, and thirdly, and with due respect, you are unlikely to know all the fine details of the stolen material considering the scope of your responsibilities.'

'My, you have done your homework,' said Caldwell with a hint of irony, 'but let me be Devil's Advocate for a moment. All information is stored on the computer system, albeit in encrypted form. If I know the relevant passwords what is to stop me downloading files onto a memory stick and simply driving out of the site with it? After all, as Research Director nobody stops me at the gates.'

'Very true,' responded Brent, 'and of course we have considered this as a possibility, not so much in your case but could someone else outside the group have done as you have described? As you have just said yourself it would be very risky for anyone to take such information out of the centre in any form whatsoever.'

A few brief moments of silence followed as Caldwell mentally reviewed images of people he thought he knew so well. How could any of these trusted colleagues be the traitor in their midst?

Brent's voice broke into his thoughts, 'I must repeat Dr Caldwell, please do not to tell Dr Jenkins or anyone else in this site about what we are doing. Also try to keep any new sensitive information to a minimum. From our experience we know that once anyone commits this sort of offense then he or she is permanently in the hands of their criminal contacts. They naively think that they can make themselves a spot of cash and then opt out. It's sad really but they soon find out that they are trapped in a vicious network of conspiracy. Any attempt to wriggle out and they have the threat of both violence and blackmail. Whoever is passing this information means that he or she is doing it on a regular basis and this gives us our best chance of catching the individual.'

Brent paused before outlining his intended course of action.

'We plan to request that officers from the Metropolitan police Special Branch maintain a programme of covert observation of every member of the research team when they are not at work. These officers are highly skilled at this type of operation and know the sort of things to look for. None of the team members will be aware that they are being watched.'

***

For the next few weeks officers from Scotland Yard's Special Branch, headed by DCI Stephen Brooks, were allocated to work in conjunction with MI5 to keep a discreet watch on the everyday activities of the twelve HGMRE team members. Stephen Brooks was an experienced police officer of middle age, six foot three inches in height with a slim athletic build. Most of the observation was carried out from unmarked police cars aided by numerous under-cover photographs. Mostly they depicted staff going about perfectly innocent everyday life, but all the photos were examined meticulously at the end of each day to see if they revealed any unexpected features.

The breakthrough occurred on the Saturday of the fourth week. One of the surveillance teams, comprising detective sergeant Harris and detective constable Thomson, was watching a male staff member, a scientific officer named Tony Crowshaw, as he parked his car outside his local library. Just one more event to be logged of the many similar ones they had covered over the past few weeks.

'Hmm,' said DC Thomson to his sergeant, 'here we go again, another boring wait.'

'Hold on,' said Harris. 'A bit odd that he wasn't carrying any books to exchange.'

'Oh, that's nothing,' responded Thomson, 'Lots of people go into libraries to check references, look for jobs, and so on.'

'I suppose I just want something a bit more exciting to happen,' said Harris with a sigh.

Minutes after Crowshaw entered the library a large black car drew up outside. The driver got out and went in.

Again this was hardly suspicious but it prompted a comment from the sergeant.

'Hmm, that's odd, another one without any books to change. I see there's another man in the car. Try and get some close-ups of him and the driver when he comes out.'

136

'Yeah, I know,' Sarge said Thomson giving his superior a meaningful look. 'That's what I'm here for.'

'Ok, ok Thomson, sorry,' responded Harris with a laugh.

Libraries were well known as places where spies exchanged information. Documents or small items such as a memory stick could be surreptitiously hidden in or around the bookshelves to be quickly retrieved by an associate without any direct contact.

As Norman Longford entered the library he noted there were several tables with chairs occupying about a quarter of one end of the room which was bordered by bookshelves.

Other bookshelves were freestanding at the other end of the room and alongside one wall were positions for consulting a variety of daily newspapers, journals and magazines.

Tony Crowshaw was standing in front of one of the newspaper positions apparently scanning the news. Longford made no attempt to talk to him; he just went directly to the bookshelves as if to browse. He moved to one of the free standing book cases out of the receptionist's line of view, and withdrew a particular book, one that had been previously named by Crowshaw. Longford opened the book after a brief look round to ensure that there were no other customers in the vicinity, and quickly withdrew the micro SDHC card taped to the inside of the back cover. He slipped it in his pocket and exited the library.

'Hmm, very odd,' said Sergeant Harris to his partner. 'This man entered the library just after Crowshaw and now he's come out without books and too soon to have done anything worthwhile. Did you get a close up face shot Thomson just in case?'

'Yes, Sarge,' responded Thomson lowering the DSLR camera with its long focus lens. 'I got a clear shot as he came out of the library and one of his passenger.'

'Good,' said the sergeant, 'we'll check it with records back at the Yard. Hang on here until Crowshaw shows his face but I can't see it telling us anything new.'

Norman Longford was not only Schmitt's general factotum, hit man, and driver, he also carried out jobs of this nature to prevent any direct contact between his boss and this particular mark. Another of his duties was to keep a keen lookout for any sign of observation wherever they went. He had a second instinct in this respect and could always tell the signs of police presence no matter how covert. He could recognise tell-tale signs such as cars parked nearby with inactive occupants. As soon as he exited the library he took a mental picture of all cars in line of sight of the library and whether or not they had occupants.

There were several cars parked nearby and one of them had two occupants. That is definitely suspicious he thought.

Longford also noticed the camera make its brief appearance through the side window of the car.

'Boss,' he said tersely as he climbed back into the driving seat, 'We are being watched and photographed from that car over there.'

'Oh bloody hell,' hissed Schmitt, 'Come on, let's get out of here.'

As they returned to the office Schmitt mused out loud, 'that means the police are keeping surveillance on members of that research team. They would photograph anyone who came out of the library while Crowshaw is in there.'

He sighed, 'Ah well it was only to be expected I suppose. The police aren't stupid. They would know that there had to be a leak and I have no doubt they will soon find the source of it.'

He was silent for a few moments before continuing, 'I'm pretty sure that we're not likely to get anything more useful from Crowshaw. If he gets arrested I'm sure he'll blab, he's just the type to break down under interrogation and that means he would name you as his contact. So Norman,' he concluded, 'It's up to you to make sure that there won't be any such confession.'

'Ay,' growled Longford in return, 'I know what to do, but hold on a minute boss. Our faces will be on their files so they will identify us anyway.'

'Too true Norman but so what?' replied Schmitt. 'There's no proof that we had anything to do with Crowshaw. It's just a coincidence that we were there at the same time. After all, it's no crime visiting a library whoever else happens to be in there.'

***

Norman Longford's association with Hans Schmitt dated back to the time when they had been joint prisoners in the same jail, Schmitt for company fraud, and Longford for robbery with violence. Schmitt soon recognised in Longford a man who could be useful to him later after their release from prison.

He believed that the field of industrial espionage could be fruitful particularly in this day and age when so much information could be moved about in small electronic memory devices. All he needed to do would be to somehow persuade people who worked in targeted companies to steal confidential information and pass it on to him so that he could sell it to rival companies at great profit.

He planned to use intermediaries who he would employ legally as liaison officers but whose function it would be to actually find such people, termed *Marks*, and persuade them to betray their employers. These liaison officers would then channel the information to Schmitt. In that way Schmitt never came into direct contact with the *Marks* so he could never be identified by them.

Often the promise of huge financial reward would be enough, but many people could have skeletons in their cupboards, such as illicit affairs or historic offenses unknown to their employers. Once hooked it would be impossible for them to withdraw without the threat of exposure, or even violence.

That's where Longford could come in and so Schmitt had set about cultivating Longford's friendship. Longford had many links to the criminal fraternity and when Schmitt discussed his proposals with him Longford was able to name several men, and even some women who he thought would be ready to act as liaison officers provided there was sufficient financial reward.

Now, years later, they had formed a firm partnership and he had enrolled several liaison officers, one of whom had been Roger Partridge. Longford was really Schmitt's partner but outwardly acted as his driver, filling in where necessary with his forceful, often violent methods of persuasion.

Schmitt's involvement with Crowshaw at the HGMRE had come about by after an approach by Longford himself who saw no difference between stealing trade or State secrets. Without Schmitt's knowledge he had been keeping an eye on the HGMRE building and had picked out Crowshaw as a likely possibility. He had noted that Crowshaw often went to a nearby public bar on his way home so Longford found it quite easy to get into conversation with him.

It turned out to be a real bonus when Longford discovered that Crowshaw was a scientific officer working on secret military projects. This was a young man in the early stages of his career but was very easily swayed by the promise of the rewards that were promised if he would do just one job.

When Longford told Schmitt about this proposed change to their usual *modus operandi* Schmitt was very doubtful about proceeding as it was a serious departure from industrial espionage. Nevertheless the potential rewards were very tempting, and could be enormous if any resulting information was sold to foreign States. He eventually agreed to proceed and it was soon met by unprecedented financial success with the anti-tank weapon control system.

The actual handing over of information from Crowshaw was far too dangerous to allow this to be done by any of Schmitt's so-called Liaison Officers. It was always Longford himself, the man who had originally approached Crowshaw, who carried out the transfers.

Chapter 11
Persuasion to Betray

As Paula drove home after work one evening she mused about the twists and turns her life had taken. She knew that she was attractive to men, even to her boss, Dr Jones. She had noticed him looking her in a certain way that most women recognise, but there was nothing new about that, in fact she enjoyed playing up to it if it could be useful to her prospects. Apart from that although she had had a number of short term liaisons none of them had been serious until *Alan Birch* appeared on the scene. She now believed that at last she had met her life's true partner in this man who had created feelings within her that she had never previously experienced.

When she arrived at their shared address she noted with some satisfaction that *Alan's* car was parked in the drive as so often he had been late returning from whatever he did in the City. Then she'd had to pass several hours alone waiting impatiently for him to return home.

As soon as she entered the house she knew something was seriously wrong. Delaney was sitting on the settee, bent forward and holding his head in apparent despair. Paula ran over to him and put her hand around his head to raise it and look into his eyes.

'Darling!' she cried out. 'Whatever's the matter?'

Delaney tried to avert his head, mumbling, 'Nothing, there's nothing wrong.'

'What do you mean, nothing,' she returned, 'Come on, darling, tell me. What is it?'

Slowly he raised his head, his eyes moist with tears, then slowly mumbled, 'I'm in trouble Paula. Lots of trouble.'

Paula moved quickly to sit beside him on the settee. She put her arm round him pulling him towards her. 'What sort of trouble *Alan*, just tell me, whatever it is we are in it together,' she said.

'It's financial,' he returned in a desperate tone of voice, 'and when you hear about it you won't want anything more to do with me, and I wouldn't blame you.'

'I'll be the judge of that, *Alan*,' she said, 'just tell me.'

'I made a stupid error of judgement,' said Delaney. 'Several months ago I borrowed a lot of money to invest in shares for a new company that had been forecast to deliver a huge profit. I was going to sell off the shares when they had increased sufficiently in value, repay the loan and be left well in pocket. Well, the bottom line is that the company has just gone bust and the shares are worthless. I've lost everything. So now I don't know what on earth I'm going to do.'

'Oh, *Alan*,' Paula looked into Delaney's eyes searchingly, 'surely it can't be that bad. I have some money put by. Perhaps that could help?'

Delaney gave a short humourless laugh. 'Oh, Paula, if only you could but the amount is far greater than you could ever imagine.'

'Why, how much is it?' she responded, dreading to know what his reply would be.

In a low voice he said, 'fifty thousand pounds.'

'Oh my God, *Alan*, whatever have you done?' Paula looked at Delaney with an expression of shock. 'There's no way I could raise that amount. Whatever are we going to do?'

She paused, looking at him as the question remained unanswered. Delaney just shook his head in mock despair.

'Who do you owe this money to?' she went on. 'Can't you just explain the position to them and ask them to let you pay it back over a period of time?'

'It's not a building society or bank loan, Paula,' he said bitterly, 'these people are not the sort you mess with. I told them this morning what had happened hoping they might give me time to pay it back even if it took a long time but they wouldn't wear it. They did offer me a way out however with a hint that I either come up with the money or I do what they suggested, otherwise I could be left short of body parts!—and still owe the money.'

Paula looked back at him horror struck. 'They sound like criminals! How did you get mixed up with people like that?'

'I didn't know what they were like at the time,' replied Delaney convincingly, 'it was from some ill-conceived advice I took from a business colleague.'

'Well, never mind about that now,' said Paula, 'what was this way out you mentioned?'

'Oh, Paula,' responded Delaney, his voice almost pleading. 'I can't really ask you to do this, but if I don't agree to their demand I don't see any future.'

He paused for a long time before continuing. 'They said that if there was some way I could get my hands on the formula for EDF301 or any of the other drugs in this range and pass it to them they would forget the loan.'

It was a masterpiece of acting by Delaney but even with this false story would it be enough get Paula to do what was necessary?

It seemed unlikely if her immediate reaction was anything to go by.

Paula's attitude changed almost immediately from one of concern to anger. 'There is no way you could get that information. It would be more than my life's worth to betray the company and it would certainly spell the end of my career. What did you have in mind, *Alan*? That somehow I should get that information and pass it on to you? You must know I would never do anything like that.'

'No,' responded Delaney, 'I know you wouldn't but you could do it indirectly. I'm desperate Paula and there's simply no other way out.'

'What do you mean *indirectly?* Just spell out what you mean.'

'I mean that if you could cultivate a relationship with that boss of yours I'm sure you could convince him to get the goods.'

Paula was horrified. 'You want me to do something to incriminate him? It would destroy his career. Anyway, how could you ask me to do that? I thought you loved me and yet you want me to do kiss and cuddle an old man I have no feelings for.'

'Paula, Paula,' said Delaney taking her gently in his arms. I love you so much it hurts, and this would just be an act for you. It won't mean anything at all either to you or me, but it would get us out of this awful mess. As for your boss, he has access to all this stuff and I'm pretty sure he could smuggle the info out in a memory chip of some sort and nobody would ever know.'

He paused to kiss her tenderly, saying, 'I'll never ask you to do anything like this again but this is important to me, so will you do it?'

'No!' she said vehemently shaking her head. 'No, I won't be party to that. It really is too much whatever the consequences.'

'Look, honey,' he said gently, 'when it's all over we can get married and that's a promise, so please do what I ask.' He held her by the shoulders and looked earnestly into her eyes, virtually pleading for her to do his bidding.

Delaney's hold over Paula was very strong and the promise of marriage weakened her resolve. Eventually she gave way, mumbling reluctantly, 'All right, *Alan*, I'll see what I can do but I'm definitely not going to sleep with him.'

Delaney gave a false laugh. 'Sleep with him! You'd better not! Just stir up an expectation that you will sleep with him if he does as you want.'

On the following afternoon Paula went into Dr Jones office for a routine discussion about work, a routine procedure. She sat facing Jones, her legs crossed making sure that enough thigh was exposed to arouse him.

He cleared his throat and used what he hoped would come over as a friendly tone. 'I need to discuss some aspects of your work, Paula. Don't worry, you are doing well. I've been keeping an eye on you and I think you have a promising career in front of you.'

Paula smiled, well aware of the effect she was having on Jones. She shifted her legs to reveal even more flesh.

'Thank you very much, Dr Jones, I try my best,' she said.

Ronald Jones had indeed been keeping an eye on Paula but in a more lascivious sense. He had noted that she looked at him from time to time in what he thought was a seductive way, reviving dormant longings. His marriage of twenty years had been fruitless of children and although he still loved his wife his life had become a dull routine devoid of excitement. Nevertheless he had remained faithful but this didn't mean that his desires were gone.

As he drove home that evening his mind was in a turmoil. The weather was dull, the sky overcast with spots of rain appearing on his windscreen, none of which helped his present mood.

His mind shifted to the present state of his career. His was well aware that the staff regarded him with some contempt as his promotion to chief chemist had been built on the backs of more able people. He owed his position by virtue of long service and by taking the plaudits for much of the successful research in the department. Years before when he had prepared and presented his PhD thesis at University he had only achieved success after two attempts. He secretly envied Tom Fields and his brilliant mind, which only tended to emphasise his own failings.

How he wished for some more excitement in his life. It was now too late to achieve anything of note in his professional life which now would just go in a humdrum way until eventually he would retire, never having achieved anything of note. Even the possibility of promotion to higher echelons of management had long since faded as he was bypassed by younger and more able people.

His thoughts turned to Paula. Why would a young attractive female like her be interested in a middle aged man like himself, or had he misinterpreted the various gestures and meaningful glances. Perhaps it was it all in his wishful imagination?

But then, he knew that young women are often attracted to older men, particularly when they were in more powerful positions. There were plenty of examples of such matches reported in the media. Why shouldn't it happen to him?

The next morning he called Paula into his office and as she sat facing him he became convinced that she was making a play for him. Her whole manner was provocative, the way she crossed her legs, and the many meaningful smiles and gestures could only be interpreted in that way.

He decided to take the bull by the horns.

'Look, Miss Kendrick, we could go over some of these things in a more relaxing way if you like. Why don't we meet up at the Flying Horse pub after work to discuss it all further?'

He swallowed hard and looked at her with a forced smile, willing her to agree. Paula smiled broadly back at him.

'That's a great idea, Dr Jones. I would be pleased to,' she said easily.

The Flying Horse was the cosy pub just down the road from the research centre where Delaney had first approached Paula, and staff members often gathered there to discuss items of mutual interest. Jones made a quick phone call to his wife telling her that he would be late home due to a meeting, something she accepted without comment as he often stayed late to finish off some work or because of an emergency meeting.

They made themselves comfortable at a table in a quiet corner of the pub and immediately Jones's tone became more familiar.

'Paula, er you don't mind me calling you Paula do you? After all we are colleagues.'

'Of course not,' she replied, 'but of course I must call you Ronnie, I hope you don't mind.'

'I don't mind in the least, but probably best not to say it at work for the sake of protocol,' said Jones. He hesitated as he took a sip from the gin and tonic in front of him.

Paula leaned towards him and said playfully, 'Oh, does that mean that I would be seeing you outside work?'

Flustered, Jones responded, 'Oh, you know what I mean, you know, if we happen to meet on social occasions.'

'Oh yes, Ronnie,' teased Paula with a laugh,' just what "social occasions" did you have in mind?'

'Look Paula,' said Jones tersely, 'Let's not beat about the bush. You know I like you and I think you like me otherwise why are you here?'

Paula leant across the table and took hold of his arm, saying in a low serious voice,

'Ronnie, we both know why we're here and yes, I do like you a lot so what are you going to do about it?'

This bolt from the blue stunned Jones as the fulfilment of his desire for this young woman suddenly became a realistic possibility. The implication of her words was clear and fed straight to his groin. He could hardly believe what she had just said but, his voice trembling with anticipation he said,

'I could get a room here if you are willing?'

Paula regarded him with a look of fake surprise.

'What do you mean Ronnie?' she said, deliberately changing her attitude. 'Surely you don't expect me to jump into bed with you? I'm not that sort of girl.'

Jones spluttered, 'but I thought that's what you meant. You just said *what am I going to do about it.* What did you mean if not that?'

Paula had to make a quick decision. She realised now that the only way she was going to coerce Jones into betraying his Company would be to go the whole hog. She was a highly sexed girl and had often satisfied her need with men in the past. In this case it was a matter of sex in the cause of duty. It wouldn't mean a thing to her.

Damn Alan! She thought. He knew perfectly well that it would come to this. Well, she would show him just how well she could perform her part. Just so long as it solved their financial problem it would be worth the sacrifice.

'Sorry, Ronnie,' she said at last. I shouldn't have led you on like that.' She lowered her voice to barely a whisper. 'Go get that room if that's what you want.'

Jones rose and approached the bar where the landlord, Jim Cartwright, was busy pulling a pint for a

150

customer. There were several minutes of quiet conversation before Jim reached behind the bar to take down a key from a board and presented it to Jones in return for several notes that he took from his wallet.

'I've arranged a room for us,' he murmured to Paula when he returned to the table, his voice trembling with the emotion of anticipation.

Paula acted her part perfectly. As an adept performer of the seductive arts she was able to cry out and moan at the appropriate times even if the man between her legs was almost inanimate. He just shuddered as he came almost as soon as he had entered her, then fell away breathing heavily with satisfaction.

'Do you know, Ronnie,' she said coquettishly as they lay side by side on that first occasion, 'I would really like a little keepsake to remind me of this wonderful experience. Something like a gold chain or a bracelet. What do you think?'

She looked at him, turning on her side and regarded him with her wide blue eyes.

Jones was still in the aftermath of ecstasy and in no condition to disagree with anything that she said at that moment. He nodded dreamily, 'Yes, OK,' he murmured.

'Thank you, darling,' she said, 'but I think it best if you give me some money for it. We can hardly go off together to pick one, can we?'

He pushed himself upright and reached for his jacket pocket, pulling out his wallet.

'Here's twenty pounds, that's OK isn't it?'

'Oh c'mon, Ronnie, don't be such a skinflint. Surely our little arrangement is worth a bit more than that. I can't buy a decent bracelet for less than fifty pounds.'

'Hang on a minute,' he responded, 'I don't carry money of that sort around with me. You'll have to wait until I can draw some more from cashpoint.'

'OK, darling, but make it soon. In fact I'd like to pick something this weekend,' she said.

The following Monday Paula appeared, immaculate as ever but now sporting a bright and shiny new gold bracelet. The evening came and the ritual to the previous week was repeated. This time however, as they lay intertwined she mentioned that it would be nice to have a nice gold necklace to go with the bracelet. Once again Jones had to dig into the bank account held jointly by him and his wife.

It wasn't long before Jones realised that he was rapidly running out of ready financial assets. In his eagerness to please his new mistress he had overlooked the fact that his wife was bound to find out sooner or later. He had simply pushed it to the back of his mind in his frantic desire for this girl.

The crunch came one week when her demand for an expensive gold watch was way beyond what he could afford.

'I'm sorry, Paula,' he said, 'I just can't stretch to that. It's out of the question.'

'Oh, come on, Ronnie darling,' she countered in her most seductive tone, her hand moving down to his groin area, 'You buy that for me and I will give you something really special.'

'No, no,' he replied firmly, 'there's no way. It's just too much. I just don't have that sort of cash.'

Her face hardened, 'Oh well, if that's the case then you can forget that *something special*.'

She paused for a few moments before adding, 'I don't believe you can be that hard up. After all you are one of the bosses at Brouchers so you must be well paid. And another thing, what about your wife? What do you think she would do if she found out about our little arrangement?'

The implied threat was obvious and Jones reacted by immediately jerking up to a seated position in the bed. 'My wife?' he exclaimed, 'why should she find out unless somebody was to tell her?'

Paula didn't reply for a few moments. then she turned back to face him, 'There is a way you could make plenty of money for us both and then we could go on meeting like this as long as you like.'

Jones' feelings of rapture from their earlier activity had now died away and he was beginning to feel rattled by the turn that the conversation had taken. 'I'm not with you,' he said tersely, 'I don't see how I could make more money without getting a better paid job but I'm OK where I am. There's no need.'

Speaking in a low and intense tone of voice she said, 'I happen to know someone who would really make it worth your while if you would agree pass on one or two details you keep in that computer of yours.'

Jones looked at her, his mouth agape with horror.

'What!' he reacted loudly, 'Are you asking me to steal confidential material?'

'No,' she returned, 'there wouldn't be any risk because you only need to do it once. All we want is a copy of the contents of one particular file. I know that these files are stored on the computer in your office. All you have to do is to copy just one of these files onto a memory stick and pass it to me.'

'You must be mad,' he said angrily, 'do you really think I would do that kind of stuff?' He hesitated as his expression turned to one of curiosity, 'just who is this "*We*" you keep mentioning?'

'That's not important,' she said brusquely, 'but you would be well paid.'

'No!' Jones said angrily. 'Not a chance.'

He glared back at her as he now realised that he had been set up. The whole affair had been bogus from the beginning. A feeling of despair settled on him and he fell forward in the bed holding his head. What a fool he had been to have been taken in like that. Why did he not realise that there was no way that a young attractive woman like Paula would be attracted to a dull middle aged man such as himself?

'It's your choice,' said Paula coldly, 'but if you refuse to cooperate then I'm afraid your darling wife will get to know of your extra-marital activities.'

'So, now we know the truth,' returned Jones bitterly. 'You are not only a spy but a blackmailer, too.'

She simply shrugged her shoulders, 'Have it your way, but I mean what I say. Get that stuff for us or else.'

Jones knew he was trapped. Either he agreed to do her bidding and risk losing his career and livelihood if caught, or he would lose his wife. However, he rationalised, if he chose to betray his company the chances are that it would not be discovered and it would only be a one off after all.

'What file is it that's so important,' he said slowly.

'It's the one describing the synthesis and intermediates for the anti-arthritic drug coded as EDF301,' replied Paula shortly.

Jones was almost speechless, 'Christ Almighty,' he gasped, 'have you any idea what you're asking me to do? I would be crucified if I was caught!'

'There's very little risk,' she said, 'all you have to do is to stay late one night and copy the file. It doesn't take a minute to do that and there's hardly any risk. The computer is on your desk and even if there was somebody in the laboratory they wouldn't be able to see what you were doing. Anyway you're getting away from the point. Will you get that stuff for me or won't you?'

He nodded slowly and reluctantly. He had no choice but to do as she asked. 'When do you want it doing?' he said dully.

'I'll bring you a memory stick tomorrow,' she said. 'It's very small so it can be easily hidden. Then you could do it tomorrow evening after work. I will be waiting for you here afterwards so you can pass it back to me and you will get paid.'

Jones nodded glumly. He had no interest in any payment but since he had already succumbed to the blackmail he may as well get what he could out of it.

The next evening after the bulk of the staff had gone home Jones entered the password into his computer which brought up a database with a listing of all the files. They contained details of chemical formulae, the synthetic processes involved, and the identity keys to the coded phials stored in the refrigerator.

He entered the code EDF301 into the 'find' window and the file title was displayed on the monitor screen with a request for a password.

As he took the memory stick out of his pocket he hesitated as the enormity of what he was about to do enveloped him like a stifling black cloak. He was on the verge of betraying his company, and not with anything trivial. The company had great hopes for this latest product and all the preliminary research into its synthesis had been completed. Obviously it was vital that all the details were kept confidential as any leakage of this information to rival companies would be very damaging.

Jones thought about all the hard work that had done during the preceding couple of years to produce this new drug. It had been a complicated process involving many stages of synthesis, the most difficult of which had been to separate the active enantiomorph from the inactive one. Enantiomorphs in pharmacology were the two forms of a drug which in most respects were identical but whose molecular structure appeared as mirror images of each other. Rather like the left and right hands of a human being. The lab separation had been achieved by the process of the fast developing method of HPLC, and he had to admit, this had been due to the work done by Tom Fields.

He gave a deep sigh of despair. He had been given no choice in the matter. He quickly plugged the memory stick into a USB slot and transferred a copy of the file into it. He then quickly disconnected the device and put it in his trousers pocket.

Paula was seated at their usual corner table and as Jones slumped down opposite her he took out the memory stick from his pocket.

'I suppose this is what you want,' he said dully.

She reached out to take the device but Jones kept it held tightly in his hand. He wanted to delay this final act of betrayal as long as possible.

'Just hold your horses,' he said. 'Let's see the colour of your money first.'

After a few tense moments Paula said, 'there's a bit of a problem. When my contact said that this would be a one-off he meant that he would want both this and an actual specimen of the drug. 'You'll have to get that for me tomorrow.'

Jones glared at her unbelievingly as he realised that there was no way that they would let him get away with this single deed.

How naive he had been! Once hooked he would be expected to continue stealing the company's secrets until they had no further use for him.

Suddenly his mind was made up. 'No! I won't do it!' he said tersely. 'You can tell your anonymous friend that he can go to hell!'

Jones pushed his chair back violently and stormed out of the pub, pushing the memory stick back into his pocket. Behind the bar Jim Cartwright noticed the little scene played out in his bar but couldn't hear any of the conversation. He sighed as he thought *'Well, that's that then. Another end to a beautiful friendship!'*

Paula sat stone faced until Jones had gone then rose slowly to go to return to her car where she used her mobile to inform Delaney of the turn of events. His reaction was totally unexpected. Instead of the sympathy and understanding that she expected she was met by a torrent of hate and abuse.

'You stupid bitch, do you realise what you've done by letting him get away!' he shouted. 'We would have made a fortune with that information!'

Paula couldn't believe what she was hearing. This was not the kind and gentle man who had professed his love for her. This was the voice of a very different character.

'Alan,' she gasped, 'why are you talking to me this way? I thought you loved me. We could always find some other way of getting the money you owe.'

'Love you!' he returned bitterly. 'Don't make me laugh. As for the money, I don't owe money to anyone. The whole idea was to get that stuff from Jones to make me a small fortune.'

With that Delaney abruptly disconnected the call leaving Paula to stare unbelievingly at her now deadmobile phone.

***

As Ron Jones drove home a thousand thoughts flashed through his mind. How could he have been so gullible, but perhaps if he acted quickly he might be able avoid any repercussions.

One thing was certain, he would report to the company security department in the morning that Paula had asked him to steal confidential information but he had refused. He was sure they would accept his word without question as a trusted senior member of the staff.

He wondered if Paula was likely to turn up for work the next day. If she did she might refute any accusations against her and turn them back on him. She could insist that he had cultivated the affair between them to gain her complicity. She had refused, and intended to report him to security, and claim that he had only gone running to security to forestall her.

There was still the danger of her threat to tell his wife about their affair and Paula might still try to use this to get him to change his mind. It was a risk he had to take but he was sure he could bluster his way out of that should it happen.

First he had to get rid of the memory stick, then there would be no evidence that could be used against him.

He pulled into a lay-by, took the memory stick out of his pocket and dropped it on the hard tarmac. He ground his heel on it, flung the remnants over the hedge bordering the lay-by and continued on his way.

The blossoming relationship between Dr Jones and Paula Kendrick had not passed un-noticed by the laboratory staff even though Jones himself remained blissfully ignorant of the many sniggering comments and Paula simply ignored them.

Tom Fields was particularly concerned as Jack Blake had told him earlier that Paula was living with one of his friends. So why was she carrying on with Dr Jones? Tom thought that he should broach the subject with Jack.

'It's really none of my business, Jack, but I thought you ought to know. I don't know this friend of yours but it does seem very odd. After all, Paula is a very attractive girl. Why would she make a play for someone like Jones?'

'No idea, Tom,' said Jack, 'but I'm pretty sure that *Alan,* that's her boyfriend who I know pretty well, would take a dim view. I think I'd prefer to leave it alone. I certainly wouldn't want to interfere. It'll probably fizzle out anyway.'

'Yeah, you're probably right,' said Tom.

Everyone in the lab had noticed that for the last couple of days Dr Jones had been looking particularly stressed. He snapped at his staff over the most trivial of matters and his attitude to Paula Kendrick had become distinctly hostile. They must have quarrelled, he thought, probably accounting for Jones's changed behaviour.

***

As Jack Blake's period of probation ended he was called for an informal chat with Jim Dawson.

'No problems, Jack,' he said shaking Jack's hand, 'you've passed your probation period with distinction. You are now a permanent member of staff.'

'Phew, that's a relief,' said Jack with a grin.

'I'm sure it is, let's have a drink on it later', said Dawson.

Every weekend Jack looked forward to getting back to Canterbury to see his family and of course Mary whenever she was there. As an engaged couple they corresponded with each other daily by mobile phone and couldn't wait to meet as frequently as possible.

One day Mary rang him her voice full of excitement.

'Oh, Jack, I got some wonderful news. I applied for a teaching job at St Leonards. It's not far away from you. I didn't tell you about it in case it fell through, but now, guess what! I've received an offer so I'll be coming to live near you.'

Jack was delighted, 'That's great, Mary,' he said, 'and you can forget the *near me* bit. What do you think about us renting a flat or something and living together? After all we'll be getting married soon.'

Mary laughed over the phone, 'Well now, Mr Blake,' she said mischievously, 'Are you suggesting we live in sin?'

'Of course I am,' replied Jack with a matching laugh. 'I want us to be as sinful as possible. Mind you, I'm a bit nervous of telling that father of yours. Are you sure he's not going to come after me with a shotgun?'

Mary laughed, 'No chance,' she returned, 'he thinks the sun shines out of you. He'll understand, provided of course that we don't leave it too long before we get married, oh, another thing, he lived with my mum for ages and only got married when yours truly was on the way.'

'I'm sure my parents will feel the same way, said Jack. 'I can imagine their faces now when I tell them. The first thing they will say is "when are you two thinking of getting married?"'

Mary laughed. 'It won't be that long, Jack. We've discussed it so often and agreed we won't rush into it. Let's just save up a little longer.'

Within the next few weeks Jack procured a modest apartment for Mary and himself not far from that of Tom Fields and his girlfriend Sally. He was also able to take out a loan to buy a second hand car.

Chapter 12
The Reckoning

As Paula Kendrick returned to the rented house she shared with *Alan Birch* she was filled with a multitude of mixed emotions. Knowing that he had no feelings for her whatsoever, and that it had all been a cruel ploy to get her to do what he wanted had left her devastated.

The false promise of marriage and his loving attitude towards her had all been a pretence, adopted only for him to achieve his objective. How could she have been so stupid? She was not a bad girl and the things *Alan* had persuaded her to do were completely out of character. She remembered the strange circumstances of their first meeting, now realising that it had been arranged solely for the purpose of using her.

It was bad enough that she had been persuaded to blackmail Dr Jones but then when she had debased herself with him she felt ashamed. And it had all been so-so unnecessary. She came from a good, well–to-do family and had a generous monthly income from her trust.

As Paula thought about the many discrete phone calls, his unexplained absences, and his evasive explanations whenever she had asked him what he did for a living it was all too now apparent what kind of business *Alan Birch* was involved in. It clearly went a lot further than this sole episode at Brouchers.

She parked outside the house and entered it with mixed feelings of trepidation and increasing anger. As soon as she got through the door Delaney confronted her, his face suffused with rage.

'Do you realise what you've done,' he shouted, 'I've been offered thousands to get that material and now it's gone down the drain you stupid bitch!'

'Oh, so now we know the truth,' responded Paula furiously. 'You bastard! This was all about you getting a payoff. It had nothing to do with any loan. You led me on to believe you loved me, but nothing could be further from the truth. You made me give up my career and do something I shall regret for the rest of my life.'

'Love you!' he sneered, 'I don't love anyone, least of all you. I could have been rich with that formula and then I would have booted you out anyway.'

He hesitated before adding venomously, 'You know there's a good chance that he'll go blabbing to the company's security and that'll be the end of you.'

'Well if that's the case it'll be the end of you, too!' she flung back.

He grabbed hold of her furiously, 'What! You would dare to implicate me! I'd kill you!'

'It doesn't matter,' she said wrenching herself away from his grasp, 'I'm not naming anyone because I'm not going back there. I'm leaving this house and that means you too, *Alan Birch*, I've had enough!'

Delaney furiously grabbed her shoulder again

'What do you mean? Where would you go?'

'It means that I have come to my senses,' she raged back, 'when I think of the things you have made me do I feel nothing but disgust, not only for you but myself, too. You've made me behave like a whore. Why I agreed to do those things I'll never know but it's come to an end now. I want nothing more to do with you.'

As she tried to wrench herself free again Delaney applied more force to retain his grip on her. 'You're not going anywhere,' he snarled, 'you think I'll let you go now after this.'

'Oh yes, and how do you propose to keep me here,' shouted Paula as she continued to struggle, 'keep me locked up here forever? All I have to do is scream loudly. We live in a little avenue, now full of people at this time of the evening. How long do you think it would be before half our neighbours came running?'

He pushed her roughly away with a snarl. 'Oh get off out of here. I don't want to see you ever again.'

'Don't worry, you won't,' she returned before hurrying away to pack her belongings.

Delaney collapsed into a chair holding his head. A mixture of violent emotions coursed through him as he thought about the consequences of this failure.

If Jones were to report Paula's actions to his company's security division he could well be named as being a suspected accessory in view of their shared address. This would put his name in the domain of known industrial pirates, information that would be shared between other companies.

Schmitt's reaction would be predictable. He would become another Roger Partridge!

***

Ron Jones had a sleepless night following the meeting with Paula Kendrick at the Swan. He rose early being careful not to disturb his wife and prepared himself for work. He knew what he had to do and with any luck none of it would rub off on him.

Of course he shouldn't have copied the file but there was no evidence that he had done so. There was the danger that when the security chief confronted Paula with his accusation she would incriminate him but he would simply deny it and his word would be believed as a senior member of staff.

He was in no mood to have breakfast but he had a quick coffee as he sat in the kitchen pondering how he was going to proceed when he arrived at work. Obviously he had to go and talk to Jim Dawson, the security manager, as soon as he reached the labs.

He shouted up to his wife,

'Bye dear, I'm off to work now. See you tonight.'

He donned his coat and hat and picked up his brief case before leaving the house and heading for his car which was parked kerbside at the bottom of the drive. He had left it there on the previous evening because his wife's car had been occupying the available space on the drive.

It was a cold morning with the threat of rain and a cool wind blowing from the west. He pulled up his coat collar as he walked briskly down his driveway and round to the driver's side of his car. He was about to open the door when he heard a sudden squeal of tyres. He looked up, startled, and to his horror saw a car accelerating rapidly towards him.

Desperately he tried to jump out of the way but it was to no avail. A strangled scream escaped his lips, cut short as the inevitable impact slammed him violently against his own car before the vehicle roared noisily away into the distance.

The noise shattered the quite stillness of the suburban avenue and within seconds neighbours came running out from nearby houses. Mrs Jones also heard the noise and grabbing her dressing gown went running down the stairs and to the front door. A soon as she saw the scene outside she screamed, 'Oh my God, it's Ron!'

She ran down the path to find her husband prone on the ground beside the slightly open door of his car. His head was covered in blood and his shattered glasses and briefcase lay strewn on the ground. One of the neighbours went running back to her house to dial 999 and within minutes a police car came tearing round the corner its siren blazing, shortly followed by a paramedic ambulance.

As the police fenced off the area two paramedics examined the inert form on the ground and soon found that life was extinct. They covered the body to await its removal to the morgue.

Next to arrive was a senior officer in the shape of detective inspector Dave Dobson, a youngish man of medium height. He wore a fawn raincoat over a smart grey suit and red tie. His light brown hair was neatly parted on one side and he was clean shaven. An outwardly pleasant man who liked to appear well groomed in spite of the early hour.

But appearances were deceptive. Dobson was a highly experienced officer, and young to have attained this level of seniority. He was accompanied by his close associate, Detective Sergeant Bob Rudding, a taller, rugged looking man in his mid-forties.

As they surveyed the scene they could see that Ron Jones's car had suffered considerable damage, mainly on the driver's side from the rear end to the front door. Particularly noticeable against the dark blue paintwork of the Mondeo were red paint contact marks certainly made by the offending vehicle.

'This was no accident,' said Dobson in a low voice to Rudding. 'Plainly a case of hit and run, Get SOCO here and start the procedure for a crime scene.'

Scene of crime officers soon arrived clad in their white overalls. They examined the scene and took photographs of the ground and Jones's car. The body was removed and the car taken away for detailed forensic examination.

In the meantime a policewoman took a distraught Mrs Jones back into the house to provide some comfort while Rudding went to question the neighbours for possible witnesses.

DI Dobson strolled slowly up to the Jones's house and entered. He had to ask Mrs Jones some basic questions but it was never an easy matter at a time like this. He had to approach her in as sympathetic way as possible.

'I'm so sorry, Mrs Jones,' he said. 'This is a dreadful matter. Is there anybody who could come and be with you for a while? A friend or relative perhaps.'

She looked at him her eyes brimming with tears and it took her a few seconds before she could find her voice.

'I don't know,' she said slowly, 'I think maybe my next door neighbour would come. We are quite friendly.'

The policewoman nodded and went off to talk to the neighbour and make the necessary arrangements.

The inspector regarded Mrs Jones compassionately and then in a gentle tone said,

'I'm not going to bother you with a lot of questions just now but I do need to know where your husband was going.'

Her voice wavered unsteadily as she replied tearfully,

'Ron was just on his way to work. He works at Brouchers, the pharmaceutical company in Hastings. It was just a normal day – Oh dear God, why? How could something like this happen?' Her voice trailed off and she buried her face in her hands as she broke down again.

The policewoman returned with the next door neighbour who quickly put her arms around Mrs Jones to embrace and comfort her.

As Dobson returned to his car his mind turned over the facts as far as he knew them so far, analysing them in his usual professional manner.

He was sure that this was a case of hit and run as he had mentioned earlier to Rudding and the driver of the vehicle would have been very aware of that.

Of course it may be a case of an irresponsible driver who panicked. But somehow Dobson had a feeling that there was more to it than that. Admittedly it wasn't a very bright morning but visibility was good. Also several of the neighbours had heard a loud squeal of tyres before the crash which had caused them to go running out of their houses to see what was happening.

This sounded as if a car had been parked up and waiting for the opportune moment when Dr Jones was about to get in his car.

Was it a deliberate act of murder, and if so, what was the motive?

Leaving Bob Rudding in charge of clearing the accident scene Dobson headed for Brouchers. He announced his identity at the main gate saying that he needed to see the Managing Director urgently.

The MD, Dr John Hesselink, was a tall commanding figure with distinguished greying hair. He was smartly dressed in a pin striped suit and modest blue tie and wore rimless steel spectacles. He was seated behind a large mahogany desk scanning the morning post that his secretary had opened earlier and deposited for his attention.

DI Dobson was ushered into the office where he delivered the grim news of Ron Jones's death.

The shock on Hesselink's face was clear. This is terrible news,' he said. 'Dr Jones was one of our most valuable employees. How did it happen?'

'I'm afraid it doesn't appear to have been an accident,' said Dobson as he recounted the salient points of the morning events. 'I will need to interview some of the staff who worked with Dr Jones,' he concluded.

'Yes of course Inspector. The staff will need to be informed first though. This will be very upsetting for everyone.'

'Who is the senior person in Dr Jones's laboratory? I should inform him or her first.'

'That would be Dr Fields,' replied the MD. 'I'll call him up right away. There's a conference room along the corridor where you can conduct any interviews.'

Tom Fields was just settling down to his tasks for the day when he received the summons to report to the MD's office immediately. Wondering what on earth could be the reason he made his way apprehensively towards the main administrative building. Members of the laboratory staff only rarely came face to face with the MD so he knew it must be for something important.

'Hello, Tom,' said Dr Hesselink. 'Sorry to have to drag you away from your work but something very serious has happened.'

He went on to tell him of the morning's events.

Tom's mind reeled when he heard the news and for a moment he was at a loss for words. He soon recovered his composure however as he realised what he had to do.

'I'll inform the rest of the staff, Dr Hesselink. I know they'll be upset and shocked, just as I am.'

'Thanks Tom,' said the MD, 'but first Inspector Dobson here would like a word with you.' He introduced Tom to the Inspector who had been standing quietly in the background.

There was little that Tom could say to throw light on the situation. As far as Tom knew Dr Jones had no particular enemies although he hadn't been very popular with his staff but that hardly merited attempts on his life.

One thing that did creep into Tom's mind during the interview was Jones's affair with Paula Kendrick and the way that the relationship had obviously deteriorated in the last two days. However it was none of his business and he didn't think that it was appropriate to mention it to the Inspector.

Dobson thanked Tom for his help and handed him his card saying, 'If you know of anyone among Dr Jones's staff who might help in this matter perhaps you will let me know, sir.'

When Tom returned to the lab he called the staff together to tell them of events. The news of the death of

Dr Jones was received with shocked disbelief and there was little work done that morning as they stood around discussing it.

'Anyone know where Paula is?' asked Tom, his eyes circulating around the group.

'She hasn't showed up this morning Tom,' said Tony Banks, one of the biologists in the team.

The absence of Paula Kendrick played on Tom's mind all day long. This seemed to be too much of a coincidence considering the well-known relationship that had developed between Paula and Dr Jones. Also it seemed strange that she had not telephoned in as required when staff members did not report for work. He decided that he would call at her address on his way home as it was not far removed from his own address.

The weather had improved during the day. The sky had cleared to give some sunshine and Tom had to lower the sun visor on his car to avoid being dazzled as he drove to Paula's address.

There were no cars parked outside the house nor in the drive. He knew that Paula normally drove a small blue Fiat 500 but there was no sign of that. He looked briefly at the front of the house and noted that the curtains were all open, no indication that perhaps Paula may be confined to bed.

As he started to walk up the drive to the front door something caught his attention. It was a large fragment of glass glittering in the late sunshine. He crouched to have a closer look and could see it was from a broken car headlight.

His eyes swivelled up to look at the garage doors but they were closed so he didn't know whether or not there was a vehicle parked inside.

He straightened and continued his way to the front door and rang the doorbell. He could hear it ringing from somewhere in the house but nobody came in response. He rang again, but there was still no response.

Very odd, he thought as he turned away to return to his car. Paula has not reported for work and she's not here, so where on earth is she and this on the same day that Dr Jones is killed in a car accident?

He had an uneasy feeling that there was more to this than mere coincidence.

Then he had another thought. What about that fragment of headlamp glass on the driveway?

He really had to see if there was a vehicle in the garage. It was a brick built building separated from the main house by a pathway leading to the back garden. A tall wrought iron gate barred the way but fortunately it was unlocked and he walked quickly through to the back. There was a large window in the rear wall of the garage which he approached over the damp turf. He peered through the window, shading his face with his hands to reduce the glare of the reflected sunlight.

A car was parked inside, a red Citroen C4 Picasso. The passenger side was severely damaged and the headlight was shattered explaining the fragment of headlight he had seen on the drive. It must have dropped out before the car had been driven into the garage. Tom could also see blue paint marks over the damaged area, contrasting sharply with the red colour of the Picasso. He could just make out the registration number which he made a note of on his mobile.

Suddenly a loud shout came from the direction of the main house.

'Hey, what do you think you are doing? This is private property.'

Tom was startled as he turned to see a man standing by the open back door. He was dishevelled and his face was contorted with anger.

'Oh, I'm sorry, sir,' said Tom, 'I thought there was no-one in. I just walked through to see if anyone was in the back garden and didn't hear me ring the bell. My name is Tom Fields and I'm a colleague of Paula Kendrick. She didn't appear for work today so I dropped by to see if she was OK.'

'She's not here,' said Frank Delaney shortly. 'Her mother was taken ill so she had to dash off. She didn't have time to think about calling in. Now, if you don't mind will you please leave.'

Tom had just seen damning evidence that the car in the garage was the car that had mown down Dr Jones earlier that day. If so then it was a remarkable coincidence that the car was at the house occupied by Paula. Did this mean that Paula had been behind the wheel at the time and was it a deliberate act? If so, why, and who was the strange man?

But the car in the garage was not Paula's so it must belong to another occupant of the house. The man he had just seen must be the owner of the car, which raised the question *is he also Paula's boyfriend?*

Tom's mind was in a turmoil as he returned to his car. If that man was the boyfriend Jack Blake had told him about he must also be Jack's long term friend *—Alan Birch*, a friend who was also a probable murderer to boot!

This is a real bag of worms, he thought. Well friend or not, it looked as though the man had been so consumed by jealous rage that he had gone out to deliberately eliminate an apparent rival for Paula's affections.

Tom knew that he had to report his findings to Inspector Dobson immediately. He fished out the card the Inspector had given to him that morning and rang the number on his mobile phone.

Luckily Dobson was still busy at his desk so was able to take Tom's call. Tom told him about the car he had seen in the garage of the house where Paula lived and the encounter with its male occupant. He refrained from mentioning Paula's affair with Dr Jones as he considered it to be the province of the police to follow up that line of enquiry.

'Thank you, Dr Fields,' said the Inspector, 'We will of course follow this up straight away.'

Tom next rang Jack's mobile to tell him about these latest developments. He knew that Jack Blake was taking a few days leave of absence from work to spend some time with his family back in Canterbury.

When Jack received the call from Tom Fields he was sitting chatting with his mother Dora and fiancée Mary in their living room.

He was stunned when he heard the news of Dr Jones's death, and the probability that Frank Delaney had been responsible. If Frank was capable of such an act then it now seemed more than likely that he really had killed Andreas Christakos in Cyprus in spite of his protestations of innocence. He had been taken in completely by Frank. How gullible he'd been!

He knew what he had to do.

'This is awful Tom,' he said, 'There are things I need to tell the police but I'll ring this Inspector Dobson myself if you'll give me his contact number. I'll also be coming back there now so I'll see you soon to fill you in.'

Both Dora and Mary had seen the change in Jack as he received the call and Mary rushed over to him, consternation showing on her face.

'That's terrible darling,' she said when he'd relayed the gist of his phone conversation. 'Of course you must go back now. You haven't got a choice really.'

Dora also came over to put her arms around her son. 'Yes, Jack, of course you must go. It's dreadful news.'

'I have to give this Inspector a ring first,' said Jack. 'After he hears what I have to say he will want to see me as soon as possible.'

Mary looked at him with alarm. 'Why will he want to see you? This is nothing to do with you surely.'

Jack reached out to put his arm around her. 'There's nothing for you to worry about, darling, but Tom thinks that Dr Jones was deliberately mown down by a man I know. You'll hear more about this when I talk to the Inspector.'

Jack duly made his call and was relieved to reach the Inspector straight away. He identified himself and said he was a colleague of Tom Fields who he had just spoken to.

'I'm afraid there's rather more to it than Tom knows Inspector. I happen to know Paula Kendrick's boyfriend who goes by the name of *Alan Birch*. In fact he is a deserter from the army and his true name is Frank Delaney. I knew him in Cyprus where we were both serving officers. He hated the army so I wasn't surprised to hear he had deserted. It's just by chance I met him back here in England when he had the assumed name.'

'Thank you, Mr Blake for telling me about this,' responded Dobson. 'This needs following up so I will contact the army authorities. Incidentally, Mr Blake,' he added curiously. 'Why didn't you report this Delaney to the military authorities when you came across him here in England?'

'Difficult to explain, Inspector. I know I should have, but he had been close friend in the past and I didn't think he was wanted for any criminal activities. I do feel a bit guilty now. It was an error of judgement.'

'OK. Mr Blake, following what Dr Field has just told me I have applied for a provisional arrest warrant for this man, but I will want to talk to both you and Dr Fields as soon as you get back to Hastings.'

'Why didn't I know any of this?' said Mary as soon as Jack had finished. 'Remember, no secrets!'

Jack laughed, 'It was hardly a secret. I just didn't think it was that important at the time.' He proceeded to give her a more accurate account of the events in Cyprus than the newspapers had published and about his friendship with Frank Delaney.

'You see, darling, what sort of friend would I have been to betray him after he confided in me? I just couldn't do it. Things have changed now though,' he added bitterly.

***

As Delaney watched the retreating figure of Tom Fields he swore violently to himself through gritted teeth. He had seen Tom peering through the garage window at the car and would have noted the damage and the registration. The police would be the next to arrive and the game would be up. What he had hoped would be attributed to a simple hit and run accident had gone completely wrong when he had hit Dr Jones's car. Forensic tests on the paint damage would soon prove that his Picasso was responsible.

One thing was clear in his mind. He had to flee from the house immediately. He was not short of cash as he had accrued a sizable bank account using his false identity, but he needed to call at a cashpoint to draw sufficient funds for his immediate needs.

He threw some vital possessions into a holdall then drove hurriedly away after checking the road to ensure that it was clear.

His immediate objective was to put as much distance between himself and the house as possible so he drove westwards keeping to minor roads and hugging the coastline, but being careful to keep within the legal speed limits to avoid attracting attention. He had no clear idea about his final destination but eventually he noted from the road signs that he was heading towards Portsmouth.

It was still daylight when he reached the outskirts of the town. He was exhausted and desperate to find somewhere to stay for the night and where he could consider his next move.

He made a brief call to an out of town Retail Park to draw cash for his immediate needs from a convenient cashpoint and to buy some sandwiches and a variety of other quick snacks. As he drove further on he saw a dilapidated looking motel with a board at the entrance stating it to be *The Rising Sun*.

Hmm, looks more like the setting sun to me, he thought as he pulled in, careful to park out of sight of the lit reception area. He looked round cautiously as he entered and noted with satisfaction that that the only occupant was a tired looking elderly man sitting at the reception desk. His name was John according to a badge attached to his lapel and he was reading the racing results in a newspaper spread out in front of him. A tiny black and white television flickered in the corner. He looked up sharply as Delaney approached the desk.

'Hello there,' said Delaney forcing a smile in an attempt to show an attitude of good humoured bonhomie. 'You don't happen to have a room available do you? I've been driving all day and I'm shattered. I'm really ready to get a shower and some sleep.'

'Right, sir,' said the receptionist looking quizzically at the dishevelled figure in front of him. 'How long to you wish to stay?'

'Oh, just one night,' replied Delaney.

'Please sign the register sir and the registration number of your car. Also I must ask you to pay in advance,' said John.

He signed and paid using his alias credit card and entered a phony registration number for his car. He thought there would be very little chance of there being a check on this as the motel appeared to be practically deserted.

He was given a key to a room at the back of the motel and went out again to park his car in an isolated position away from the few other cars that were to be seen.

The room, although somewhat dingy, did at least boast a separate wash area with a walk-in shower, wash basin and toilet. There was a TV set in one corner of the room and a single bed.

Delaney threw himself onto the bed and looked up at the off-white cracked ceiling as he contemplated the desperation of his present plight. He knew that before long police forces throughout the country would be on the lookout for him. His only realistic option would be to escape the country somehow.

But how? His passport would identify him immediately.

The alternative would be to somehow stow away on one of the many container lorries crossing the Channel from Portsmouth to the continental mainland.

But wasn't this precisely what the police would expect him to do, particularly if they succeeded in tracing his whereabouts to the Portsmouth area? They would automatically focus their efforts on the docks and he would stand little chance of escape.

What he needed to do was to get away from the area altogether. He had made a number of rather shady contacts in recent months, one of whom was particularly adept at forging documents. If he could get a passport in another name he would have a good chance of escaping the country from one of the lesser known ports.

There was now the even greater danger from Schmitt. There was no doubt in his mind that once Schmitt got to know of the previous day's events he would waste no time in attempting to eliminate him.

He turned on the TV set as he knew that Jones death would certainly be reported in the news. It was an early report noting only that Dr Jones, a scientist working for a company in Hastings had been killed by a hit and run driver that morning. Thankfully there was no mention of himself or indeed whether the police were on the lookout for him. He guessed that things were bound to change very quickly so he need to get away as soon as possible.

He needed a different car and he knew precisely where it could be obtained, but first he had to vacate the motel without attracting attention. Police forces would soon be on the lookout for his present car so he would have to abandon it and set off on foot until he was far enough away to risk using public transport.

After a quick shower, he donned a dark grey hip length Parka coat over his white T shirt and jeans, an item which he was glad he had remembered to bring as it was still quite chilly at night. It had an attached hood pulled up to hide as much of his face as possible.

Delaney left the motel at dusk, cautiously keeping out of sight of the reception area. At the last minute he decided not to encumber himself with his holdall. He wouldn't need it if his plan worked out as he hoped.

He walked quickly in a direction away from the city keeping close to the main A3 arterial road heading north. It was a busy road and a number of buses passed him going in both directions. Eventually he boarded a bus that would take him on the first stage of his journey to his intended destination.

Chapter 13
The Investigation

Dobson's first action after Jack Blake's phone call was to call the military police branch of the Provost Marshal's headquarters to pass on the information about Frank Delaney. As it was now a murder case he insisted that the Hastings police remain in charge of the investigation and to postpone his inevitable arrest by the military police, but he requested them to email him a photograph of Delaney together with a summary if his army record.

Inspector Dobson then accessed the police national computer to identify the registered owners of the damaged car seen by Dr Fields in Delaney's garage. It was a care hire firm based in Hastings and a further call quickly established that a man by the name of *Alan Birch* was the current hirer of the vehicle, hence confirming what Tom Fields had already told him.

The revelation that Paula Kendrick lived at the same address as *Alan Birch*, now known to be Frank Delaney, and that she worked for Dr Jones, steered Dobson to the same tentative conclusion to that already reached by Tom Fields.

Was it a crime of passion?

To substantiate this Dobson needed to establish that *Birch* and Kendrick were in a relationship, and if there had been an affair going on between Paula Kendrick and Dr Jones. Surely someone in the laboratory would have noticed and the most likely person to approach was Tom Fields, Jones's second in command. He wondered why Dr Fields had not mentioned this during his call.

The following morning he rang Brouchers and asked to be put through to Tom Fields.

'How can I help you, Inspector?' said Tom.

'Hello, Dr Fields,' said Dobson. 'I'm sorry to bother you again so soon after our chat but I would like to ask you a few more questions regarding Paula Kendrick. You told me last night that you visited the house to see her and to find out why she had not turned up for work. That's when you saw the damaged car and the man who told you she was not there as she was visiting her sick mother.'

'That's right inspector,' said Tom, 'is there something else I can help you with?'

'I hope so,' responded Dobson. 'I am just about to set off to the address for a detailed search. The house has already been secured by some of my officers but the man you saw is apparently not there now. However there is something we need to follow up on. Do you know if Dr Jones and Miss Kendrick were having an affair?'

Tom had been expecting this. It was such an obvious thing for Dobson to ask although he probably knew the answer already.

'It was well known in the lab, Inspector,' he replied. 'We were all rather surprised by their lack of discretion considering their very different positions here and that Dr Jones was married.'

Tom paused before continuing reluctantly, 'Look inspector, I don't feel very comfortable about this. I feel as if I'm just reporting lab gossip.'

'Not at all, Dr Fields,' said Dobson. 'It could be very relevant to the case. We have to ask ourselves if Dr Jones's apparent accident had anything to do with his affair with Miss Kendrick. I'm sure that thought must have crossed your mind too, so anything you can tell me could be very important.'

'There is one thing that was very noticeable to everyone,' said Tom, 'only two days ago they suddenly started behaving very differently towards each other. It looked as if their affair had suddenly ended. We wondered if they'd had a quarrel. That's about all I can tell you, Inspector.'

'Do you know if Miss Kendrick had any other relationships?' said Dobson. 'She's a young attractive woman. It seems so strange that she would go for a man much older than herself,'

'I'm afraid not,' Tom replied. 'She's never mentioned anybody, but from what Mr Blake told me I think she was in a relationship with *Alan Birch*. I have to say inspector that Paula is a bit of a mystery to everyone here. She obviously comes from a wealthy family and she has had a privileged education. Not only that, but her clothes are expensive, hardly typical of those worn by other laboratory staff at work. She didn't look the type who needed to work here.'

'Who knows why people do what they do, Dr Fields,' responded Dobson, 'maybe she wasn't interested in the money, just a career. Anyway, we will need to find her for interview. Do you have any idea as to where she might have gone?'

'We do have her parents' address and phone number on file Inspector. I'll get it from the personnel department and ring you back with it.'

'That's very helpful, thank you, Dr Fields.'

Dobson knew he had to act quickly. He decided not to contact Paula's address by phone just in case she decided to run away again. It would be better to handle it more delicately. After contacting the Berkshire police they agreed to instigate an immediate covert watch on the Kendrick household.

Dobson next course of action was to obtain a police search warrant, then during the drive to Delaney's address, he brought Rudding up to date on *Birch*'s true identity.

'My God, sir!' exclaimed Rudding, 'this guy's a real bag of tricks, and as slippery as an eel.'

'You can say that again Bob,' responded Dobson, 'apparently he's also wanted for a suspected murder of a Greek Cypriot civilian in Cyprus before he deserted.'

The two uniformed officers he had dispatched earlier were waiting on the front drive of Delaney's house.

'I'm afraid the car's gone, sir,' said one pointing to the open door of the garage, 'and there are no occupants in the house now. They must have left in a hurry as they left the front door unlocked.'

'Damn!' swore Dobson turning to Rudding, 'Delaney probably has probably flown the coop in panic after Dr Fields visit. Let's get in the house and see what we can find. First call the station and get them to put out an all Ports warning (APW) for a red Citroen C4 Picasso with its registration number and give details of the damage. We also want to trace these two persons who can help with our enquiries.'

He handed the sergeant his notebook in which he had written down the number as reported to him by Tom Fields. Next to the number he had written down two names, one being Frank Delaney, and the other that of Paula Kendrick who was the known tenant of the house.

The Inspector then walked slowly down the drive scanning the ground and soon came across the glass headlamp fragment seen earlier by Tom Fields. He carefully picked it up to put it into an evidence bag for forensic examination.

After ringing the doorbell several times to ensure that the house was unoccupied Dobson and Rudding entered to carry out a search. Their aim was to find evidence for motive or where Delaney or Paula Kendrick may be heading.

They found nothing of interest downstairs so their attention shifted to the bedrooms upstairs, one of which had been converted to a study.

'There's a laptop computer Bob?' said Dobson, pointing at the desk. 'If there's anything of interest here it's got to be on that.'

'Looks like a recent model, sir,' replied Bob Rudding as he bent down to peer at it.

'You're the computer whizz, Bob. I'll let you start it up,' said Dobson.

Rudding positioned himself in front of the computer and switched it on. After a short wait the monitor screen showed the usual Windows opening screen displaying a range of programme icons. Dobson crouched down to peer over Rudding's shoulder looking eagerly for anything that might be relevant to their enquiries.

'I think we need to look at a database, or possibly a word processor,' said Rudding as he manipulated the touchpad to scan the programme icons. 'Ah, there is one.' he exclaimed highlighting one labelled 'WORD'.

He double clicked the touchpad to start up the programme and scanned the list of files displayed to see if any would be relevant. Most of the files were related to games, routine domestic affairs, and copies of letters, none of them of any interest. However their attention was drawn one file simply labelled with Delaney's initials *E:/FD*.

Rudding attempted to open the file but a popup window appeared with the stark words *cannot open E:/FD*

'What does that mean, Bob,' said Dobson. 'Does it mean we're stymied?'

'No,' replied Rudding, 'it means that the programme is looking for a file that is not actually stored on the computer. It is stored on an external memory device which you have to plug in. That probably means there is information on the device that Delaney did not want to be seen by anyone other than himself.'

There was a box of DVD's standing alongside the computer and Dobson riffled through them to see if any of the labels could be the one required.

Most of them were for computer games, others for programmes which were already on the computer. There were several others with indeterminate contents and Rudding put them in turn into the CD bay of the computer but without any reaction.

'It's unlikely that what we are looking for would be on a disc,' said Rudding, 'it's more likely to be either on a memory stick or an SD card.'

'Well, whatever the device is, it's got to be somewhere here,' said Dobson.

There was a small bookshelf in the study and Dobson took down every book to examine the pages, known to be a common hiding place, but again without a result.

Photographs in frames were another possible hiding place but there were none on show but there were several pictures hanging on the wall. Rudding took them down one by one and dismantled the frames.

Suddenly he exclaimed, 'Hey, look at this sir! '

He held up a piece of paper that he had just retrieved from the space inside the back cover of the frame.

'There's something written on it,' said Rudding. 'It has two rows of letters and numbers.'

'What on earth is it?' said Dobson, 'doesn't make any sense. There must be some reason why it was so carefully hidden.'

'I think I know what it is, sir,' said Rudding. 'I believe they are passwords for a computer file. Now all we have to do is to find the file.'

They continued the search looking in drawers and cupboards until Rudding attracted Dobson's attention with a sudden shout.

'I don't believe it, sir, look at this!'

He was holding a cigar holder in the air with a wide triumphant grin. Inside the holder he had found a memory stick, and it had been stacked upright along with a number of biros and pencils on the desk in full view.

'Bob,' said Dobson with a wide grin. 'We are bloody idiots. Of course *Birch* didn't hide the stick itself because it would be useless to anyone not knowing the password. OK, let's see if it works before we start crowing.'

Rudding carefully plugged the stick into a USB slot and entered the two passwords depicted on the paper. A file opened on the database showing a list of names, telephone numbers and information relating to their places of employment.

'These people must have meant something to Delaney,' said Dobson. 'Look at the places where these people work. They are the type of companies where industrial espionage can be fruitful for competitors. I'll bet that's what Delaney was into.'

He turned towards his sergeant, 'My God, Bob, do you realise what this means? If Delaney is heading some sort of espionage ring, and he's murdered this Dr Jones, there must be more to it than a simple crime of passion.'

'Yes, sir,' said Rudding thoughtfully, 'but there's no evidence that Jones was involved in that business and *his* name is not on that list.'

'No, but look at the company he worked for,' said Dobson. 'It's the same sort of company as some of those on this list. They are highly competitive companies that develop drugs or other products.'

'I agree, sir,' said Rudding, 'this case seems to be taking an unexpected turn.'

'That's true, Bob,' said Dobson with a frown, 'we seem to be getting into rather murky waters. Anyway, let's not jump to conclusions. We need firm evidence. Get the names on this list checked out against our records to see if they are associated with any known criminal activity.'

'Hang on a minute, sir,' said Rudding, as they scanned the list of names on the screen, 'I'm sure I recognise that name.'

He pointed to the name of Schmitt, 'A few years back before I was transferred to Hastings from London I remember a fraud case that involved someone of that name. It's a few years ago now but I'm wondering if this is the same fellow.'

The file gave a mobile phone number for Schmitt but with no other comments in relation to place or type of work, in contrast to the other names on the list.

'That's odd,' exclaimed Dobson. 'Why should Schmitt's name be the only one without any other details? He must be someone special.'

'That's true,' said Rudding, 'maybe he's *Birch's* boss. Easy enough to check up on.'

'OK Bob,' said Dobson, 'that's a start. It's lucky that the list gives these people's telephone numbers so we can trace them easily. We'll start with this Mr Schmitt, particularly if we find he is one and the same person as your fraudster.'

The news media were quick to report the incident, with mid-day television news bulletins describing it as a hit and run accident resulting in the death of a local scientist. Dr Jones's photograph was shown in late newspaper editions.

Then in an early evening television broadcast Inspector Dobson came on the screen to appeal for witnesses.

'We are anxious to trace the two tenants of a house in St Leonards near to where this dreadful accident occurred. One is Miss Paula Kendrick, who works at the pharmaceutical company Brouchers in Hastings but did not report for work this morning. She might be driving a small blue Fiat 500 The other is *Mr Alan Birch* who is believed to be driving a red Citroen C4 Picasso.'

He proceeded to give details of both registration numbers and the damage to the Vauxhall.

He added, 'If either of these two people is watching this broadcast, or if anyone knows of their whereabouts, will you please contact the police immediately on the number to be shown after this broadcast.'

Records of the earlier fraud case involving Hans Schmitt, were emailed by the Metropolitan police and were waiting for Dobson when he returned to the station.

They showed that twelve years earlier, Hans Schmitt, a Swiss national, had been brought to trial for embezzlement while working as Finance Director for a Company at its London headquarters. He had been found guilty and sentenced to five years in jail.

As they sifted through the records they found a photograph of Schmitt which evoked a satisfactory grunt from Dobson.

'Right,' he said, 'first things first. I'll ring that number first thing tomorrow morning. If we're lucky we might get an answer straight away.'

The following day Dobson rang the mobile number they had found on the computer list hoping that it had not been changed.

'Hello, Hans Schmitt here,' said a voice in response to Dobson's call.

'Ah, Mr Schmitt,' said Dobson, 'sorry to trouble you but my name is DI Dobson of the Hastings CID. I'm investigating a case involving a Mr *Alan Birch*, and we believe that he is an associate of yours. Is that correct?'

There was a brief silence before Schmitt replied, 'Yes of course. Mr *Birch* is an employee of mine and I know you are looking for him from last night's broadcast. This is a dreadful matter. I'll help you in whatever way I can.'

'Thank you Mr Schmitt. We knew you were associated with him in some way as we found your name amongst a list of his associates and we would really like to discuss the matter with you in person. Would it be convenient to pay you a visit later this morning, say eleven o'clock?'

Schmitt's reluctance showed clearly in his voice as he agreed to the visit and gave details of his office address in the Northern suburbs of London.

'Hmm, the Brevington Employment Agency,' murmured Dobson reflectively. 'Sounds very proper and above board. Of course, it could just be a front for some kind of subversive operation, or it may be genuine and Schmitt's telling the truth. This address is in the London Metropolitan area so we can't go poking our noses in without their permission. I'll ring them now.'

A brief phone call to a senior officer at New Scotland Yard procured the necessary permission once it was explained that it was connected with the much publicised murder of Dr Jones.

The Brevington Employment Agency was located in in a busy area of Palmers Green, North London. The two officers parked comfortably just outside the address after a two and a half hour drive from Hastings. A plaque mounted outside the entrance to the building listed the businesses inside and they noted that their destination was located on the top floor of the three storey building.

They entered a reception area of what appeared to be a smart modern office. A young lady sat behind a desk typing and she looked up quizzically.

'Hello, can I help you?' she said with a pleasant smile.

'Yes, young lady,' said Dobson, giving her an equally pleasant smile in return. 'My name is detective inspector Dobson and this is detective sergeant Rudding. We have an appointment to see Mr Schmitt.'

The girl's smile was quickly replaced by a look of consternation. 'Oh yes, I'll let him know.'

She pressed an intercom button and relayed the message. After a short delay a muffled voice replied, 'OK, Jane, you'd better show them in.'

Schmitt was seated at a large oak desk operating a desk top computer. He looked up at the two officers and gave them what appeared to be a forced smile.

'Please sit down,' he said indicating towards several spare chairs at the back of the office.

As soon as the two officers had entered Schmitt's office they recognised Schmitt as an older version of the man in the photograph. He was the man who had served a term of imprisonment for embezzlement.

'We are investigating circumstances relating to the death of Dr Jones in Hastings a few days ago, sir,' said Dobson. 'As I told you over the phone yesterday, we are trying to trace Mr *Birch* to help with our enquiries, and your name was found on a concealed list in his house. You said that he was one of your employees but I am puzzled to know why *Birch* went to so much trouble to conceal the fact.'

'As I told you on the phone Inspector,' said Schmitt, 'I know about Dr Jones because it's been plastered all over the media. As to why *Birch* concealed the fact that he worked for me, well his work does involve handling confidential information about our clients who come to us looking for employment. His main function was to carry out background checks on them, so that's probably the reason.'

'Look, Mr Schmitt,' responded Dobson more brusquely, 'that list was very carefully hidden and *Birch* is suspected of not only being involved in Dr Jones's death but also of criminal activities involving industrial espionage. We think that the other names on that list were his contacts and we are checking up on this now. Are you telling me that you had no idea about these activities?'

'Yes I am,' said Schmitt tightly. 'I've no knowledge of these activities if they are true. It's nothing to do with me.'

He hesitated for a few moments before adding,

'Look, Inspector, I know perfectly well that you will have done a check on me and you will have dug up my previous conviction. I paid the penalty and it is now in the past. I now run a perfectly legitimate business so I'm afraid you have wasted your time by coming here.'

'Yes, of course we know about your previous conviction,' responded Dobson, 'but you must realise that it was because we had your name on file that we established a connection with your name on this list.'

He turned to Rudding. 'Sergeant, show Mr Schmitt the list.'

Rudding took a printout from his pocket and proffered it to Schmitt.

Schmitt took a brief look then shook his head as he handed the paper back to Rudding,

'Sorry, Sergeant, but apart from my own these names mean nothing to me. I really can't help you. I can only assume that if *Birch* was doing these things it was unknown to me.'

'Well, that may be the case,' interjected Dobson, 'but I must warn you sir that concealing information from us is treated very seriously. If anything should come to mind please contact me immediately.'

He fumbled in his coat pocket and produced a business card which he handed over to Schmitt.

As they exited the building Rudding murmured, 'Yes, that's the same man I remembered all those years ago and the photograph from police records confirms it.'

'There's no doubt about that,' responded Dobson. 'Of course we need to interview the other names on that list but I don't think it will lead anywhere. They will all deny knowing either Schmitt or Delaney and will claim to have no knowledge as to why their names are on it.'

'That's true, sir,' said Rudding, 'but it's pretty clear that this is all about industrial espionage. Apart from Schmitt all those names work for vulnerable companies such as research divisions of pharmaceuticals, chemical, medical, and so on. We must check with those companies to see if they have suffered any losses of information. They can then carry out their own investigations of their employees.'

'Yes, I agree,' concurred Dobson. 'It's not our job to investigate industrial espionage but it could be the motive for the disposal of Dr Jones, but how Schmitt comes into it is not at all clear. It might be just a dead end. Let's just focus on finding Delaney. I think we can be pretty sure now that Jones's murder was no crime of passion!'

As the two officers left his office Schmitt sat angrily behind his desk breathing heavily.

'Damn *Birch*,' he thought, 'he's added my name to that list and that has led the police to my door. Now he's on the run who knows what might come out when the police catch him, or what they might dig out from the other names on the list.'

Birch was just one of several primary informants who satisfied the side of his business that relied on industrial espionage. However there was that other far more risky side to their activities which required them to be particularly vigilant; the theft of secret government information from the Hammond Grange Military Research Establishment.

Longford's recruiting of Tony Crowshaw and the information they had obtained about secret projects at that establishment had already reaped rich rewards so, he reasoned, the risk was justified. Anyway, he was a Swiss citizen so it could hardly be called treason.

Chapter 14
The Kendricks

Rural Berkshire is home to many well-to-do families, many of whom earn their living in the city of London. The Kendricks were one such family with John Kendrick being a prosperous merchant banker and his wife Patricia, still attractive in middle age. Paula was their only daughter and both parents lavished both love in abundance and a good proportion of their material wealth on her.

They had ensured that she had received a good education at an exclusive girl's school during her teenage years. She had gone on to university achieving an honours degree in biochemical sciences. Although she could have lived comfortably at her parents' expense she preferred to get a good position and to make her own way pursuing her chosen subject.

At aged eighteen Paula had accessed a sizable trust fund left to her by her grandmother who had died when she was an infant and this provided an income sufficient to supplement a comfortable lifestyle. Her one weakness was men. She'd had a variety of unsuitable relationships with unscrupulous men most of whom had only been interested in her money. Luckily she had recognised this fact in time and had consequently ditched each one before any serious damage had been done.

Her parents were of course distressed by her choice of men but they entertained the hope that one day she would settle down and find a steady relationship that they could approve of.

When *Alan Birch* appeared on the scene and moved in with Paula John Kendrick was less than happy. On the face of it, it would appear to be a good match. *Birch* was a well-spoken young man with an easy charm and Paula was clearly besotted, but when John had met him during a rare visit he had become distinctly uneasy. There was just something about him which was disturbing.

His suspicions now turned out to be justified when a distressed Paula told her parents that she had fallen out with *Birch* but she omitted to tell them about what had actually happened. It was too much to admit to them about what he had persuaded her to do.

How ashamed she felt over her behaviour while under Delaney's spell but she had now come to her senses and was determined to put the past behind her.

She was now relaxing with her parents in the living room, idling watching the television news, her mind elsewhere when the face of Inspector Dobson appeared to deliver the facts and the appeal for the vital witnesses.

On hearing the news of Dr Jones's death and that both she and *Alan* were being sought by the police, Paula gave a gasp of horror,

'Oh my God!' she cried.

Her parents both looked at her in consternation.

'Paula, what is this about? Why are the police looking for you?' said her mother in a distressed voice.

'Dr Jones is my boss at Brouchers, and that house is the one I shared with *Alan Birch* in St Leonards. Oh my God. What am I going to do...and *Alan's* gone missing!' Realisation dawned on her with a terrifying certainty.

'Oh God! *Alan* must have done this. He killed Dr Jones!'

'You must ring that number and contact the police immediately,' said her father urgently. 'This is a dreadful affair but you are not responsible. You must tell the police everything you know....and Paula, darling, you know that you will always have our backing.'

Paula promptly went to the house phone and, her hands shaking, she lifted the receiver and dialled the number broadcast in the television programme.

Her call was received by a sergeant in the incident room at the police station and her parents' address and telephone number were logged.

'Thank you for contacting us, Miss,' said the officer. 'We would be obliged if you could stay where you are for the time being. Inspector Dobson is in charge of this investigation and he will be in touch with you later tonight.'

Less than an hour later Dobson phoned back.

'It's important that I come to see you as soon as possible, Miss Kendrick, but first I must ask you about *Mr Birch.*'

'I was in a relationship with him,' responded Paula, 'but we fell out yesterday so I finished with him and came straight here to my parents' house.'

'Do you know where he's likely to be now?' said the Inspector. 'He's not at the house and we are anxious to find him to help with our enquiries.'

'I don't know,' said Paula. 'I wish I could help you Inspector but I honestly don't know. He never told me who his parents were or if he had any relatives.'

'Look, miss,' said the Inspector, 'this is a very serious matter and I commend you for contacting us so quickly. I will come and see you first thing tomorrow morning Also if you can find a recent photograph I can pick it up when I see you.'

After the call Inspector Dobson sat his elbows resting on his desk, hands interlocked in front of his face, contemplating this latest turn of events.

Clearly Paula could now be eliminated as a suspect because her parents would verify that she had been at their house since the previous day. Nevertheless she may be able to provide vital evidence against the man now known to be Frank Delaney.

Tom Fields statement about the car he had seen in the garage and the red paint marks around the damaged area of Dr Jones's car were also vital evidence. Delaney had to be apprehended quickly.

***

Behind the reception desk at the Rising Sun motel John Worthington yawned and glanced with little interest towards the TV as the evening news was broadcast. The time for his shift would soon be over and as soon as Charley, his replacement, arrived he would be able to go home and enjoy a nice evening meal with his wife.

It was during the appeal by Inspector Dobson when he described the car that they were looking for was a damaged red Citroen C4 Picasso that John suddenly sat bolt upright in his chair. His mind immediately went back to the earlier arrival of the unkempt stranger as he remembered getting a brief glimpse of a red car as it turned into forecourt of the hotel before going just out of sight round the corner. He remembered being a bit puzzled at the time as most new arrivals parked immediately outside the reception entrance before going on to their allocated rooms.

He made a quick note of the registration and telephone numbers given out by the Inspector and waited impatiently for Charley to appear.

'Have you heard about that hit and run accident over near Hastings this morning?' he said to Charley when he arrived. 'It's just been on the telly. Apparently a man was killed and they're looking for the bloke and the car that did it.'

'No,' said Charley, 'haven't seen any news today, why?'

'Cos I think he might be here,' said John. 'I'm just going have a walk round to have a look at his car just to check, won't be a sec.'

He slipped out the door and walked quickly round the motel to the back where the room leased to the stranger was situated. There were several cars parked belonging to the few residents of the motel but one was parked well away from the others in an unobtrusive position.

It was a red Citroen Picasso, damaged as described in the TV bulletin and its registration number matched.

So the man who had signed in to the motel earlier must be the one the police are looking for!

John's heart was beating fast as he returned to reception and told Charley of his discovery before ringing the contact number to report his discovery.

'Right, sir,' said the PC receiving the call. 'Please stay where you are in case the man leaves. Do not intervene in any way as we believe he may be dangerous. The police will be with you shortly.'

Within twenty minute a police car pulled into the motel grounds and four uniformed officers emerged, an inspector, a sergeant and two constables from the Portsmouth division. After a word with John they borrowed a pass key then moved quickly to where he had reported the position of the car. A quick check soon verified that it was the car that they were looking for.

They approached the apartment which had been leased to the driver. It was on the ground floor of the motel but appeared to be in darkness. The inspector knocked sharply on the door, but there was no response so the inspector inserted the pass key and they entered the apartment.

It was deserted although there were a few belongings scattered around the room and on the bed was a holdall but it only contained items of toiletry. Obviously the occupant had left in a hurry, leaving his car knowing that it could be easily traced.

'It looks like he's done a runner,' said the inspector, 'but he can't have got very far because his car is still here. He must either be on foot or using public transport.'

He turned to his sergeant. 'An APW has already been issued for this man, but I want the search to be intensified for the area between here and the docks. Alert the customs at Portsmouth. And remember, he will be desperate and probably dangerous.'

***

The day after the phone call from Paula, Dobson sat opposite her in the privacy of her father's study, his manner professional, but not unduly brusque.

'Miss Kendrick, thank you for contacting us so quickly yesterday. Any information you can give us will be very helpful at this stage of our investigations. Now I know you are employed by Brouchers in Hastings and you will have seen the report of the death of Dr Jones who was your superior there. It is in connection with this matter that we need to find *Alan Birch* to assist in our enquiries and you told me that you shared a house with him.'

Paula nodded, her face pale, evidence of a sleepless night. Her recent brazen attitude had gone now replaced by one of shock and nervousness.

'He was my boyfriend,' she replied. 'We lived together but last night we had a terrible row so I left him and came here. I was too upset to turn in for work,' she finished miserably.

'Mr *Birch* has now left the house and we are very anxious to find him. Have you any idea about where he is likely to be?' said Dobson.

'I've no idea, Inspector,' she replied, 'I really knew very little about him. He never spoke about any friends or family in all the time I knew him.'

'I'm sure I don't have to tell you Miss Kendrick that Dr Jones was almost certainly knocked down by Mr Birch's car,' said the inspector. 'Of course it may have been an unfortunate accident but the fact that the car was garaged at your address and you worked for Dr Jones is a remarkable coincidence. I know now that you were not driving it as you were here with your parents at the time of the accident but I'm sure you can see that there are some things that need some explanation. For a start perhaps you can tell me what your quarrel was about as it does seem to have some bearing on the case.'

Paula was silent for a while, looking down at her lap, struggling to find an appropriate response. Then emotion started to overtake her as tears rolled down her face. She realised she would have to reveal the truth. In any case her relationship with Dr Jones would soon be made known to the inspector when he questioned the laboratory staff.

'Are you telling me that you were having an affair with Dr Jones at the same time you were living with your boyfriend?' said the inspector. 'If Mr *Birch* found out about this wouldn't he have been very angry. Angry enough perhaps to wreak revenge on Dr Jones?'

'No! It wasn't like that,' said Paula. 'It was arranged, *Alan* wanted me to do it.'

'He wanted you to do it?' A note of incredulity crept into the inspector's voice. 'Why, Miss Kendrick. Why would your boyfriend want you to have an affair with your boss?'

After what seemed like an eternity Paula eventually raised her eyes to meet those of the inspector, murmuring in a barely audible voice.

'He wanted me to get information about our work at the lab. He told me that he was desperately in debt and anyway it wasn't illegal. I didn't want to do it, but he was so persuasive so eventually I went along with it as it seemed to be the only way out. I admit that I did get Dr Jones to copy some secret documents from the computer about an important drug Brouchers is developing, but then *Alan* wanted an actual sample of the drug. Dr Jones refused to go that far and he destroyed the information he had already got so *Alan* blamed me for not putting enough pressure on Dr Jones.'

'By pressure do you mean blackmail?' interjected the Inspector sternly.

Paula nodded, but added quickly, 'Yes I had threatened to tell Dr Jones's wife about our affair. That's what made him copy the information in the first place but the second stage of getting a drug sample was too much for him in spite of the threat. It was *Alan's* reaction when I told him that made me realise he had only been using me all along. I was so angry when I realised the truth. We had a colossal row then I left and came straight here.

The inspector was silent as he digested this new information. He knew about industrial espionage but hadn't for one moment thought that it played a role in the present case.

'Miss Kendrick,' he said firmly, 'you have been very foolish. What Mr *Birch* told you about your role in this matter not being illegal is quite wrong. You have committed a quite serious offence with your admitted threat of blackmail. However my concern is to get to the bottom of this crime and find who was responsible for Dr Jones's death. Also I respect the fact that you have been very honest with me and are showing remorse for what you have done.'

'I want to ask you one more thing,' pressed Dobson. 'Was Mr *Birch* concerned that his part in all this was about to be revealed by Dr Jones?'

Paula nodded, 'Yes, he was furious that the chance of a good financial reward had gone, but he was sure that Dr Jones was going to tell the security department about me and that I would reveal that *Alan* was behind it all when confronted.'

She paused again, choosing her words carefully.

'I'm sure that *Alan* had other people working for him who were feeding him confidential information because I overheard him several times on his phone. Nothing specific, just bits and pieces that I heard over the past few months, also he got quite a lot of mail which I was forbidden to open.'

'Whatever else he was involved with, Miss Kendrick, may come to light during the investigation, but for the moment I have to concentrate on the matter in hand, in other words anything directly connected with Dr Jones's death.'

Inspector Dobson remained silent for a few seconds, regarding her stricken face grimly.

'Oh dear, young lady,' he said eventually, 'you've really been led up the garden path by this character. He doesn't sound like a very nice person does he?'

'Look Inspector,' said Paula, her voice faltering, 'I know I have done wrong, something I shall regret for the rest of my life, but am I likely to get into trouble? I mean will I be charged with anything?'

As Dobson looked at her pale face with her deep blue eyes and frightened expression he felt a twinge of compassion. He was a seasoned professional and had no truck with criminal wrongdoing but somehow this girl did not fit the usual mould. He could see that she had been completely besotted by *Birch*. He shook his head briefly as he responded.

'There is quite a lot you don't seem to know about *Birch*, Miss Kendrick,' said Dobson looking at her intently. 'For instance, did you know that *Alan Birch* is not his real name?'

'Not his real name, what do you mean? I've known him for months,' replied Paula with a look of complete shock.

'His name is Frank Delaney and he is a deserter from the army. He's also wanted for other things,' said Dobson.

'I don't understand,' responded Paula. 'A deserter?—and what other things?'

'You needn't be concerned about those things. They are irrelevant to the investigation, but of course it means that the army are after him as well as us.'

Paula was silent for a few moments as she tried to absorb what she had just been told.

'How stupid I've been,' she said eventually. 'How could I have been taken in so easily? It looks as if I was set up deliberately. He never thought anything about me from the start. I was just a target for him to get what he wanted from the company.'

Dobson nodded, 'I'm afraid that looks to have been the case, miss. As far as any criminal culpability, well you have done wrong but there is nothing that could be proved in your case. Nevertheless your career will be at an end and that will be a severe punishment in itself. The attempt at blackmail is of course illegal but the victim is no longer here to complain. There are some things that you must do, however, which may go some way to rectify things. First write a letter of apology to your employers and inform them of the facts. As no financial damage has actually been incurred by them as a result of your actions I'm sure that they won't take any action against you except that you will no longer be in their employment. Big companies are not very happy about this sort of publicity.'

Paula nodded miserably, 'I shall get on with that straight away, Inspector, it's been on my conscience ever since it happened.'

'That's the least you can do, young lady,' said the Inspector. 'Oh, by the way, you don't happen to have found a recent photograph of Mr *Birch* do you?'

'Why yes, will this do?' said Paula reaching for her handbag. She pulled out a small black and white snap showing *Alan Birch* smiling back at the camera in relaxed mood. 'It's one I took during a day out in Hastings a couple of months ago.'

The inspector regarded the snap thoughtfully for a few seconds. It was clearly the same man that had now been identified as Frank Delaney.

His manner became more formal as he looked up at her to speak, his voice serious.

'You must inform me immediately if Delaney contacts you in any way, Miss Kendrick. Also I would like you to keep me informed of your whereabouts if you should decide to move away from here. You would be an important witness in any proceedings against Delaney, you do realise that, don't you?'

Paula nodded, 'I think I shall be staying here for a while Inspector. I've no intention of going anywhere else now.'

'There is another thing you must be aware of Miss Kendrick,' said Dobson, 'All the time that Delaney is at large you could be in danger. I shall be asking the Berkshire CID to keep an eye on this house just in case he tries to approach you.'

'Yes, I'm aware of that, Inspector,' said Paula. 'In fact when I left the house he did try to restrain me but I threatened to scream so loudly that the neighbourhood would have come running.'

'Right, Miss Kendrick I think we have finished here for now but you will have to make a formal statement of the facts you have revealed to me and sign it,' said Dobson as he rose to go but then, as an afterthought added,

'Oh by the way, Miss Kendrick, have you ever heard of a man by the name of Schmitt? Did you ever hear Mr Delaney mention the name for instance?'

'No,' replied Paula after a moment's thought, 'I can't recall ever hearing that name, sorry.'

Sometime later Paula sat talking to her parents in the sitting room, her mind in a turmoil.

'I've been such a fool. How could I have been taken in by that man? He just pulled the wool over my eyes in making me think that there was nothing really wrong with what we were doing. How could I have been so stupid!'

Her mother regarded her with compassion. 'We all make mistakes in life, darling, and you can't go back on them. The important thing is to move forward. In this case you must help the police as much as possible. Your dad and I are just relieved that you can now see that man for what he is and the sooner he is behind bars the better.'

'Yes,' said her father, 'I agree with your mother. It's no secret that we didn't like him when we met him for the first time but at the end of the day your life is your own. You will have some difficult times ahead but be rest assured that your mother and I are both behind you.'

'Thanks, Mum and Dad,' said Paula slowly, her eyes glistening with tears. 'I just love you both so much. You've both done so much for me and yet I've let you down badly. How can I make it up to you?'

'You don't have to make anything up to us,' said her father. 'Obviously we have been very worried about the path you were taking, particularly after you met this ghastly man, but that's in the past now. As far as the immediate future is concerned, well, you can stay here for as long as you like, at least until you have sorted yourself out and decided what you want to do in the future. Your first task of course is to write to Brouchers; they deserve a very humble apology from you.'

'I'll do that now, Dad,' said his daughter, 'I need to think about what I am going to say in my letter so I'm going out to the summer house for a while. It's nice and quiet out there and I can put my thoughts together in what I hope will be the right way.'

A large patio doorway led out from the sitting room onto a terrace fronting a huge lawn and Paula exited the house after donning a wool wrap as it was a dull cloudy day with a chill in the air. The summer house was a large timber constructed building situated on the far side the lawn. A tall hedge and cleverly sited shrubs hid the summer house discretely at the boundary of the garden and out of sight of the main house. It was an ideal spot for quiet contemplation and this is where Paula headed.

She opened the door and entered the building, intending to make herself comfortable in one of the two wicker chairs inside, but as she set foot over the threshold a hand appeared out of nowhere and clamped itself over her mouth stifling the scream that started to rise in her throat. She twisted round frantically, trying to escape, but to no avail. In the next instant a voice whispered hoarsely,

'Be quiet, bitch or I'll kill you.'

Paula instantly recognised the owner of the voice.

Alan Birch!

Her panic turned to anger and she wrenched herself free and turned to face him.

'*Alan*!' she gasped, 'or should I say Frank Delaney. That's your proper name isn't it? Not just a thief and murderer but a cowardly deserter as well. The police are looking for you everywhere? They've already been here.'

Delaney glared at her malevolently, 'I know that, I've just seen that man arrive and leave, who, I assume, was a copper. No doubt you gave him every assistance. I knew that you would be high on their list for a visit, that's why I've been hiding away in here since yesterday and keeping watch. I've a good mind to kill you now you bitch, but for the moment you are more use to me alive. Whether you like it or not you are going to help me get away.'

Paula looked at him with disbelief written all over her face. 'You must be mad. Do you think I would help you after what you have done? Why don't you just give yourself up? It'll be easier on you in the long run.'

'Don't make me laugh,' he said, 'once they get their hands on me they'll throw away the key. Anyway, you don't have a choice. You will help me whether you like it or not.'

With that Delaney drew a gun from his pocket and pointed it menacingly at her.

Paula recoiled in horror at the sight of the weapon. 'You fool, *Alan*. You'll only make things worse for yourself.'

'Listen,' he hissed, 'I need a car to get me to the coast. I have a contact there who can get me a passport and help me get away to the continent. Just turn around and lead me into the house.'

Paula had no choice but to obey. She looked pleadingly at Delaney. '*Alan*, please don't hurt them. They will do what you want, but please don't hurt them.'

'No-one's going to get hurt provided everyone just does as they are told. Now just move it,' he snarled waving the gun in front of him.

They made their way back to the patio doors which Paula had left slightly ajar, and stepped inside the sitting room to confront her parents. As soon as they took in the scene her mother's hands flew up to her face in shock.

Her father reacted differently.

'What's the meaning of this,' he said angrily. 'What do you mean by coming here and threatening my family?'

'It's all right, Dad,' said Paula. 'I don't think he means to harm us provided we do what he wants.'

'And what may that be! The only thing I want to do is to get the police to come and arrest you for what you are, a bloody murderer!' said her father.

'Never mind all that,' said Delaney tersely. 'You will do what I want or else someone will get hurt. Remember I'm already wanted for murder so another one wouldn't make much difference.'

'So what do you want from us,' muttered her father.

'I want transport,' said Delaney. 'Paula's car will do me fine. I noticed it was parked outside and the cops won't be looking for that.'

'And what's to stop me ringing the police the moment you've gone?' responded Paula's father.

'That's easy,' said Delaney with menace. 'Paula will be with me. In fact she will drive me, and if I see any sign of police then you can say goodbye to your precious daughter, so don't try ringing them the minute we have left.'

He turned towards Paula, 'get your coat and bring your car keys and your passport.' he said menacingly.

A short time later Paula's car turned out of the driveway of the Kendrick's house with Paula driving and Delaney in the passenger seat. Delaney looked around urgently as they turned into the road to assure himself that they were not being observed. There were a few parked cars further down the road but they seemed innocent enough so he felt sure that there were no police units keeping watch.

But Paula's car was seen by an alert detective constable sitting in a car parked unobtrusively among those seen by Delaney. DC Murdock was one of the covert officers who had been posted there the previous day to watch out for Delaney should he appear. However Delaney had not been seen when he had entered the grounds at the rear of the house on the previous day by climbing over a garden wall backing on to a field. The appearance of Paula Kendrick's car took Murdoch by surprise, but he had a long enough impression of Delaney to recognise him from the photograph he had seen earlier. He started his own car and followed at a discreet distance, at the same time radioing in to the incident room that had been set up at the Hastings station. The call was relayed directly to DI Dobson who was returning to Hastings following his interview with Paula. 'It was him, sir, leaving in a blue Fiat and it was Miss Kendrick driving. I'm following some way behind and it looks as though they are heading east.'

'Right Murdock, good work. Keep me informed of your position until another of our cars makes contact with you. Then you can return to the station.'

Dobson then made calls to several other patrol cars in the area to keep track of the Fiat but not to apprehend in case Delaney threatened Paula, using her as a hostage. He was quite sure that Paula was driving the car under duress and that her life could be in danger if Delaney was cornered. He stressed the importance of keeping a low profile and under no circumstances to allow Delaney to realise he was being followed.

It soon became clear that Delaney was heading for the east coast, never realising that several innocent looking cars driven by CID officers had been observing his route.

DI Dobson quickly turned round to change his course. He presumed that Delaney was heading for one of the ferry termini to make his escape to the continent, probably Holland, and that he daren't risk releasing Paula until he was out of the country for fear of her raising the alarm. Dobson decided that it would be better for groups of police to be waiting at all the ferry ports on that stretch of the coast, and made the appropriate calls for such assistance at the local CID centres.

Some two hours later Paula's Fiat drew up outside an unprepossessing terrace house in the middle of Harwich. The house belonged to a character well known to the local CID by his nickname of "Ossie" who had already served several goal sentences for forgery. Delaney had got to know him for insurance purposes to be used in just such a situation as he now found himself.

'Right,' said Delaney, 'Just do as you're told and you won't get hurt. Try anything and I'll kill you. Now just get out of the car and walk in front of me to that front door.'

Terrified, Paula did as she was told and the door was opened in response to Delaney's knock. Ossie was a short middle-aged man of scruffy appearance, wearing wrinkled grey flannel trousers with braces and a grubby white shirt. He blinked at them briefly over the top of reading glasses perched over the end of his nose before ushering them into a shabby room equipped with forlorn items of dated furniture.

'OK, *Birch*,' he said in a high pitched but coarse voice, 'I've got what you want but I need to take a photo of you and print it so it'll take about another half hour.'

'Right, just get a move on,' grunted Delaney.

'Oh, and another thing. This'll cost you. I don't do this sort of thing for charity,' said Ossie.

'All right, all right,' Delaney said impatiently, 'just get on with it.'

'Hold on, *Birch*,' said Ossie, 'payment first if you don't mind. I want a grand for this job.'

Delaney glared at the man. He needed all the cash he had drawn from cashpoint to pay for his passage on the ferry and to live off for a while.

'A grand! You must be joking, just for half an hour's work!' he said hotly.

'I don't think you've got a lot of choice,' said Ossie with an unpleasant leer, 'I know you're on the run and if you try using the fake passport you've already got in the name of *Alan Birch* you would be arrested the minute you try to get out of the country.'

'Look, mate,' said Delaney using a more conciliatory tone. 'I really don't have that sort of cash on me but there's a perfectly good set of wheels outside which I'm sure with your connections you could turn into a nice profit on a thousand pounds. How about it?'

Ossie hesitated briefly then nodded, 'OK, where are the keys?'

Delaney turned to Paula. 'Give him the keys,' he said menacingly.

Paula was still holding the car keys and she handed them over to the man without hesitation. She was far too frightened to be concerned that it was her car that was being so freely donated. She looked at Delaney imploringly.

'Please, let me go now. I promise I won't tell the police.'

'Huh, you think I'm stupid,' said Delaney. 'You'd go running straight to the police. 'You will stay right here by my side until we get to Holland.'

Half an hour later they exited the house with Delaney now in possession of his new fake passport. He turned to walk in the direction of the ferry terminal.

'Don't try to make a run for it or I will shoot you before you've gone three steps,' Delaney hissed.

He was unaware that they were under observation from several CID officers hidden in positions around the area. They were under strict instruction not to interfere but to track Delaney's movements carefully.

The way to the International ferry terminal was clearly signposted and they reached the foot passenger entrance within twenty minutes through a maze of back streets. Delaney glanced around the reception hall and found what he was looking for, a kiosk on the far side advertising the ferry company and manned by an attractive young woman in a blue uniform. Delaney gave her one of his most charming miles.

'Hello, miss, when is the next ferry due to leave for the Hook of Holland?'

'That will be the overnight sailing leaving at 10 p.m sir,' she replied with a smile.

'Can I book two return tickets please?'

As the girl bent to prepare the tickets she glanced up at them quizzically, 'Don't you have any baggage, sir?'

'Oh no,' replied Delaney, 'we are going on to The Hague to do some shopping as soon as we get to Holland. In the meantime we just wanted to travel light. We can get what we need tonight on board.'

'That's OK, sir, you won't need baggage retrieval tickets then. Can I see your passports please?'

'Yes of course.' said Delaney. He handed his recently manufactured passport to the receptionist and turned to Paula.

'The young lady needs your passport, too, honey,' he said with a false smile, giving an outward impression of a close loving relationship.

There was no return smile from Paula. Her face was devoid of any expression as she withdrew the passport from her handbag and handed it to the receptionist.

As soon as she opened the passport the young woman's face creased in a frown.

'There must be some mistake, madam. This is not your photograph and it's in the name of a Patricia Kendrick, your name is Paula. You can't travel on this.'

Patricia Kendrick was Paula's mother, of course, Paula had taken it knowing that it would prevent her from travelling.

Delaney's false mile evaporated, turning towards her with an expression of fury.

'You bitch! You did that deliberately!'

His arm shot out and grabbed Paula around her neck pulling her towards him backwards. The young lady behind the desk screamed and other passengers in the hall looked on in horror.

'Stay away! Stay away or she's dead!' Delaney shouted as he pulled his gun from one of the large side pockets of his Parka and started to back towards the exit doors, dragging Paula with him.

'My God, he's got a gun!' shouted someone.

Then another voice rang out, a commanding voice.

'Delaney, I am a police officer and there are other officers both in here and outside. You cannot escape. Let the girl go and put your weapon on the floor!'

Desperately, Delaney looked towards the source of the voice as he became aware that he was under surveillance and probably had been for some time.

'Stay away!' he shouted in desperation, 'Stay away or I will shoot her.'

He pointed the gun at Paula's head. Terrified, she tried desperately to pull away from him but his hold on her was too tight.

The officer's voice rang out again.

'Don't be such a fool, Delaney! If you harm that girl things will be so much the worse for you. You must realise that!'

Delaney looked wildly around and saw several uniformed police covering the main exit doors. Realising that the game was up he gave a loud gasp of anger and pushed Paula violently way from him to send her sprawling on the floor. He then backed away with his gun pointing in front of him.

'Keep off me!' he shouted in desperation.

'Delaney! Don't be a fool. There's no way you can escape. Throw your gun on the floor and give yourself up,' said the officer.

Realising that there was no possibility of escape Delaney threw his gun on the floor as two men detached themselves from the group of passengers. One of them went to Paula to pull her to safety and the other approached Delaney.

'Frank Delaney, my name is Detective Sergeant Dunne of the Essex CID. I am arresting you on suspicion of the murder of Ronald Jones.'

He proceeded to give Delaney the formal caution on arrest then turned to beckon one of several uniformed police officers. A sergeant stepped forward to handcuff him and he was led quickly outside to a police car.

At almost the same time, Inspector Dobson reached the Harwich police station. He had been kept informed of the progress of events but the sudden way it had ended had taken him by surprise. He had expected the arrest to be made as the pair went through customs where it would have been comparatively easy and without any harm coming to Paula.

Delaney had in fact been tracked at every stage from the Kendrick's house. When they had turned onto the A120 from the A12 the police knew that they would be heading for Harwich rather than Felixstowe and had acted accordingly, setting up police observation units at the ferry terminal.

Paula was given separate transport back to her parents' home. They had been notified earlier of her safe release and were waiting anxiously when she arrived. She ran tearfully into their arms.

'Oh darling, thank God you're safe,' said her mother. 'We've been so worried.'

'Yes,' said her father, 'but you know as soon as you left here this young lady came and told us that they were being followed and that it was only a matter of time before they arrested Delaney. She assured us that your safety was their main concern.'

He turned to smile at a young woman in police uniform who was standing in the background.

The following morning Dobson and Rudding faced Delaney in an interview room where he maintained that his car's collision with Dr Jones had been an accident. He claimed that he had been on his way to confront Dr Jones because of his affair with Paula. When he saw Jones about to enter his car he had wanted to encounter him before Jones drove away, but in his haste he had accidentally struck him. He had run away in panic and now felt full of remorse for Jones's death but he never had any intention to harm him.

With regard to the accusation in Paula's statement of industrial espionage he protested complete innocence.

'It's pure fiction to cover up what she was doing at Brouchers,' said Delaney. 'She wanted to get that information and sell it to competing companies. I knew nothing about it but now this has happened she is trying to pass the buck onto me. I admit that I did act foolishly by running away and of course I shouldn't have abducted Paula but I emphasise, I did not murder Dr Jones!'

Delaney was formally charged with murder and held in custody to face the magistrates Court where he was remanded in custody to await a Crown Court trial.

Chapter 15
Inquest at Brouchers

There was a tense atmosphere in Dr Hesselink's office where several figures were sat listening to Dobson's account of the latest events. Brouchers had been his first port of call the following morning after the arrest of Delaney. His audience consisted of Hesselink, Jim Dawson, and Jack Blake.

'I think it's clear to you now why I requested that senior members of your security department be present, Dr Hesselink,' concluded Dobson. 'Your staff member Dr Jones was being blackmailed by Paula Kendrick to steal confidential information from your Company. From what Miss Kendrick has told me this morning, Dr Jones reneged at the last minute so, fortunately for you, the operation was unsuccessful, but unhappily for him it resulted in his death. We think her live-in boyfriend Frank Delaney was behind the plot and he is now under arrest.

Jack Blake was the first to speak. He was still suffering remorse for not having revealed Delaney's identity after having met him in that London wine bar. 'Inspector Dobson has not told you this so I think it's up to me to do so. Frank Delaney was an old friend of mine from our army days. He deserted when we were serving in Cyprus and somehow managed to get himself back to the UK under an assumed name. Then I came across him in a bar in London and promised not to reveal his true identity because of our friendship, a misplaced sense of loyalty I suppose. I really had no idea that he was engaged in these sorts of activities. Obviously if I had known about what he was doing I would have gone straight to the police.'

Jack turned in his seat to address Dr Hesselink directly. 'None of these terrible events would have happened had I reported him at the time. I therefore offer you my resignation.'

Hesselink opened his mouth to speak but was forestalled by Jim Dawson.

'You'll do nothing of the kind, Jack!' he responded sharply. 'You had no way of knowing that Delaney was engaged in this kind of piracy, or that he was capable of murder. I think any honourable person would be loyal to a close friend under similar circumstances, and that is a valuable asset. The fact that you were quick to ring the Inspector here to tell him about Delaney as soon as you found out what he had been doing is a measure of your integrity, so no! There will be no resignation.'

Dr Hesselink nodded his head, 'Yes, Mr Blake, I agree with Mr Dawson. I need you to continue to work in our security department and the first thing we need to do is to review our security arrangements.'

Dobson rose from his chair, 'I've said all I came here for and now I have to go to continue with the investigation. I know that industrial espionage is a terrible scourge for companies such as yours but there is little the police can do about it as long as no actual crime is committed.'

As Dobson left Hesselink looked grimly at Jim Dawson and Jack Blake.

'Well, gentlemen,' he said, 'you know the score. As I've just said we need to review our security measures. I don't need to tell you what it would mean to Brouchers if any details regarding EDF301 got out to any of our competitors. It seems we can't guarantee the loyalty of senior staff members particularly if they are under extreme duress. However Jones probably copied the documents after working hours when he was alone in his office. It would have been more difficult for him to do this during the working day with so many other staff members about. For a start I think we must restrict the presence of all staff to working hours only.'

***

In the upper floor office that masqueraded as Brevington's Employment Agency, Carl Schmitt sat behind his desk facing Norman Longford.

'Bloody hell,' said Schmitt angrily gripping the arms of his chair. 'That bloody fool *Birch*. Why the hell did he have to kill that Dr Jones? Now he's been caught trying to escape the country and that puts us at risk if he squeals.'

Longford scowled back. 'How can we be sure he won't?'

'He won't,' countered Schmitt confidently. *'Birch* is not that stupid. He knows that if he did he wouldn't live long with your connections.'

Schmitt was referring to Longford's primary function that he could call on if there was any danger of his organisation being exposed. It was not unknown for individuals to be violently attacked to ensure their silence even when confined on remand. He had a long arm which stretched when needed to inside most of the UK prisons.

'But what about the girl?' said Longford. 'She's the one who was used by *Birch* for bait. Did she know about his connection to us?'

'I don't think so,' replied Schmitt. His face took on a cynical expression as he added, 'She thought *Birch* was in it alone and that they were going to make pots of money, go off and live happily ever after.'

'That's all very well,' said Longford, 'but there's a trial to come and she will be one of the main witnesses. How can we be sure that nothing will come out?'

'You worry too much,' responded Schmitt. 'You can bet your bottom dollar that she's already squealed to the police about *Birch* and what went on at Brouchers but she wouldn't know anything about us and our operation. That's why we take so much care when we select our operatives and make it clear to them that their lives depend on keeping any association with us completely secret. It isn't as if we haven't been here before. We can't run this business if we have to panic every time some silly sod gets caught, and we can't go around leaving a trail of bodies everywhere. That would be far too risky, so relax!'

Schmitt sat back in his chair with a smile on his face.

'None of it matters anyway Norman,' he said smugly. 'We've already got all we need to know about EDF301 from Palmer, who's a lot more reliable than *Birch*. He does it for the sheer pleasure of the risks involved, unlike *Birch* who does it under duress. Anyway he passed the formula on directly to the company we work with and I understand they are now working on their own version of it.'

'I've just received very substantial payoff from them,' he went on, 'but I've told Palmer that we need to know more about Brouchers research. He's got one of their senior staff in the palm of his hand so we can expect a lot more in the future.'

Chapter 16
Industrial Piracy

Several months had passed since the tragic death of Dr Jones and in the main Brouchers conference room a group of solemn people sat round the long highly polished oak table. The group included the personnel manager Nigel Brody, Dr Anne Garbot, the head of the pilot plant facility, Dr Angela Freeman, head of the fundamental studies laboratory, and Tom fields, now head of Research and Development laboratory number two. Security was represented by Jim Dawson and Jack Blake, and Hesselink sat at one end of the table, a portentous look on his face.

'Ladies and gentlemen,' he said, 'you will all know by now about the latest news with regard to the death of Dr Jones, and the role of Paula Kendrick, one of our employees. She wrote me a letter confessing everything about what she had done in collusion with Dr Jones, but it's clear she had nothing to do with his death. Unfortunately for her any career she was hoping for in this industry is now gone. Whatever was behind it she betrayed this company so now she would be unemployable. It was fortunate for us at the time that the scheme was unsuccessful they did not succeed in stealing information about our work.'

Hesselink paused, a hard look on his face before continuing, 'unfortunately, in spite of all our efforts and the failed plot involving Kendrick and Jones, vital information about this product has been leaked and with serious results for our company.'

He put his hand in his pocket to withdraw a small bottle containing white tablets which he placed on the table in front of him. It was labelled *parostamine.*

'This product has just been introduced to the market by Naismith's,' he said tersely. 'These tablets are claimed to be a new effective relief from the pain of osteoarthritis, just like the product that we are in the final stages of marketing. We've had them analysed and the formulation is identical to our product, the one you all know as EDF301.'

There was a combined gasp from the assembled staff as they realised the implication of the news. 'My God,' exclaimed Dr Freeman, 'it's obviously been stolen from us, but how? We've tightened up so much recently since that business with Dr Jones.'

'Be that as it may,' said Hesselink grimly, 'the fact remains that our formula has been stolen and I've no need to tell you that the Board is going to be very critical of us and this division of Brouchers. We have to do something about it very quickly so it is essential we find the source of this leak before we get a repeat with any of our other products.'

Hesselink paused to look round the table at the array of concerned faces before continuing.

'Now it may be a coincidence that EDF301 is the same drug that was involved with the recent regrettable business with Dr Jones. He is no longer with us and I have no intention of vilifying his actions now, but I do have a deep suspicion that Naismith's is the same company that was behind that unfortunate matter. The coincidence is just too great. It now seems that whoever is behind this have made up for their previous failure, resulting in a considerable financial loss to our company. You all know that Naismith's has a dubious reputation in the industry and have been suspected by other companies of receiving confidential information in order to market competitive products. Maybe they use planted agents to do the dirty work, or maybe they work through some kind of organiser to prevent their name being directly implicated.'

'It's probable that the theft of the formula was stolen before we tightened up after Dr Jones's unfortunate death. It's even possible that it was taken before that terrible event but whatever is the case it looks as if we could have another rogue staff member.'

The assembled staff gave a collected groan.

'It seems almost unbelievable,' said Nigel Brody. 'All new staff are subjected to such a vigorous vetting process. I find it difficult to believe that our confidential information is being so freely leaked.'

'I suppose it depends on the circumstances,' said Hesselink wearily. 'It's possible the perpetrators look for weak links in our staff's background. Could be down to blackmail as it was in the case of Dr Jones, or there may be an addiction such as gambling, or just plain and simple greed with the promise of lucrative rewards.'

'Anyway ladies and gentlemen,' he continued, thumping his clenched fist on the table, 'whatever the reasons we have put considerable resources into the development of this range of new drugs and I intend to put a stop to it! Not only that but we will find the culprit and we will get the company responsible for marketing this stolen product to withdraw it.'

'That's a promise!' he said firmly.

He looked round at his collected staff as he concluded, 'the main onus is on our security department and I ask you and your staff to cooperate with them fully.'

Amidst the barrage of questions one voice from Dr Anne Garbot commented, 'What about patent cover? Can't we sue them?'

'We do cover much of the process by patent,' said Hesselink, 'and our product EDF301 is patented but we can't cover standard chemical processes used to make it. It's a bit of a minefield really and it's very difficult to prove that they haven't just hit on the same product from their own research. Anyway I can see you all have plenty of suggestions. Please will you write them down and pass them to either Jim or Jack. They will collate the results and submit recommendations to me. Mind you there are things you can do in your respective departments if you see areas for improvement.'

After the meeting broke up Jim Dawson and Jack returned to their office to discuss the matter.

'Well Jack,' said Dawson, 'what a sickener. It seems that in spite of all our efforts recently there must still be a spy in our midst. What else can we do about it?'

'Look, Jim,' said Jack, 'up to now we've been focussing on the staff who work in the laboratories. They are already subjected to a high level of security checks, even more than before the Jones affair. What about outsiders who go in and out of these areas and may not be subjected to these checks to the same degree?'

'You mean people like carpenters, plumbers, and electricians,' said Jim doubtfully. 'They know little or nothing about the research being done so I would find it hard to believe that any of them could be responsible. Anyway how would they know how to access anything. All the information is stored on our computer system and you have to know all the important security passwords which only the very senior staff know. Even if someone like that did get hold of a password it would look extremely odd if they were to be seen sitting illicitly in front of one of the computer terminals.'

'Yes, that may be the case,' said Jack, 'but remember that they often work in the various units after the staff have gone home. They would have ample opportunity provided they knew how to access the computer system. Even if they didn't know it's still possible that the information was stolen from filing cabinets. An expert thief might not know a lot about computers, or science but he might know how to break into a digitally locked filing cabinet.'

'Well I suppose we should include it as a possibility,' responded Dawson, 'but what do we do about it? We couldn't very well have a guard standing there every time a maintenance worker goes into a lab to do essential work. There is one thing we could do though,' he added after a brief pause. 'I will see Dr Hesselink about installing close circuit TV cameras in all the sensitive areas but without the knowledge of the staff or maintenance crew. It's something we should have done earlier. We have CCTV cameras covering all the main building entrances but no interior ones. There are companies who specialise in the installation of this type of equipment. They use very small discrete cameras which can be effectively concealed from view. I know that the work can be done in a few hours so it could be carried out during the night when the laboratories are inaccessible.'

'This material could have been stolen from our computer network just as Dr Jones did,' said Jack. 'We know that's how Dr Jones did it because Paula Kendrick said so in her statement to Inspector Dobson. Let's face it Jim all important research results are logged onto our central computer system but can be accessed by any of our network computers by the use of the appropriate passwords.'

'We could cover this possibility by installing security software into the computer system, This will send an audible or visible warning to a remote station if any attempt is made to copy sensitive information from one of the satellite computers. That would probably limit the identification of the person to one in that section. It wouldn't be sufficient simply to block all the USB ports because that wouldn't tell us the person's identity.'

'Oh dear,' said Jim, 'I hate to consider that as a possibility, but yes, you're right. Dr Jones would have been the last person we would suspect of doing what he did so it's not beyond the realms of possibility that someone else on the staff could be bribed. Well Jack,' he concluded with a grim smile, 'there's a lot to think about and there's no doubt that Dr Hesselink expects results judging by what he's just said. First we will step up security with regard to non-scientific staff, install the internal cameras, and the additional computer software and hardware as you suggest. Mind you it's a bit like bolting the stable door after the horse has gone,' he added ruefully.

'That may be the case,' responded Jack, 'but let's suppose that it is a senior member of staff. They have already betrayed the company for money, probably at the behest of someone outside. They certainly wouldn't stop now.'

Within days the new CCTV system was duly installed with a special multichannel recorder placed unobtrusively in Dawson's office where the tapes could be reviewed. Similarly the company computer system was upgraded by a firm of IT consultants as suggested by Jack with the warning system also placed on a desk in the office. It was rather like a desk top computer but any illicit attempts to copy files would cause a red light to flash and a loud pulsating buzz would be heard. In addition the site of the computer terminal where the copying was being carried out would be shown on the screen hence enabling the probable offender to be identified.

Jack and Jim Dawson took it in turns to review the tapes at regular intervals. It was something of a chore but for the most part each tape could be viewed in a fast forward mode, at least until there were signs of human presence. These were due to occasional visits by maintenance workers doing routine jobs or members of the staff going about their normal work.

Suddenly Jack sat bolt upright in his seat. But it wasn't anything on the tapes. It was a red flashing light and a low buzzing sound coming from the box on the wall.

Somebody was copying files! A quick check showed it to be in Dr Garbot's office attached to the pilot plant facility.

Jack quickly rang Jim Dawson who was out of the office, to tell him.

'OK, Jack,' said Dawson, 'we need to get over to that office now. Meet me there.'

When they arrived Garbot's office was empty and all staff in the section were busy in the pilot plant area which was out of sight of the office. Dawson then approached the senior assistant, Dr Hudson, to ask him if anyone had just used the computer in Dr Garbot's office. Hudson responded by saying that several staff including himself had used it in the past half hour as it was essential for logging their work. He couldn't say who had been the last one to use it and he was certainly not aware of any attempts to copy data.

Hesselink gave a sigh of exasperation when told of the incident. 'Are you sure this new system of yours is reliable?'

'The system is well tried and completely reliable,' said Jack. 'Also there's no doubt that it was the computer in Dr Garbot's office. It can't have been Dr Garbot herself because she's on leave of absence at the moment. There were several other persons cleared to use that computer as it was necessary for their everyday work and we can't find out who used it at the time we got the alarm. When we spoke to Dr Hudson about it he seemed a bit evasive. I'm pretty sure it was he who had used the computer when it alarmed.'

'We need to be careful here,' intervened Jim Dawson in a cautious tone of voice. 'We can't just go barging in and accusing people of wrongdoing without firm proof.'

'Don't rush into anything,' interjected Hesselink, 'I don't want whoever is responsible to have any suspicion that he or she has been rumbled. Let us for the moment assume that it was the senior assistant Dr Hudson. What I propose is to have him followed discretely when he leaves work this evening.'

Jack nodded uncertainly, saying, 'sounds fine to me Dr Hesselink, but how do we do this? None of us are qualified to that kind of detective work. We'd probably give ourselves away in no time.'

Hesselink smiled, 'Yes Mr Blake, that's very true. We will use a firm of professional private detectives who specialise in this kind of work.' He turned to Jim Dawson, 'You remember that case a few years ago, Jim, when we had a staff member embezzling cash from the accounts division?'

'I remember it well,' said Dawson. 'The firm was excellent. They tracked down the culprit very quickly. I was impressed by their expertise and efficiency.'

'That settles it then,' said Hesselink. 'I'll get them on board immediately. 'Thank you, gentlemen, your measures seem to be doing the trick.'

Just after 5 p.m. that same day Hudson was seen to exit the centre in his car as usual but just a short distance along the road he stopped behind a stationary Peugeot car and went to speak briefly to its driver and quickly handed over a small envelope. He returned to his car and drove home. The covert observer, a highly experienced female investigator named Sheila, discretely photographed the event and rang the car's registration number through to her HQ. She then proceeded to follow the car.

It travelled a short distance to a semi-detached house and parked on the drive, presumably that of the driver's house.

The driver of the Peugeot was soon identified both from the car's registration number and the address of the house. His name was Bill Palmer and he lived there with his wife and two children.

What wasn't revealed was Palmer's main occupation as one of Hans Schmitt's so-called liaison officers.

These facts were reported back to Hesselink who discussed with Dawson and Jack Blake what further action should be taken.

'Well, that settles it,' said Dawson. 'Hudson was the one copying that material. He has to be faced with this immediately and dismissed.'

'Sorry, Jim, I don't agree,' said Hesselink. 'My priority is to get that pirated product off the market and the only way to do that is to keep surveillance on this Bill Palmer. At some stage he has to transfer the material to whoever pulls his strings, whether it be Naismith's themselves or someone else. In the meantime I don't want Hudson to know that we are on to him.'

Further observation of Palmer's movements showed him to be those of any ordinary family man. Most evenings he spent with them at home, occasionally visiting his local public house to socialise with friends. He was also observed to make a number of trips up and down the country but Sheila had been instructed to only follow if he appeared to be heading in the direction of Leicester where Naismith's were situated.

Things changed on the Monday. He came out of his house early in the morning carrying a small brief case and drove away in his car. He was followed by Sheila as he drove to Watford Gap service station on the motorway to have a bite to eat and then on in the direction of Leicester. He eventually pulled up at the main gate of Naismith's where Palmer was seen to talk briefly to the uniformed security guard just outside the gate. After a few minutes an elderly man appeared and approached Palmer to be handed a padded envelope from his briefcase. Palmer did not enter the gate probably to avoid his visit being logged. The event was photographed from Sheila's viewing point and the elderly man was later identified as one of the directors of the company. After the handover Palmer climbed back into his car and returned home.

'We've got them haven't we?' said Dawson. 'Enough to go to court with surely.'

'Almost,' returned Hesselink, 'but we need definite proof that the briefcase contains our material. It's fortunate that the stuff he took this time was fairly unimportant and until this business is cleared up that will have to remain so. Palmer must be in the employ of someone bigger who doesn't make these deliveries personally.

'So how are we going to get that proof,' said Dawson. 'I would have thought that the evidence we have now is indisputable.'

'Don't forget that if this comes to court they will engage the very best of barristers,' countered Hesselink. 'Circumstantial evidence will not be sufficient. I've thought about this and come to the conclusion that the only way we can prove that what's in his briefcase originates from us is to take it from his car after he sets off to deliver it. That means taking it while he is in the restaurant at Watford Gap. I'll talk to our firm of consultants see how this can be done.'

Hesselink rang the head of the firm, a man he had known for many years and trusted implicitly, and put forward his idea.

'I agree,' said the voice over the phone. 'We had already thought about that as the next step. Of course, breaking into and entering a car and taking material from it is illegal but I think we can deal with it in our own way. Leave it to us Dr Hesselink.'

Surveillance continued as before and during the course of the next few weeks Palmer was seen to go through the same routine once more. It seemed that he would have no knowledge of the significance of the material he was stealing but would be required by his paymaster to deliver on a routine basis.

***

Bill Palmer pulled in to Watford Gap service station looking forward to his breakfast and morning coffee. His usual excuse to his wife on these occasions was that he had an extra shift to work, and indeed this was quite common so there were no raised eyebrows or objections from her.

When he emerged from the restaurant he was surprised to see a young woman waiting beside his car.

'Hello,' he said. 'Do you want something?'

'Hello, Mr Palmer,' replied Sheila, 'could I have a word with you?'

'Why? Who are you?' responded Palmer sharply.

'I am an investigator working for Brouchers, the Hastings pharmaceutical company. Let me come straight to the point. We believe you have been conveying confidential information to a company in Leicester, a pharmaceutical company known as S.W.Naismith and Sons.'

'What the hell are you talking about,' said Palmer sharply, 'you're not a cop. You have no powers over me and I don't have to answer your questions.'

'No, sir, that's true,' replied Sheila, 'but I would ask you to indulge me just for a little while. Do you have anything to say about what you are suspected of doing?'

'I'm just a PR man,' said Palmer calmly, 'I work for a company in London so I've no idea what you are talking about. I know nothing about this Hastings company and I wouldn't know how to even start doing anything like that.'

'Oh, I think you do, Mr Palmer. In fact I have photographic evidence that you are in regular contact with one of the scientists there by the name of Dr Ron Hudson, and you have been seen to be handed something from him several times. Our surveillance of you recently has shown that you deliver the item, which we believe is a computer memory device, to Naismith's, and that's where you are going now.'

'Looks like you've got me stitched up good and proper,' doesn't it,' said Palmer, raising his hands briefly as if in surrender. 'So what do you expect me to do if you can't arrest me?'

'No,' replied Sheila, 'that's not our job. Our job is to gather and provide information. In stopping you now I am acting under the aegis of my employers. They want to give you a choice.'

'Oh yes, and what's that?' said Palmer.

'They want you to hand over that briefcase to me.'

'Why should I do that?' responded Palmer quickly. 'It would just be even more evidence to use against me.'

'For one very good reason,' said Sheila. 'Hand it over now and we lose any further interest in you. If you don't then the police will be informed and we will hand over all the evidence we have gathered. There are many aspects of industrial espionage that are illegal, particularly when it involves extortion of any kind.'

'Well, how surprising,' said Palmer sardonically, then he sighed, 'Oh, very well, just so long as you don't pester me again.' Palmer knew that private detectives had no power of arrest but then he remembered how he had coerced Dr Hudson to cooperate in the first place.

He reached inside his car, withdrew the case, and handed it over to Sheila. As he did so thoughts coursed through his mind about what Schmitt would say. He wouldn't be pleased! But Palmer was too valuable to Schmitt to be 'disposed of.' He had already passed information from Dr Hudson which had enabled Naismith's to replicate an important drug. Naismith's had paid Schmitt very well for that information, a handsome slice of which had landed back in Palmer's pocket. He had *Mar*ks in other companies to concentrate on. The loss of this one was no big deal. Anyway, best do the right thing he thought. He took out his mobile phone and rang Ron Hudson to warn him.

Hesselink was handed the briefcase personally by Sheila along with a written report of the operation. He soon ascertained that the case contained an envelope with an SD card, and it was full of Broucher's confidential information.

'There's something else we have found out that you should know,' said Sheila. 'We have done background checks on Dr Hudson and found that he has a severe gambling problem. He initially borrowed money from the bank, but then soon lost it all so he now finds himself in debt. We believe he was recruited by Palmer who found out these things and consequently coerced him to smuggle out confidential information with the promise of considerable financial reward.'

'It seems that Hudson has already been told that we know about him,' said Hesselink succinctly. 'He apparently left the premises a few hours ago in a hurry and he's not been seen since. We know where he lives but I don't think we'll pursue the matter. He certainly will not be back here. It's just not in our interest to publicise this sort of thing.'

'Now comes the tricky part,' said Hesselink later to Jim Dawson and Jack Blake. 'I intend to send a letter from our legal department to the chief executive of Naismith's. It will point out that unless they withdraw their product parostamine from the market immediately we will pursue them in the civil court on a charge of patent violation. That would not only damage their reputation even more severely than the way it stands now, but would cost them a crippling amount in compensation'.

'Sounds fair enough,' said Dawson. 'I would think they'd have little choice when they get to know the evidence.'

'I don't know,' said Hesselink. 'They could always argue that their product was developed fairly and that it had nothing to do with their association with Palmer. However gentlemen, I've not been completely idle since Palmer's name came up. We know that the unfortunate affair with Dr Jones was concerned with an attempt to steal information about the same drug, and it doesn't take a great leap of our intelligence to suspect that Naismith's was the intended destination for that information too. That implies that two separate agents, Delaney and Palmer, have tried to corrupt our staff on behalf of this Naismith's company and I think they were both working for, what we call in common parlance, a "Mr Big". Whatever is the case, it's very important that we block any more sabotaging of our work. Our Board of Directors must already think our security is like a leaky sieve.'

In a matter of days Hesselink was closeted with the company solicitor who showed him a letter just received from Naismith's legal department. It claimed that in order to avoid embarrassment to both companies they did not wish to pursue the matter in court. They agreed to discontinue their marketing of parostamine forthwith whilst denying wilful wrongdoing.

'Just look at the last sentence,' said the solicitor. 'What a nerve!'

The sentence read – *Finally our Board of Directors wishes to express its sincere regrets about this unfortunate coincidence but hopes that your Company will enjoy success with your own product.*

Chapter 17
Crowshaw

In DCI Brook's office at New Scotland Yard two men, Brooks and Senior Agent Tony Brent, were bent over a table studying a number of photographs laid out in a row. They were the close-ups shots taken by DC Thomson during the earlier library surveillance of Tony Crowshaw. The photos of both Schmitt and Longford were recovered from police records so establishing their identities as the two men seen at the library whilst Crowshaw had been inside.

'We still don't have enough evidence to arrest these characters,' said Brooks, 'We can't arrest them because they happen to visit a library at the same time as the man under surveillance, but in view of their criminal records the coincidence is highly suspicious. If they are receiving government information from Crowshaw they must have some way of selling it on, that's how we'll get them.'

'No,' agreed Brent, 'we can't afford to take any chances but if they are the men who are receiving the information, our first priority is to get the one who is procuring it in the first place.'

'I'm pretty sure that Crowshaw is the one who's doing it,' said Brooks. 'As a matter of national security I am going to question him to deliberately put him on his guard. That should be enough to warn him off for now. Then when we secure proof that Schmitt and Longford are guilty then that would be enough to justify charging Crowshaw for violation of the Official Secrets Act.'

'What if Crowshaw takes fright knowing he is under suspicion and tries to run away?' said Brent.

'No chance,' responded Brooks, 'we shall keep watching him very closely indeed.'

He paused for a few moments before saying, 'something else has cropped up which I think you will find interesting. Schmitt's name has come up recently in a murder case investigated by the Hastings CID. Apparently it involved an army deserter by the name of Frank Delaney who was involved in industrial espionage. It came out during the investigation that Delaney was legitimately employed by Hans Schmitt in his employment agency business. It's almost certain that Schmitt was also involved with this type of activity. Is it that much of a jump to go from industrial espionage to trafficking in government secrets?'

'That's very interesting,' responded Brent. 'If Schmitt *is* involved in that game it adds grist to our mill I suppose. All we need now is confirmatory evidence.'

'I've told Inspector Dobson who was the officer in charge of that investigation to hold off any surveillance of Schmitt,' said Brooks. 'The ball is firmly in our court from now on.'

Brooks moved quickly as these events came to light. His first priority was to deal with Tony Crowshaw in spite of no firm evidence. All that had been established so far was that he had been observed at the same time and place as Schmitt and Longford, but there had been no direct contact and nothing had been observed to change hands. Nevertheless this was a serious case of treasonable activity and they couldn't afford to take any chances.

The following morning a car drew up outside the apartment block housing Crowshaw's apartment. Brooks and DS Harris emerged, their mission being to interview Crowshaw after telling him that it was a routine spot check being carried out on all staff at HGMRE in the interests of security.

They ascended the stairs to the apartment and knocked sharply at the door.

There was no response so they knocked again more loudly but the door continued to remain closed.

'That's funny,' grunted the Brooks. 'It's Sunday morning. 'Surely he can't be out.'

Frowning, he tried the door expecting it to be locked, but to his surprise it opened easily.

'Now why would he go out and leave the door unlocked?' he said.

'It could be that he is still in bed. After all it is Sunday morning,' responded Harris. 'He wouldn't be expecting us and the door might just be a careless oversight.'

They entered the flat cautiously to be faced with a small entrance hall and two inner doors. Brooks called out loudly,

'Hello, is anyone here?'

Once again there was no response, just an uncanny silence, generating an uneasy feeling in the two officers as they contemplated the two doors, one of which was wide open. Beyond the open door lay a living space and cooking area. Remnants of a meal were scattered on a table.

'Hmm, looks like last night's takeaway,' said Harris.

'Let's check the other room,' said Brooks. 'It must be the bedroom. Be funny if he is still in bed,' he muttered uneasily.

He opened the door to the bedroom and peered in warily. There was a bed on the far side of the room and it was occupied by an inert figure.

'Mr Crowshaw, are you awake?' he called out, but there was no movement or response from the figure. With an increasing feeling of foreboding the two officers walked quickly over to the bed.

A chilling sight met their eyes, one that would remain with both officers for the rest of their lives. Crowshaw's body lay face upwards on a blood-soaked pillow.

He had been shot in the head.

Chapter 18
Schmitt

The post mortem revealed that Crowshaw had been shot in the early hours of the morning, seemingly a victim of a professional execution. The investigation team found that there were no signs of forced entry but concluded that it would have been a simple matter for the assassin to pick the lock of the front door, enter the apartment, and carry out the killing using a silenced weapon.

As far as Tony Brent was concerned it was now certain that Crowshaw was source of the information leak and he had been removed to avoid him being arrested and revealing the identity of his accomplices.

The incident at the library indicated that Schmitt and Longford were definitely the contacts and in all probability Crowshaw had left the information in an agreed hiding place as soon as he had entered the library, somewhere in a bookshelf or a book perhaps, out of sight of the librarian or other clients. It could then be retrieved by Schmitt's agent Longford without any need for direct contact between the two.

It was clear to both DCI Brooks and Agent Brent that Crowshaw's murder had been carried out by Longford by order of Schmitt, but the evidence for this was based only on supposition. Nevertheless it was sufficient to justify an application for warrants to search the private residences of both men, but nothing incriminating had been found. Furthermore nothing suspicious had been heard or seen by the other residents of Crowshaw's apartment block at the time of the murder.

Following these fruitless searches both Schmitt and Longford were asked to attend for interrogation in London where Brooks proceeded to question them. Both men assumed an outward mantle of innocence and denied knowing Crowshaw. When he was asked about his visit to the library when Crowshaw was inside Schmitt said that it was simply a coincidence. They had gone there to check on job vacancies for the employment agency records.

Brooks knew that this was an unlikely coincidence but as there had been no observed contact between Longford and Crowshaw, there was no firm evidence of any collusion between the two.

During his investigation of Schmitt's activities Brooks noted that he was a frequent traveller abroad. When Schmitt was questioned about the purpose and frequency of these trips he had affirmed that it was part of his legitimate business, involved the recruiting of staff for companies throughout the world.

As Longford drove Schmitt back to their office following the police interview he gave a humourless grin,

'Bloody pigs, they've got nothing on us. I'm pretty sure we're in the clear, Boss.'

'Don't you be so sure,' responded Schmitt sharply. 'They are not stupid. It's a good job that we are very careful not to leave a trail behind us. Just be on your guard. In fact I think you had better lie very low for a while because you know what will happen if you get tied to murder, and it will bring them down on me like a ton of bricks. Another thing, I've got to take some pretty hot stuff to you know where next week and I know damn well that the coppers will try to trip me up at the airport. I just have to outwit them – but I have ways and means,' he concluded with a grin and tapping the side of his nose.

Several weeks later Brent received a message from Brooks that Schmitt was on his way to Heathrow airport and, acting jointly, they should both go there immediately. Brooks instructed the head of security at the airport to detain Schmitt at the check-in point. If Schmitt was carrying illegal information then he would be most vulnerable at the point of departure from the UK.

En-route to the airport Brent received a further message that Schmitt had reached Terminal three and then a short time later he was informed that he had been detained *'for security reasons'* on reaching the first class desk to check in for a flight to Singapore.

When Schmitt emerged from his apartment carrying a suitcase and briefcase he was aware that he was being watched, but he had an important assignment in the far East which he hoped would be extremely lucrative. He just had to be very careful as it involved passing important defence information to a far eastern country but he was confident that his methods of concealment would be undetectable. The information revealed more details about weapons guidance systems being developed at HGMRE as passed on to them earlier by Tony Crowshaw. Previous information had been sold very profitably to a certain State and Schmitt was hoping this current overseas trip would prove to be even more so.

Longford was waiting outside to drive him to terminal three at London Heathrow airport where he headed for the first class check-in desk. A uniformed security officer was standing near to the desk but Schmitt was not alarmed at this. He knew that he would be stopped but was quite sure that after a search they would have to let him proceed on his way.

'Excuse me, sir, I will have to ask you to come this way,' said the security officer. 'We have been requested by the police to detain you on a routine security matter. We won't keep you long so you will still make your flight.'

For a moment Schmitt looked startled then quickly assumed an attitude of bemused innocence.

'Er what's the matter? I don't understand. What do you want with me?'

'I'm sure we can clear this up quite quickly, sir, but will you please come this way,' repeated the officer stiffly.

Schmitt was escorted to a small interview room on the second floor of the arrivals hall. His luggage was placed on a table and he was asked to sit and wait. Very shortly Senior Agent Brent arrived accompanied by CDI Brooks. Schmitt was startled as he recognised the two men who had interviewed him only a week ago.

The security officer was dismissed and Brooks turned his attention to Schmitt.

'Right, Mr Schmitt, I think you will be aware of our reasons for detaining you. I am, as you know, Detective Chief Inspector Brooks of the Metropolitan Police and I'm sure you recognise Senior Agent Brent from MI5.

You are under suspicion for being involved in activities in contravention of the Official Secrets Act. Pending further enquiries you are under arrest and you are being taken to New Scotland yard for a search of you and your belongings.'

Schmitt was shaken by this turn of events as he thought he would simply be searched and allowed to continue on his way when nothing incriminating was found.

He responded irately, 'I've got important business abroad, legitimate business I might add and certainly nothing illegal. You arrest me and you prevent me from attending important meetings abroad and my business suffers.'

'Sorry, Mr Schmitt,' responded Brooks, 'but the circumstantial evidence against you is too strong and that will be explained to you later. Please come willingly as I'm sure you don't want to be seen in the terminal wearing handcuffs.'

Yes, I'm not going to make a fuss,' said Schmitt, 'but I will certainly be making a very strong complaint about this. I suppose I must expect to be victimized after the last time I saw you two. You were wasting your time then and you are wasting your time now.'

'OK, sir, that's your privilege,' replied Brooks.

On arrival at Scotland Yard they went to a small room adjoining the Metropolitan Police Forensic science unit.

'Senior Agent Brent has been given police authority to search you and your belongings, Mr Schmitt,' said DCI Brooks.

Brent was well versed in the kinds of places that small items could be hidden. He started by donning a pair of rubber gloves from a small case containing variety of search implements. Other items included a powerful magnifying glass and tweezers.

He started with the suitcase and its contents but he knew that it would be unlikely that anything incriminating would be found because of the time it spent separated from its owner. Brent turned his attention to the briefcase which was locked requiring two three digit numbers to open the two latches.

'Open this, sir, if you please, said Brent.

Schmitt opened the briefcase as demanded but all it contained were files of Schmitt's clients, presumably those who were looking for situations abroad but again nothing suspicious was found, neither in the main compartment nor the document pockets at the back.

Brent used the magnifying glass to examine every square inch of the case for hidden pockets, false base, and even the grip. He then had a close look at the two latches with their digital locks. His expert eye had noticed that there must be a false bottom to the case, albeit a very slim one.

'Could you now please open the other part of your case for me Mr Schmitt,' said Brent.

Schmitt made a show of glaring at Brent as he input another set of digits into the two locks. He pulled the latches and the bottom part of the case sprang open to reveal a file. If Brent was feeling any element of expectation he didn't show it. He opened the file which contained several sheets of paper containing what appeared to be financial data.

'That is private and confidential data relating to my business, said Schmitt with an inward smirk. 'I keep it in a separate compartment for obvious reasons. I don't think there's anything illegal about that is there?'

'No, sir,' said Brent politely, but I had to look.'

The negative result of this search was of no surprise to Brent. He was an experienced agent and he knew that if Schmitt was carrying sensitive information it was more likely to be found on his person. Apart from the usual paraphernalia of money, wallet, flight documents and mobile phone he had a locket hung by a gold chain around his neck, a watch on his left wrist and a signet ring on his right little finger.

Brent knew that Schmitt had to be concealing a memory chip of some sort with the objective of taking it abroad to sell the information to a foreign country. He would find it no matter how long it took.

A cursory examination of the watch and ring revealed nothing suspicious but the locket had a spring opening. Inside was an image of an elderly woman.

'That is my mother,' said Schmitt angrily. 'I don't think that it's illegal to carry photos of one's family, is it?'

Brent shook his head saying calmly, 'Of course not, sir.'

'Are you happy now that you've wasted my time?' growled Schmitt. 'If you don't mind I would rather like to go and catch my flight.'

'Just doing my job, sir, but before you go could I just have another look at that ring of yours?'

Brent had been closely observing Schmitt's body language during the search. In his experience suspects often showed guilt by certain involuntary actions. He had noticed that Schmitt wore a signet ring on his right hand little finger and that he seemed to keep covering it up in a less than natural way.

Schmitt was visibly shocked. He glared back at Brent muttering, 'What! It's just a signet ring.'

'Well if that's the case you've nothing to worry about,' said Brent. 'Please pass it over.'

Schmitt wrenched the ring angrily from his finger and passed it over to Brent who took it carefully between his thumb and forefinger and proceeded to examine it with a magnifying glass. It was an ordinary gold men's signet ring with a rectangular shaped surface on which the letter capital H was engraved. On looking more closely now with the magnifying glass he could just make out an almost invisible discontinuity around the circumference of the surface where it joined the main body of the ring, imperceptible to the naked eye.

'Hmm, that's interesting,' he said, looking over at Schmitt, 'can you tell me, sir if this ring is made in two parts.'

'Two parts? That's rubbish,' protested Schmitt in a distinctly shaky voice, 'it's just a ring with my initial engraved on it. Why would it be made in two parts?'

'It looks as though the top part can be removed. I know that such rings can be made by specialist craftsmen and can be opened quite easily if you know how. Do you want to open it for me?'

Schmitt looked back at Brent defiantly, 'I've just told you, it's just a ring. There aren't any secret compartments.' He looked increasingly uneasy and beads of perspiration were appearing on his brow.

Brent continued with his examination of the ring, then, on the back of the projecting part bearing the H monogram, there was a tiny recess, not much bigger than a human hair. From his case he withdrew a special tool consisting of bunch of fine wires of various diameters. It provoked an immediate reaction from Schmitt who sprang out of the chair and made an attempt to grab the ring from Brent.

'No!' he yelled, 'that's my personal property and you could damage it doing that. You've no right!'

He was easily restrained by CDI Brooks who stepped in front of him grabbing his shoulders and forcing him back onto the chair.

'We have every right' said the officer firmly. 'When it comes to matters of National Security we have the power to detain you and carry out whatever search we deem necessary. If you are innocent then you have nothing to worry about so please remain seated until we have completed our job.'

It was very thinnest of the wires that penetrated the tiny recess and it released a tiny catch which allowed the top part of the ring to be rotated. It fell away to reveal a micro SD card lying snugly in the revealed space of only one millimetre in depth.

The card was removed using the tweezers by Brent and taken into a different room where a computer sat on a desk. The card was plugged into a suitable slot via an adapter and the contents displayed on the screen.

It contained pages of information which was incomprehensible to Brent, but each sheet was headed by the bold statement,

TOP SECRET
HAMMOND GRANGE MILITARY RESEARCH ESTABLISHMENT

'We have to verify this material with HGMRE,' said Brent later to DCI Brooks, 'but I think it's clear what it is and it's certainly enough to arrest Schmitt.'

Schmitt sat under the watchful eye of a uniformed police officer growing increasingly fretful as the time passed. Eventually Brent returned, again accompanied by CDI Brooks who confronted Schmitt.

'Mr Schmitt, we have found evidence of a serious breach of the Official Secrets Act in your ring. You will be charged and detained to face a magistrate's court tomorrow. I'm cautioning you now and we will record a further interview with a solicitor of your choice in attendance, do you understand?'

'I understand you,' Schmitt replied tersely, 'but I am a Swiss National. You don't have any right to arrest me.'

'Oh yes, sir, we do,' retorted Brooks sharply. 'Your nationality is irrelevant when it comes to matters of National Security. I advise you to phone your solicitor now so we can progress with a recorded formal interview under caution.'

A short time later Schmitt sat grim faced at a table beside his solicitor, a short sandy haired man in his late forties. CDI Brooks sat beside Tony Brent on the other side of the table facing the pair.

'Mr Schmitt,' said Brooks, 'your ring contained material which would be sufficient for us to charge you now. The evidence is irrefutable and would most certainly be sufficient for a conviction. We know where this material originated from and that it was Mr Crowshaw who passed it on to you, and we believe that you used Norman Longford, your employee, as the in-between. Do you have anything to say to that?'

Brooks paused and glanced questioningly at Schmitt but received no response, just a sullen glare.

'Of course you have the right to remain silent but there are two other matters I want to bring to your attention,' he continued. 'We interviewed you recently about the murder of Mr Crowshaw who worked at HMGRE. You denied knowing Mr Crowshaw, claiming that your observed presence at the same place and time as him was just a remarkable coincidence.'

Brooks paused, slowly shaking his head from side to side disbelievingly. 'Really, Mr Schmitt,' he went on, 'you really expect us to believe that? Look at the facts. You and Longford were both observed to be present in the library at the same time. We know that Crowshaw was involved in the business of stealing defence information and you have just been caught in possession of a memory chip containing highly confidential dossier originating from HGMRE where he worked. Crowshaw has now paid a severe price for his betrayal no doubt to ensure his silence. We will find his killer have no fear.'

Brooks looked pointedly at Schmitt as he made the last comment before adding,

'Have you anything to say now?'

Again there was no reaction from Schmitt.

'Another thing, Mr Schmitt,' continued Brooks, 'we know from the Hastings police that your name was found on a hidden list of contacts found in the house of a Frank Delaney who is being held on a charge of murder. You've already been interviewed by the Hastings police about that and we are aware that Delaney was involved with industrial espionage. Amazing isn't it how your name keeps cropping up?'

Schmitt simply glared back at Brooks and hissed, 'No comment!'

'OK, Schmitt,' said Brooks, deliberately dropping the "Mr" title, 'let me put it to you this way. You can continue to maintain your silence, as of course you are legally entitled to, and you will be charged and I've no doubt you will be found guilty because the evidence is irrefutable. You will certainly go to prison for a long time.'

There was a further lengthy pause as Brooks regarded Schmitt impassively, waiting to see if he would break his silence, but to no avail. Schmitt continued to stare back at him defiantly.

'You must understand the gravity of your situation,' said Brooks seriously. 'The business that you have been engaged in is a serious threat to the security of this country. In fact if this was wartime and you were to be found guilty, you would be shot as a spy. Mr Brent here is a member of our Intelligence services and he will now take over this interview.'

'Mr Schmitt,' said Brent in a formal tone of voice, 'let me say first that we are not interested in those activities of yours concerned with industrial espionage, serious though they might be. Our concern is national security and you will be charged with receiving information from Crowshaw who stole it in breach of the Official Secrets Act which he had signed as a condition of his employment. If you agree to cooperate with us and confess your part in this it could have a mitigating effect on your sentence. Any other information you give us would also help particularly by confirming to us that it was Longford who was the direct contact with Crowshaw. I would advise you to think about this very seriously. That's all I have to say, I'll pass you back to CDI Brooks.'

'Right, Mr Schmitt,' said Brooks, 'you've heard what Mr Brent had to say. Do you have anything to say to me now?'

Schmitt simply growled back again, 'No comment.'

'I think you need to talk to your solicitor,' said Brooks. 'Mr Brent and I will leave you for a while to discuss it.'

The two men returned some time later and Brooks looked at Schmitt expectantly.

'Well, Mr Schmitt, have you anything to say to me?'

Schmitt nodded, a look of defeat on his face. 'OK, you win. I'll tell you what you want to know but I need some assurance from you that it will help me in court.'

'I can't give you any guarantees,' responded Brooks, 'but the judge may look favourably on your willingness to cooperate. That's all I can say.'

Schmitt subsequently made a full statement passing much of the blame onto Norman Longford saying that he was the one responsible for recruiting Crowshaw and receiving information from him. He had nothing to do with Crowshaw's murder. That must have been carried out by Longford to avoid his name being revealed.

Schmitt was consequently charged with receiving stolen State confidential information with the intent to pass it on to a foreign power. He was remanded in custody to await trial by Crown Court.

The information supplied by Schmitt admitted the involvement of Tony Crowshaw in the theft of defence secrets from HGMRE on several occasions, the most serious being that relating to the weapons guidance system which had marked Brent's entry to the case.

Schmitt's office was the next focus for attention and Brooks and Brent accompanied by other Special Branch officers ascended the stairs to the reception area. Brooks flashed his search warrant to the shocked secretary and the group dispersed to carry out their task, one of which was to impound all items likely to be of interest.

Longford was sitting behind Schmitt's desk having returned from taking Schmitt to the airport. He was lounging with his feet propped up on the desk and reading an issue of the Racing Times. He looked up in alarm as the officers burst into the study.

'What the hell!' he exclaimed vehemently.

'Mr Longford?' said Brooks abruptly.

'Yes, that's me, what do you want?' returned Longford furiously. 'What do you mean by barging in here?'

'Norman Longford,' said Brooks calmly. 'You are under arrest under suspicion that you have received State confidential information with a view to passing it on to a foreign power.' Brooks proceeded to issue him with the usual arrest caution.

Longford was shocked as he realised that Schmitt had been caught with this material at the Airport, and that he had been named by Schmitt. Nevertheless he protested his innocence vigorously, shouting, 'What! That's nonsense. I'm just Mr Schmitt's driver. I don't know what you're talking about.'

'Mr Longford', said Brooks, 'you will of course be interviewed in the presence of a lawyer so you will have ample opportunity to rebuff this accusation, but there is another very serious matter relating to the killing of the person who we suspect passed you this information. So we are also holding you under suspicion of the murder of Tony Crowshaw.'

In spite of his protests Longford was handcuffed by one of the officers and taken to wait in one of the police cars outside. The remaining officers carried out a comprehensive search of the premises.

One item had caught their immediate attention as soon as they had entered the office. It was a desktop computer with its printer and keyboard alongside. It was already turned on in its sleep mode and Brooks alerted it to show the usual collection of programmes.

Nothing suspicious could be found on them, they merely contained details of Schmitt's legitimate business such as lists of clients and companies looking for employees. However one file caught Brook's eye on the word processor, it was labelled simply *ad hoc*. When he tried to open it a popup window appeared asking for a password.

'Now why would Schmitt have one file with an innocuous label be under password protection?' said Brooks thoughtfully.

'Well, no matter,' said Brooks. 'It'll be a simple matter for our forensics to break into it.'

There were two filing cabinets in the office as well but they yielded nothing of interest, just normal office files again relating to Schmitt's legitimate business.

The computer was impounded and conveyed to Scotland Yard's Forensic department to await expert examination.

The next port of call for the officers was Longford's home address. Brooks knew only too well that they had no firm evidence to charge Longford for murder even though they were quite sure that he was the killer so a search of Longford's apartment was a top priority. The police car with Brooks, Brent, and Longford handcuffed to a third officer, set off to drive the short distance from Schmitt's office to his apartment. The address was a block of flats looking as if they were ready for demolition. Longford reluctantly showed them the way to a lift which took them up to a dingy apartment on the fourth floor.

'I don't know why you are doing this,' moaned Longford. 'You lot have already searched this flat. You found nothing then and you'll find nothing now because I've done nothing wrong.'

The previous search of the property had been with the objective of finding hidden documents which had proved to be fruitless. This time the focus was on a more subtly hidden item, the murder weapon, and the search was carried out by highly experienced officers.

Eventually one of the officers called out, 'I think we may have something here, sir.'

He was looking into a nondescript built-in cupboard in the kitchen area. It was part of a unit comprising several cupboards secured into the wall. Behind the conglomerate of food items the officer was pointing to the back of the cupboard.

'This looks like a false back,' said the officer. It doesn't look as if it's part of the rest of the cupboard but there are four screws holding it to the wall. Do you know of any reason for that Mr Longford?'

Longford was visibly shaken as he denied any knowledge of the apparently false back.

'It's always been like that since before I moved here. Probably put in like that to make it fit with the rest of the unit. It's certainly nothing to do with me.'

The officer proceeded to remove the four screws which allowed the cupboard back to come away from the rest of the unit. It revealed a recess in the wall and inside was a gun fitted with a silencer. The officer was wearing rubber gloves and he carefully withdrew the gun to avoid disturbing any fingerprints.

'Well, Mr Longford,' said Brooks, 'how do you explain this?'

Longford was clearly stunned by the discovery. 'I don't know anything about that. I didn't know it was there,' he said, his voice shaking with the shock of discovery.

'We shall see,' responded Brooks grimly.

He turned to his sergeant. 'OK sergeant, we've finished here. Let's go.'

Later forensic tests showed the presence of Longford's fingerprints all over the weapon and comparison with bullets taken from the scene of Crowshaw's murder proved that it was the weapon used. Longford was subsequently charged both with illegally receiving State information and murder. He was remanded in custody at a magistrate's court the following day to await trial for both charges.

The examination of the hard drive contents from Schmitt's office enabled the password encrypted file to be opened. It revealed a list of all of Schmitt's Liaison Officers involved in the business of industrial espionage. Also listed were commercial companies, Borough Councils, Government research establishments and a host of other information relating to their primary activities.

'These are all places where you might expect to see some kind of espionage going on,' said Brent. 'They mostly deal with research and development of commercial products, privileged information that would be very lucrative to competitive companies, or even other countries.'

They continued to scan the list of names until Brooks came across one that led to a surprised exclamation.

'This is interesting,' said Brooks, pointing to an entry which read:

Frank Delaney, known as Alan Birch. Replacement for Roger Partridge.

'Remember we heard about this Delaney character from Hastings police and Schmitt's name had been found on one of his files during their investigation of the murder of a Dr Jones for which he has already been charged.'

Then they came across the name of Len Parker, listed as an "overseas contact exchanging information about arms transfers and other matters".

When they saw that Parker lived near Larnaca in Cyprus it produced a gasp of surprise from Brooks.

'This is too much of a coincidence,' he said. 'Parker lives in Cyprus, not far from the Dhekalia army base where Delaney was a serving officer and from where he deserted. The odd thing was that Delaney deserted at the same time that a Greek Cypriot civilian at the base was shot dead and there is some suspicion that it was Delaney who did it. Now we find that both Delaney and Parker are listed on Schmitt's files so they must have known each other, and I'd go further to say that they were both involved with thefts of arms and other materials from that base. There is also the possibility that Parker might have had something to do with the murder of Christakos as well.'

'We must alert the Cypriot authorities about this information. They are very likely to institute extradition proceedings. The ball is very much in their court.'

The list included some of the information provided by Schmitt in his statement but the computer file was more valuable. Schmitt obviously did not discriminate between his state espionage activities and his less lucrative commercial ones.

'My God,' said Brooks finally, 'this business is taking more twists and turns than any maze. These files give us the clearance to interrogate a hell of a lot of people. Who knows how far this stretches. It might well include other cells with a host of other agents who may be operating in our state research departments. It's a gold mine of information and it is vital that we get to work on it immediately.'

'I agree,' said Brent, 'but I think my function in all this is finished. My remit was to find the source of the leaks from HGMRE and that, with your help, has been done. It's a purely police matter now so I'll wish you luck and take my leave.'

Brooks smile back and shook Brent's hand. 'Yes, it's been a very successful joint effort and thank you for your help as well.'

Chapter 19
Cyprus

Many miles away in Cyprus, Len Parker sat relaxing on his patio savouring his elevated view overlooking Larnaca bay. His face relaxed into a smug self-satisfied smile as he reviewed in his mind's eye his present good fortune. His trading of small arms stolen from various army bases, both British and Cypriot, had paid rich rewards and continued to do so. The operation was made possible by using Greek Cypriot civilians who worked in these depots and who he had been able to bribe or entice to carry out the thefts. A bonus was that there were occasions when he had also been able to recruit army personnel as well as they were more likely to have access to their respective armouries. The other aspect of trading in goods such as NAAFI stores was less remunerative but still worth the effort.

He reflected on the events leading to the death of Andreas Christakos. He had congratulated himself when he succeeded in getting Frank Delaney on side. A British army officer; what could be better than that; someone who would have access to most of the army buildings in the Camp without question. However Delaney had only promised to assist him for a limited time provided that

Parker arranged for his escape from the army and Cyprus. The problem was that Christakos would surely panic as soon as he knew that Delaney, the one who organised his activities, had gone. He could not afford the risk that Christakos would confess and reveal his name.

The loss of Delaney from his direct control was of little consequence. He had simply been passed on to Hans Schmitt who was a vital contact for the interchange of information about buyers, sellers, and other matters from which he made considerable profits.

As Parker sat savouring his luxurious life he heard the slamming of car doors outside his villa. He sat up with a frown. Who could this be? That didn't sound like any of his usual visitors who came discretely making as little noise as possible, and usually under cover of darkness.

The next minute there was a loud knocking at his front door and Parker went to open it with an increasing feeling of apprehension. Two uniformed officers stood facing him and he recognised the insignia of an inspector and sergeant in the Cypriot police.

'Mr Leonard Parker?' said the inspector.

'Yes, that's me, what do you want?' replied Parker.

'Mr Parker, we have a warrant to search these premises.'

'What the hell for!' protested Parker. 'I've done nothing wrong. What are you looking for?'

'We just have to do our job, sir,' said the officer. 'Please don't try to obstruct us.'

The two officers pushed past Parker to carry out their search while Parker stood helpless, a look of desperation on his face.

Within minutes the officers had found the locked cellar and he was forced into giving them the keys. There was no point in resisting as they would have forced the lock anyway. Inside they found his extensive stock of stolen weapons and other goods.

The inspector faced the now distraught Parker, 'Mr Parker, based on what has been found in your house, and from other information we have received, you are under arrest for the possession of stolen arms and other materials with the objective of illegal arms trading.'

He gave Parker a formal warning of his rights, handcuffed him and promptly led him from the house to be driven to the police station in Larnaca for formal questioning.

Later Parker sat in the interview room with his solicitor, a tall-red headed man named Kenneth Drew, a long standing friend also from England who lived not far from Parker. He was also an ex-pat who practiced from an office in the town, and they often socialised together as part of the British community.

The same two officers who had arrested him faced him across the table. A recording machine sat on a nearby stand.

The inspector leaned forward towards Parker to say, 'You cannot deny that you knew that you had a considerable volume of arms hidden in your cellar. These have all been identified as having been stolen both from British army bases here in Cyprus, and also from Cypriot bases. Can you admit to me that you knew they were there?'

Parker knew it would be futile to deny that he knew of their presence in his house. He was the owner and the only occupier.

He nodded glumly.

'Please say yes or no Mr Parker for the recorder,' said the inspector.

'Yes, he mumbled. 'They are my property.'

'How did they come to be in your possession when they have been stolen?'

'I bought them,' said Parker. 'I'm interested in collecting weapons. I didn't know they were stolen.'

'Do you also happen to collect cigarettes, alcoholic drinks, and that electronic gear we found?' persisted he inspector.

Parker looked round desperately at his solicitor for advice and received the unspoken message.

'No comment,' he said.

Later he sat in his cell with his solicitor to discuss the charges against him and what his chances were during his trial.

'Len,' said Drew, regarding him with solemnly, 'the evidence against you is pretty damning and if you plead not guilty it could go very badly for you. On the other hand if you cooperate with the police, plead guilty, and name some of the people who supplied you with these things, I believe it would lighten your sentence. What do you think?'

'I don't know,' said Parker slowly, 'do you really think that would help me?'

'Look, Len, I shall have a word with the prosecution and see what I can do. If there were a number of people who supplied you and they could be identified it would alleviate one of our main problems on this island. Both the British and Cypriot Governments have known about these thefts for years so I'm sure that it would result in a lighter sentence for you. Another thing, your name would not be used openly in evidence against them, for your own protection.'

The following day Drew appeared to tell him that the prosecution had agreed some limited leniency provided that he made a compete confession and named all of his accomplices.

'Do you know how the police got onto me?' said Parker. 'They must have had some valid reason to search my house.'

'I don't know all the details,' replied Drew, 'but I understand they received information from the UK which tied you in to a known criminal by the name of Hans Schmitt.

'Bloody hell!' swore Parker, 'Schmitt!'

'Yes,' said his solicitor, 'he is in prison awaiting trial for contravening the official Secrets Act in Britain. Apparently you name was found on his computer as an accomplice in illegal trading.'

'How can you be sure the same thing's not going to happen to me?' challenged Parker. 'I've never had anything to do with that sort of stuff. I am not a traitor!'

'Let me be the Devil's Advocate for a moment, Len,' said Drew. 'The prosecution could well argue that stealing weapons from army bases and selling them to possible enemies could well be interpreted as an act of betrayal of your country. I will argue against this of course and stress that your customers were chosen with care and none of them posed a threat either to Cyprus or Britain.'

'What about the people I name in my confession?' said Parker. 'They are likely to come after me aren't they?'

'The prison service will do it's best to protect you,' said Drew, 'but if and when you come out my advice would be to get out of Cyprus and live somewhere under an assumed name. You might even be eligible to be treated as a protected witness and be given a false identity and place to live.'

'Another thing, the Cypriot government has applied to the UK for the extradition of someone else you seem to have known. Frank Delaney, the army deserter, who I believe was yet another of your associates. He is suspected of shooting Andreas Christakos who worked at the base and was thieving from it. Delaney will be tried for murder back here if his extradition is granted.'

'My God,' groaned Parker. 'If that happens Delaney will try to pass the blame onto me as an accessory. Let's hope the extradition application fails.'

Chapter 20
Court Martial and Extradition

Frank Delaney paced his remand cell furiously. After hearing about Schmitt's arrest and then learning in addition that Schmitt had been arrested for attempting to export state defence secrets he was horror struck. As a contact he could be accused of being involved and that would make his situation even worse.

His mind was in turmoil. The prospect of a lifetime in jail was unbearable and, from his distorted point of view, that was down to that bitch Paula Kendrick. He was determined to wreak revenge on her somehow, no matter how long it took.

There was a sudden rattle of keys from the cell door and it swung open to reveal one of the wardens.

'There are two visitors waiting to see you in the interview room Delaney. I'll take you there now.'

When Delaney entered the room he was amazed to see his father sitting at the table next to a distinguished grey haired man who regarded him dispassionately. In contrast his father glared at him, his face set in hard lines.

Without any greeting, his father said abruptly, 'I said before that I wanted nothing more to do with you and that hasn't changed. You are a disgrace to the family and I have disowned you. However, you are my son whether I like it or not and I can't abandon you altogether. I have engaged Mr Matthews here to act in your defence. He is a QC and highly experienced. That's all I have to say to you, and let me add that after this I never want to set eyes on you again.'

With that he rose from the table and departed from the room.

'Well,' breathed Delaney, 'that was short and sweet, so much for family ties.'

'Mr Delaney,' said Matthews, 'I'm sorry about your family problems but my job is to defend you to the best of my ability. I have already reviewed all the facts of the case and read the statements by Miss Kendrick and from information found on a list in Mr Schmitt's office tying you to acts of industrial sabotage. The prosecution's case is based on a supposed motive that you killed Dr Jones to prevent him from revealing your role in the attempted theft of confidential information. Do you have anything to say to that Mr Delaney?'

Delaney responded acrimoniously,

'If they believe everything that bitch has told them then I suppose that's so, but I repeat, I did not set out to kill Dr Jones. As I told the police it was an accident. I wanted to confront him about his affair with my girlfriend. You will have seen all of this in my statement.'

'Yes, I've read your statement and as you know the burden of proof rests with the prosecution,' said Matthews. 'Frankly I think that the proof in this case is more circumstantial than solid whatever they bring up as a motive. There is no doubt that your car struck Dr Jones causing his death, and you were driving the car at the time, but I would argue that you wished to confront him before he drove off to try to convince him not to go running to his company's security people. That means that you would have to admit that you were behind the attempted theft of secret information from Brouchers. This is substantiated by evidence we found on Schmitt's computer which ties you in to this kind of activity. There is far too much evidence against you for you to go on denying it.'

Matthews paused and regarded Delaney with a querying look.

Delaney nodded slowly and reluctantly. 'OK, yes, it's true. I did get caught up in that business and yes, I admit that it involved Dr Jones. Things went wrong so I was on my way to see him but when I saw him getting into his car I tried to stop beside him so I could talk to him. Unfortunately I misjudged it and struck him so I panicked and ran off.'

'You are not on trial for industrial espionage,' said Matthews,' and it's not my job to comment on that, but I do have a proposal. If you are found guilty as charged you would of course get a life sentence but if I can convince the prosecution to accept a plea of guilty of involuntary manslaughter then the sentence would be much lighter, only a few years in fact. What do you say to that?'

Delaney looked dubious, 'What if they find me not guilty of murder. Wouldn't I get off?'

'No,' replied Matthews, 'Even if it was a pure accident as you claim you are still guilty of involuntary manslaughter according to the law, but the sentence would be more severe than if you pleaded guilty to that charge to start with. Also you would not have to undergo the ordeal of a prolonged trial. If you agree I will go to the prosecution and see if they would accept that alternative.'

His voice took on warning tone, 'I wouldn't let your hopes go too high, Mr Delaney. They do have good reasons to pursue their case for murder, not least your action in kidnapping Miss Kendrick and threatening her with a gun. That won't go down too well with the jury will it?'

Delaney raised his hands in an expression of resigned submission. 'Yes I know, it was stupid of me but it was all done out of panic. I just wanted to get away. All I can do is to say sorry to everyone involved, and yes, I will do as you say provided the prosecution accepts it. There is something else that I'm worried about, though, Mr Matthews.'

'Oh yes, what's that?' said Matthews raising his eyebrows quizzically.

'Yes I admit I was passing stuff to Schmitt but I had absolutely nothing to do with pinching state secrets. Whatever else I am, I am not a traitor.'

'You've no need to worry about that,' said Matthews, 'Schmitt has made a full confession and it is clear that his involvement in industrial espionage was quite separate from the activity for which he has been charged. We have interviewed him about the people named on that file from his office and he made it clear that you and the others were only involved in industrial espionage which is not essentially a criminal offense. Of course there will be occasions where criminal acts are performed in pursuance of that occupation so the situation is not clear cut, but I repeat, you have nothing to worry about as far as the official secrets act is concerned.'

This was something of a relief to Delaney who had been expecting a life sentence so he thought that given remission for good behaviour he would now be out in only a few years.

'There is another complication,' said Matthews slowly. 'You are a deserter from the army and we have been informed that they want you to face a general court martial. At the moment you are awaiting trial, but your court martial will take place during that period. Consequently you will be transferred to an army detention centre in Colchester until the army have finished with you. Obviously I can't be involved in that process but I will continue to be your brief for the primary charge.'

The news of Schmitt's arrest, and that Frank Delaney's name had been found on a hidden file, soon reached DI Dobson of the Hastings CID. Dobson knew from Paula's statement that the motive for this act had been to avoid his role in industrial espionage in Brouchers being revealed.

But now something even more serious had turned up following a series of communications from the Ministry of Defence. Delaney was summoned to the Governor's office to find DI Dobson waiting there with two military police officers.

Delaney looked at Dobson in surprise. 'Why are you here again?' he said with some annoyance in his voice.

'There have been some important new developments Delaney,' said Dobson. 'We now have evidence from Schmitt's files that you were involved in industrial espionage so your story that you knew nothing about anything like that going on is not likely to hold much water. What I've come here to tell you is that the Greek Cypriot authorities have contacted us to say that they have firm evidence that you were concerned with the shooting of a Greek Cypriot National by the name of Andreas Christakos. They want you extradited to Nicosia in Cyprus to be tried for that murder. You have already been informed by your brief that a court-martial is being convened and these military police officers are here to transport you to the military prison in Colchester. The army wants you to be a civilian before being transported back to Cyprus, because there's no doubt that's what you will be after the court martial. Our government has allowed the extradition application so you will be transported back to Cyprus straight after your court martial. This has been agreed because the charge you are to face there is one of murder, a more serious charge than the one here which would probably one of manslaughter. You would face that charge back here at a later date.'

A look of complete despair was on Delaney's face as he heard of these developments. There seemed to be no way out. It looked as if he was going to spend many years in prison.

'What is this nonsense about me murdering someone in Cyprus?' he muttered.

Dobson shook his head. 'I can't tell you anything about that Delaney. I only know that the Cypriot embassy has presented our government with that evidence and it was sufficient to persuade them to grant the request of extradition.'

'It must be that rat Parker,' hissed Delaney, 'who else could it be?'

'That will probably come out during your trial,' responded Dobson as the prison Governor signed the necessary release document allowing Delaney to be transferred.

Delaney was promptly transported handcuffed to HM military prison, Colchester. As an unconvicted prisoner on remand, he was officially still Lieutenant Delaney, and had to wear the appropriate uniform for weeks until a general court martial could be convened.

When Jack Blake heard that Delaney was now on remand he felt he should visit him in jail, but when he spoke to Mary about it she shook her head vigorously.

'No, darling, I think it's a bad idea,' she said, 'can't you see that he's a bad lot. Just look at all the stuff he's been involved with, and don't forget what he did to that girl, Paula Kendrick.'

'I'm not likely to forget her,' retorted Jack, 'but I'm not waving any flags for her after what she did. No, it's just that he was my closest friend at one time. We did everything together when we were out there in Cyprus. I was shattered when all that happened. I suppose I want some form of closure. Of course he might refuse to see me, in fact he probably will, but I must try.'

'Well, if you must, but don't say I didn't warn you,' she said, 'and be very careful, it could stir up some nasty feelings, particularly that he'll know that you told the police about his true identity. You never know what he might do.'

'It's unlikely,' said Jack dismissively. 'I think he will know that I had no choice. Anyway I feel it's something I must do whatever the outcome.'

Jack applied to the Military prison to see if Delaney would accept a visit by him, not expecting a favourable response. He was surprised to hear several days later that Delaney had agreed to see him and he was given a date and time for the following week. When the time arrived, Jack entered an antechamber with a throng of other visitors. He was body searched before being allowed to walk through into a long room filled with wooden tables and chairs, all arranged to allow one visitor per inmate. Military police officers were standing at the sides of the room and many of the tables were occupied by inmates looking expectantly towards the entrance. The sounds of scraping chairs echoed throughout the room as visitors took their places, adding to Jack's feeling of apprehension.

He scanned the table occupants, looking for Delaney. He spotted him seated about halfway down the hall and his heart beat a little faster as he made his way towards him. Delaney seemed little changed except that his fair hair was rather longer and he had a strained look about his face, a very different man from the carefree one that Jack had known so well.

Delaney looked at him as he approached with no hint of recognition, and certainly no hint of a smile of welcome.

'Hello, Frank,' said Jack pulling back the chair to sit down to face his one-time friend.

Without preamble Delaney said shortly, 'What are you doing here? I would have thought I was the last person you would want to see.'

'I must admit that it's taken me a long time to pluck up the courage,' said Jack, 'but it's something I've been wanting to do. We've been such good friends in the past.'

'You've just said it yourself,' responded Delaney tensely, 'we were good friends. That's what made it worse. I really felt bad when I heard you had told the police about me.' He paused for a few moments and then his face relaxed into the semblance of a smile and he shook his head slowly from side to side before he continued.

'You know, Jack, you are one of the best things to happen in my life and I do treasure that friendship we had. You are what you are, an honest and good man, something that I could never be. I know once you learned that I was behind that business with Paula Kendrick you had to do the right thing and tell the police. It would have come out anyway in time. Just as well. Things have caught up with me now so I have to face the music.'

Jack looked back at Delaney not knowing just how to respond to him. Eventually he said, 'I'm really sorry to see you like this, Frank, but whatever you've done I just wanted to see you. Maybe it's for old time's sake, I don't know, it just seemed to be the right thing to do.' He paused momentarily before adding, 'Look, Frank, if you don't want me to visit you just say so and I'll leave you alone, but I will visit you again if you want me to.'

Delaney shrugged, saying, 'That may not be possible but yes, I would like it if there is time. It takes quite a while to set up a General Court Martial so I could be here for weeks. I know what will happen because I shall be pleading guilty to desertion, and then I'll be transported to Cyprus to face the charge of Christakos's murder.'

Jack decided not to pursue this matter. He was quite certain now that Delaney had been responsible for shooting Christakos but thought it better to change the subject.

'Do you get any other visitors?' he said looking at Delaney searchingly.

'Visitors! You must be joking!' replied Delaney bitterly. 'Who the hell would want to visit me? Apart from Rose my family have all disowned me and whatever friends I had want nothing to do with me, probably because they cringe at the idea of visiting a prison. Maybe it brings back unpleasant memories,' he concluded with a sarcastic smirk.

'What about Rose?' said Jack, 'doesn't she want to come and see you?'

'She does,' replied Delaney, 'but I put her off. I don't want her coming here to see me like this.'

'I'll talk to her,' responded Jack. 'I'll tell her that I've been to see you and you are well, and I'll explain to her the reasons why you don't want her visiting you here.'

They continued to chat about some of the things they did in the past and Jack felt he had managed to raise Frank's spirits just a little. He knew that Frank Delaney was a bad lot but he was still his friend, for better or worse. He couldn't condone any of the things Frank was accused of, but Jack simply could not abandon him altogether.

Anyway,' Jack concluded as he rose to leave, 'I'll try and visit you again.'

'Yes,' said Delaney, 'I'd like that, but it's unlikely there'll be enough time. Just hope you're happy with that girl of yours, Jack. I'm quite jealous really; just wish I could have been more like you.'

That final comment was said in a genuine tone of regret and showed one of the very few moments in Delaney's life when he had expressed a true feeling.

A further visit was destined not to take place as Delaney received notification that his Court Martial hearing was due to take place only days later. As a matter of course he had been appointed an attorney by the military court, another officer of the same rank whose only function would be to enter Delaney's admission of guilt and to offer any mitigating evidence.

So the day arrived and Delaney stood in front of a board of five senior officers seated behind a long table who were to listen to evidence and to pronounce judgement. Seated separately was a senior barrister known as the judge advocate whose presence was necessary to ensure that the correct legal procedures were followed.

The facts of the case against Delaney were presented to the court by the prosecuting officer, who stood to face the board. He spoke confidently to say that on the specific date named in the charge sheet two years ago, second lieutenant Delaney failed to report for duty at his base in Dhekalia, Cyprus.

Further investigation showed that he was not present in the base, nor did he turn up later. He was later found to have returned to the UK and to be using a false name, i.e. *Alan Birch*. This is a clear case of desertion and the prosecution asks that the maximum penalty for this offense in peacetime be applied, that is for second lieutenant Delaney to be cashiered and discharged from the army with disgrace.

The lead member of the Board was a distinguished Colonel of the Scots Guards with a row of campaign medals. His name was Colonel McGregor, a blue-eyed Scotsman in his early forties.

He regarded Delaney for several seconds without expression before speaking in a rich Scottish accent.

'Lieutenant Delaney, you have already entered a plea of guilty to this charge and your attorney has provided the court with a written statement which offers very little in the way of mitigation for your actions. However there are additional things that must be said. We know that you stand accused of much more serious matters and they will be dealt with by other courts. We also know that we could have included additional charges of theft from the armoury at the Dhekalia base where you were stationed. A very serious matter for which you could serve many years in prison, but on consideration of your extradition to Cyprus the Board has decided not to include these at the present time. The Board has already considered the charge as it stands and only one penalty is possible. You are stripped forthwith of your commission; you will be discharged with disgrace from the British army and delivered into civilian custody for immediate transportation to Cyprus to face further charges.'

Delaney received his sentence without any appearance of emotion. He had pleaded guilty so he knew what would happen but he was surprised to see two armed RAF police officers appear. They had been standing by to receive him into custody. His uniform was exchanged for his civilian clothes before he was transported to a holding cell at a large RAF station in East Sussex.

At her parents' home in rural Berkshire Paula Kendrick gave a huge sigh of relief when she heard that she did not have to appear in court to testify against

Delaney, at least not at any time in the near future. She had been dreading the thought of having to face his malevolent glare, and the knowledge that he would vow to wreak his revenge on her. Hopefully he would be confined in Cyprus for an indefinite time.

She continued to feel disgusted with herself for what she had done and felt herself responsible for Dr Jones's death. It was something that she could never forgive herself for. She would pay for it as she had lost a promising career. One that she would never be able to resume. She now had to look round to find another career but there she was fortunate in having a private income and wealthy parents.

Within months she was able to start up her own small company in fashion design which quickly proved to be successful and so she moved on with her life, putting the past events well behind her.

Chapter 21

Act of Revenge

Within hours of Norman Longford's arrest CDI Brooks arrived again to confront Schmitt where he brooded in his prison cell. Desperate to avoid the further charge of being an accessory to the murder Schmitt had earlier protested his innocence in his statement. Longford was one of his employees in his legitimate business at Brevingtons employment agency but in his earlier confession he had put the blame firmly on Longford's shoulders and that he certainly he was not behind Longford's killing of Crowshaw.

Brooks gave Schmitt a long hard look. 'I have difficulty in believing much of what you say,' he said. 'Apart from the charge you are now on we know that you have also been involved in industrial espionage. You have admitted to this and Longford has been closely involved as well. That is not my concern. What *is* my concern is the murder of Crowshaw who we know was the one who passed the information to you via Norman Longford. You said in your initial statement that you thought Longford was behind that murder but I believe that you instigated it. Do you still maintain that you had nothing to do with it?'

'Of course,' said Schmitt. 'OK. I've held my hands up to what I've already been charged with, but murder. No!'

'We'll see about that,' said Brooks. 'I have to caution you that you will be charged for being an accessory to murder but the CPS want to delay the trial for that until much later.'

In his subsequent Crown Court trial Schmitt pleaded guilty to the charge of trading in secret State information contrary to the Official Secrets Act. He was given a lengthy term of imprisonment and promptly removed to a high security prison.

Within months Longford was tried for the murder of Crowshaw. His defence counsel argued that his client was completely under the thumb of Schmitt and, as Schmitt's employee, he had only been carrying out his instructions. The evidence against him was conclusive however and he was given a life sentence for murder. He was to face the additional charge of trading in State secrets at a later date.

Longford's naturally violent disposition had already led to several jail sentences for robbery with violence in recent years, so prison life was familiar to him although since being employed by Schmitt he had been more shielded from justice by the blanket of security that his employer maintained over his organisation. To all appearances Longford was Schmitt's driver but in reality he was Schmitt's hit man having already dealt with numerous instances where persuasive techniques had been required.

The strongest evidence against him was Schmitt's statement which tried to shift the blame entirely onto Longford's shoulders. He had an inborn instinct for retribution dating from the days when as a common street thug he would inflict physical violence on anyone who crossed him. That instinct now resurfaced to direct itself against Hans Schmitt.

As a member of the so-called criminal fraternity Longford knew many other individuals like himself who were able to communicate with each other whether or not they were in confinement. They tended to have an inexplicable loyalty towards each other, a kind of criminal code which could be called upon when necessary using a very efficient network of communication, either via corrupt wardens susceptible to bribery, or from well-hidden mobile phones.

Retribution was what Longford had in mind now and Schmitt would pay for his betrayal. That night he took his mobile phone from its discrete hiding place and proceeded to send several texts. He had to wait some time to get replies but finally he laid back on his bunk smiling in smug satisfaction.

**

In a northern prison far removed from Longford's place of confinement, Schmitt was a very miserable and lonely man. He could not adjust to the severe change in his lifestyle and he remained aloof from other inmates who consequently regarded him with hostility. Also, many prisoners, whatever their crimes, had an odd sense of patriotism, and knowing that Schmitt had been selling their country's secrets to foreign powers augmented that hostility. The fact that Longford himself was awaiting a similar charge was as yet unknown to them.

Schmitt was often pushed and jostled roughly when standing in meal queues, and on one occasion he was tripped over when carrying his meal, sending him sprawling on the floor with the contents of his tray.

There were several occasions when inmates were required to attend educational films intended to educate them about important issues that could help to rehabilitate them. The films were shown in a room with bench seats and a warden sat watchfully by the door.

Schmitt reluctantly took his place on one such occasion thinking it was such a waste of time considering the length of time that would elapse before there was any chance of his release. He found himself squeezed on either side by two burly prisoners he recognised as being among the most hostile towards him, and his heart started to beat faster with fear and apprehension. He tried to move to a different position but one of his neighbours hissed from the side of his mouth, 'Stay where you are, Schmitt, and don't make a noise or you will be dead.'

The film started and the lights dimmed but within seconds there was a loud scream ending with a gurgle, then a moment of silence before pandemonium broke out. The prisoners jumped up shouting from their seats as the guard frantically turned the lights back on. All the prisoners were crowded around the area where Schmitt was sitting. The guard blew his whistle to summons assistance and shouted for the prisoners to move away. Other guards came rushing in and as they re-established order the reason for the mayhem became apparent.

Schmitt lay slumped on the wooden bench seat with blood trickling from his open mouth set in the rictus of death. A knife handle projected from his abdomen.

The subsequent investigation found it impossible to prove which of the prisoners had carried out the killing. No fingerprints were found on the knife, and not surprisingly, there were no witnesses. The coroner's inquest concluded that the death of Hans Schmitt was due to *murder by person or persons unknown*.

Chapter 22
Marriage

The marriage between Jack Blake and Mary Charlesworth took place one Saturday morning the following spring in their home town of Canterbury. It was a balmy day with spells of warm sunshine dodging between cotton wool clouds pushed by a light breeze which ruffled the long dresses of the bride and bridesmaids. Mary entered the church holding on to the arm of her proud father dressed resplendently in a smart wedding suit.

Jack had chosen Tom Fields as his best man and as he saw his bride coming down the aisle he felt an overwhelming surge of love and pride. He smiled as she approached him, a smile that she returned, a little nervously at first then with confidence as she stopped beside him.

After the service he lined up beside his new wife and other close relatives. His father, mother, Mary's parents, and not least, Jenny who had been the first one to run up to them with her congratulations as soon as they has emerged from the church.

'So you've beaten me to it, you rotter,' she said with an assumed look of petulance which immediately transformed into a broad smile as she gave them both an affectionate kiss and hug. Jenny looked round at her fiancé Alistair who was standing next to her.

'We've been keeping it quiet, but I want you to be the first to know apart from Mum and Dad. Alistair and I are getting married next month.'

'Oh, Jen,' said Jack as he bent forward to hug her. 'I am so pleased for you. Anyway, it's about time,' he concluded in mock admonishment.

Mary's parents, were next to congratulate them warmly. 'So pleased for you both,' said Tom. 'As for you, Jack, I hear you are doing well and you're in the same line of business as myself. I was very pleased when I heard that. I'm sure you will be successful and we wish you both every happiness for your future.'

Jack then hugged his parents and thanked them for their support.

'Proud of you, son,' said Fred. 'I know you've had some difficult times over the past months but you have handled it well. Congratulations to you both.'

The reception was held in a nearby hostelry that Jack had known from his teenage years. Tom, as Jack's best man, gave a humorous speech, followed by one given by Jack with the usual thanks to everyone who had contributed to their happy day.

While the reception was still in progress the couple disappeared to a separate room to change quickly and then dash away in Jack's car for a honeymoon in the Lake District. They waited until they had put some distance between them and the hostelry before untying all the paraphernalia that had been trailing behind them.

They had agreed earlier that they would not go abroad for their honeymoon to reserve their cash resources for more important items with which to start their married life. A deposit for a modern semi-detached house in the suburbs of Hastings had been the first stage in the process.

The honeymoon was over all too soon and the couple returned to their respective jobs.

On Jack's first day back Jim Dawson took him aside.

'I've something rather important to tell you, Jack,' he said.

'Oh yes Jim,' said Jack curiously, 'What is it?'

'I've got another job,' said Dawson briefly. 'It's as Group Security Manager for Williamsons. It means more money and better prospects for me and my family. I wanted you to be the first to know particularly as it will surely mean promotion for you.'

Williamsons was a huge industrial concern with headquarters in the north of England and branches in a number of European countries.

'That's great, Jim,' said Jack, grabbing Dawson's hand to pump it enthusiastically. 'I'll be sorry to see you go though. I think we've developed a good partnership here.'

'Yes we have, responded Dawson, 'and in a way I shall be sorry to go. But I think you will do well, Jack, just keep on the way you have so far.'

'I'll certainly do my best,' said Jack with a grin, 'but your shoes are big ones to fill.'

Dawson laughed, 'If you mean that I have big feet then that's probably true!'

After Dawson departed Jack was duly promoted as head of security and one of the first to congratulate him was Tom Fields. Now with a higher salary Jack was able to buy a better car; a new silver Ford Focus. Mary already had her own car which she needed to commute to her place of work.

Life progressed uneventfully and Jack enjoyed his new responsibilities. He was well respected by the staff who understood the increased restrictions that were placed upon them in the interests of improved security.

He tightened up in a number of areas, particularly in the handling of sensitive material. Events of the recent past became a distant memory, but the increasing demands of health and safety legislation took up a great deal of his time.

He was settled in his domestic life and within a year Mary gave birth to a little girl. She was named Tina Jane at her christening.

Chapter 23
Retribution

As Delaney sat brooding in the RAF holding cell awaiting transport to Cyprus he was on the verge of despair. Even if he was found not guilty in Cyprus he still had the prospect of facing trial back in the UK for Jones's murder, even if it was ultimately reduced to one of manslaughter. After that he could face a further charge of arms theft from the army base in Cyprus. It seemed as if the powers that be had considered the range of possible charges and decided that they should be dealt with in order of severity.

When he heard what had happened to Schmitt he received it with mixed feelings. In spite of the plethora of charges hovering over him he had been walking in fear of Schmitt ever since it became known that the police were after him. Now Schmitt was out of the picture that particular danger was no longer there, but Delaney had little doubt that Longford was the one responsible for Schmitt's sudden demise. Could he be next in line?

Whenever he had come face to face with Longford he was always very wary, realising that this was a very dangerous man. He was only too well aware of

Longford's function in the organisation. However he could think of no reason why Longford should bear him any hostility. Longford was already in prison and serving a life sentence for murder so there was nothing that he could do to make things any worse for him.

The following day after his transfer to the RAF station, Delaney was driven to an awaiting a C17 RAF transport plane parked on the tarmac. He sat in one of row of inward facing seats guarded by two RAF police officers. In spite of his desperate circumstances Delaney had a natural outgoing personality and he had tried to engage his guards in conversation during the long flight but their responses had been very brief and non-committal. It seemed as if they were under instructions not to communicate with him for whatever reason.

Four hours later the plane landed at RAF Akrotiri, the premier sovereign base in Cyprus where once again he was transferred to the base prison, He was given a meal and a sparse bed for the night. He was also given some lightweight plain clothing more suited to the hot climate. It seemed to consist of an aircraftsman uniform but stripped completely of any insignia.

The next morning he was awakened by the clanging sound of the metal prison doors being opened and shut.

Three men entered his cell, two of them obviously Greek Cypriots, the third, an RAF Wing Commander. The Greek Cypriots were introduced as plain clothed police officers and one, without preamble said, 'We are here to drive you to the main prison in Nicosia and you will be handed over to the Cypriot prison authority as agreed according to the terms of your extradition. Do you understand?'

Delaney nodded with a sarcastic smirk. 'Yes, I understand. Let's keep you lot happy so we can keep the good old Union Jack flying here.'

The remark fell on deaf ears as the officer signed a form clipped to a board that was proffered by the RAF officer to confirm the transfer of Delaney to the hands of Cypriot authorities.

His wrists were handcuffed together and he was led outside to a waiting police car, easily recognised by its white colour and surrounding blue stripe.

As he emerged from his cell, even though it was still early in the morning, the bright Cypriot sunshine caused him squint. He raised his cuffed arms to shade his eyes, muttering, 'bloody hell, I'd forgotten how sodding hot it gets here.'

Delaney was made to sit in the back of the car beside one of the police officers. The other man drove the car.

The journey was due to take the A1 motorway from Limassol directly to Nicosia, a journey of about one hour. Before that however they had to reach the start of the motorway, some seven miles away from the RAF base, which would take them through the Limassol suburbs, a maze of streets and housing.

As Delaney sat with his handcuffed wrists in front of him he gazed out of the window but only vaguely conscious of the passing scene. He was filled with despair at his likely prospects as he knew he could expect no leniency from any Greek Cypriot jury.

Then suddenly he became aware that it seemed to be taking an abnormally long time to reach the motorway, a familiar road from his army days. Instead of the expected conglomeration of housing and buildings as would be expected in the outskirts of Limassol, the scenery outside was increasingly bleak with more and more vegetation by the roadside. They were also going uphill.

'Are you sure you're on the right road?' he uttered tersely.

'Just keep your mouth shut, Delaney,' said the man beside him.

It began to dawn on Delaney that things were not right. Why would they be heading up into the mountains?

And the attitude of his guard did not seem to be that of a professional policeman.

He realised with a sudden shock that he was being kidnapped!

'You're not police officers. What the hell are you doing?' he yelled.

'I said, keep your mouth shut,' repeated his captor. With that he produced a gun which he prodded into Delaney's side, 'If you don't you'll be shot.'

Delaney shrank back in his seat, his mind in complete disarray. Why would anyone want to kidnap him?

Perhaps he was being allowed to escape.

Could Len Parker be behind this to stop him from testifying in court that he had been acting under Parker's instructions in the shooting of Christakos?

Yes! That must be it. It was the only explanation.

'Are you working for Len Parker?' he ventured, his voice shaking with dread, 'Is that what this is all about?'

The remark was met by a sharp painful jab in the ribs from the weapon pointed at him, but there was no verbal response from the man sitting beside him.

Delaney lapsed into a terrified silence as he pondered what his intended fate was to be.

The car continued its ascent into the Troodos Mountains, and in spite of his present plight it brought to his mind those far off days that he had enjoyed with Jack Blake. It had been a strange friendship as they were so different from each other. He knew that *straight as a dye Jack* was doing well in his career and good luck to him.

But he knew he could never have been like that. It simply was not part of his character.

He was jerked out of his reverie as the car turned sharply off the main road onto a single track unsurfaced road into a pine forest.

After several hundred yards of a very bumpy ride they came to rest by a small stone building. There was no sign of any other buildings in the vicinity so it appeared to be some sort of overnight lodge, perhaps for trekkers.

As Delaney was bungled out of the car he noticed that there was another car parked just by the entrance. He was pushed into a small room and forced to sit in a chair.

He looked around wildly not knowing what to expect. Then a door facing him opened and another man entered and stood regarding him.

Delaney recognised the man instantly. A few years older and with a significant moustache and longer hair but his identity was unmistakable.

'Dimitri!' he gasped, 'Dimitri Christakos!'

'Yes, that's me, Mr Delaney,' replied Dimitri with a grim smile and with a mocking emphasis on the term *Mr*. 'So pleased you recognise one of your old friends from your days with us.'

'What do you want with me, Dimitri? Why have you gone to all this trouble to kidnap me? Don't you realise that the entire Cypriot police force will be out searching for you?'

'We know what we are doing,' replied Dimitri.

Turning to one of the other men guarding Delaney he said, 'Better get on your mobile to the Limassol police and tell them where their colleagues are. Wouldn't want any harm to come to them would we.'

He turned his attention back to Delaney.

'Now, Mr Delaney, the reason you are here. I know you have been returned here to face trial for the murder of my brother. Then no doubt you will be found guilty and imprisoned for a long time.'

Dimitri paused for a few seconds, shaking his head slowly before continuing.

'That's not good enough for us is it?' The last rhetorical remark was addressed to the two other men in the room.

'Oh, sorry, Mr Delaney, you've not been introduced to my two cousins. Say Hello to Nikolas and Stephas.'

Delaney made no response. His heart was beating wildly as he realised what was about to happen to him.

'Oh well, no matter,' said Dimitri turning his attention back to Delaney, 'to continue what I was saying, I know that you shot my brother.'

'No, no Dimitri, that wasn't me!' shouted Delaney in protest. 'All I wanted to do was to get away from the army. That must have been somebody else who did that!'

'Don't waste your breath, Delaney,' said Dimitri in a calm controlled voice, then, choosing his words carefully, he continued, 'We know it was you and we have held our own trial in *absentia*, I believe that's what you call it. Here we believe in the age old credo of an eye for an eye, so the verdict was guilty.'

'No!' shouted Delaney, 'you can't do that. You have no power to try me for anything, let alone find me guilty!'

Dimitri stood regarding his prisoner without expression as Delaney continued to protest and struggle but the two cousins restrained him by holding him firmly in the chair.

'Frank Delaney,' said Dimitri suddenly in a loud voice, causing Delaney to stop struggling and look back at him in dread. 'The sentence is for you to be executed forthwith. Therefore you will be taken out of here and shot.'

'No!' shouted Delaney again. 'You can't do that! It would be murder!'

He tried to struggle to his feet in protest but his guards pushed him violently back into the chair.

'You can't do this, Dimitri,' he went on desperately. 'Look, if you release me I'll plead guilty in court and I'll be punished by your own people.'

'Take him outside,' said Dimitri to his cousins. 'Let's get this over with.'

Delaney, struggling violently, was hustled out and tied by ropes around his chest to the trunk of a nearby pine tree. He knew then all hope was lost, but in spite of everything he had done in the past, he was no coward. He stopped struggling and looked ahead with a frozen expression.

Dimitri strode out of the building holding an automatic weapon. He raised it, carefully took aim at Delaney's chest area and fired a single shot.

'For you Andreas,' he breathed.

Delaney's body was taken down and placed inside the stolen police car. Both cars were then driven back to the mountain road, and the police car with Delaney's body inside it was abandoned by the roadside.

Inside the central police station in Limassol the desk sergeant received the mobile message to say that two of their officers were tied up at a locked garage several miles away. The station had already received a call from Nicosia that Delaney had not been delivered on time, but it was thought that perhaps they had been delayed for some reason. But then, why had they not rung in? It was now clear that the police car had been hijacked and Delaney kidnapped, so an immediate search was activated by police and military units. The assistance of the RAF was requested and helicopters from the Akrotiri base were deployed to search the extensive mountainous regions.

The stolen police car with Delaney's body inside was soon found but there was no indication of who had killed him and, in spite of an extensive investigation, no arrests were made. On release the two hijacked policemen said that they had been ambushed in a quiet street in the suburbs of Limassol. It had been early morning with no-one about, when two hooded men had appeared in front of them brandishing automatic weapons, forcing them to stop. There had been no time to radio for assistance, and all means of communication had been removed from them. The hijacking had taken place immediately outside the locked garage from where they were eventually released.

Chapter 24
Finale

Frank Delaney's parents were the first to hear of their son's death via a private phone call to their landline from a government source. Delaney's father, Patrick, picked up the phone and as soon as he heard the words from the caller, he collapsed into a chair a look of shock on his face,

'Oh my God,' he gasped, 'but how?'

Both Dorothy Delaney and Rose, presently on vacation from university, looked at him in shocked surprise.

'What is it Dad?' said Rose. 'What's the matter?'

'It's Frank, he's been found dead in Cyprus,' said her father shortly.

'Oh God!' said Dorothy, her hands flying up to her face, 'surely not Frank, it can't be possible.'

'They haven't said how,' said Patrick. 'They said the matter is still being investigated, but they offered their deep regrets and that his body would be returned to us for burial after a post mortem.'

The family, of course, knew about Frank's situation and why he was in Cyprus and Mr Delaney's attitude had never softened. If anything it had hardened on hearing about the murder charges and the reasons for the extradition. But now, on hearing about his son's sudden death, a surge of emotion overtook him and he collapsed forward in his chair, holding his head in grief. His wife and Rose rushed over to him and the three of them hugged each other in silence.

The events very quickly reached the worlds media. It was just another chapter in the saga of Delaney's activities that had been widely reported both in the press and television news broadcasts since the events leading up to his initial arrest.

Paula Kendrick was at home with her parents watching television when the basic facts were given. There was no mention of how it had happened.

She sat up sharply with a gasp as soon as she heard Delaney's name.

'Oh Mum and Dad, that's the man who kidnapped me. The one you knew as *Alan Birch*!'

'That's him is it,' said her father sharply, 'a really nasty case. I'll never forget what he put you through so I can't say I'm sorry. Looks to me like he's got his just desserts. Mind you I don't approve of cold-blooded murder however evil the victim. He should have faced justice in the Courts,' he paused then added grimly, 'then I would have put him up against a wall and had him shot!'

'I know dad,' said Paula feelingly, 'I feel a bit the same way but there is just a tiny bit of me that remembers what he was like when I first met him. Stupid me, I really fell for him and I was completely under his spell when he made me do those horrible things. It was only later that I woke up to the truth about him. I agree that he deserved to pay for his crimes but I'm sorry that it had to end that way.'

Some miles away in Hastings Jack and Mary Blake heard the news at the same time.

'My God,' said Jack. 'What the hell, I don't believe it. Frank, you poor sod.'

'I think he's been asking for it,' said Mary. 'I'm sorry for your sake though, darling, knowing what close friends you both were at one time.'

'Yes, that's true,' said Jack, 'I'm devastated if the truth be known. I realised he was a bit of a rogue when we were in Cyprus but I never thought he would do all those terrible things he's been accused of.'

He shook his head in frustration.

'Well, whatever. I must go to his funeral assuming it's going to be back here in the UK. I'll have to ring Rose, his sister. She'll know.'

'That's all right Jack,' said Mary. 'You go, but I'll stay here if you don't mind. I never met Frank Delaney and it wouldn't mean anything to me to be there.'

'Of course not darling,' responded Jack. 'I wouldn't expect you to be there. To be honest I don't know why I need to go. I suppose it's to bring some sort of closure to everything.'

Three weeks later Jack Blake was at the Delaney household waiting with them for the cortege that would take them to the crematorium. Jack Blake expressed condolences to Delaney's parents before turning to Rose who greeted him with a sad smile.

'Hello, Jack,' she said, 'thank you for coming. I really believe that the friendship between you and Frank was one of the most treasured things to him. It was genuine and he often mentioned you in his messages to me.'

'Yes, I believe that's true,' responded Jack. 'We were close during those days in Cyprus. I just can't understand the way things turned out.'

'What about you, Rose, how are you keeping?'

'I'm fine,' she said brightly. 'I should be finishing my studies this year and then get an internship at a hospital.'

'I'm sure you'll be very successful,' said Jack, 'but Mary and I would really like you to visit us down in Hastings. You would be very welcome.'

'Thank you, Jack. I will definitely do that,' she said.

It was a dismal cloudy day with spots of rain, in fitting with the occasion as they entered the cars comprising the cortege. There were a few news photographers and members of the press waiting to report on this finale to the life of someone who had become so notorious in the locale. Also waiting were several family friends and others, probably curiosity seekers.

The non-religious service was brief with no mention of Delaney's life or events that had led to his death. A hapless affair that Jack Blake was glad to see over.

Later, as he drove home, the drizzle stopped and a hint of sunshine appeared from behind the grey clouds. His mood brightened and he smiled at the thought of getting back home to Mary and baby Tina.